PROMISE of a LIFETIME

To all the Elliot Stabler and Derek Morgan lovers.

Also by N. Alikyan

Buttercup Baby

Promise of A Lifetime

Also by Nelly Alikyan

Whittle Magic Series

Alluring Darkness

Beholding Darkness

Claiming Darkness

Desiring Darkness

Catchers Series

With the Flames Catching Midnight

With the Rains Catching Dawn

With the Ice Catching Twilight

With the Storms Catching Dusk

With the Winds Catching Sunlight

With the Ashes Catching Daybreak

Soundtrack

Million Scarlet Roses - Alla Pugacheva

(Миллио́н а́лых роз - Алла Пугачева)

·

Bring Me to Life - Evanescence

·

(Kissed You) Good Night - Gloriana

·

The Few Things - JP Saxe & Charlotte Lawrence

·

This I Promise You - *NSYNC

·

Promise of a Lifetime - Kutless

·

Heaven's Telephone - Forest Blakk

*..............Six parts ballad,
seven parts finale..............*

Part One

"*I don't want to be at the mercy of my emotions. I want to use them, to enjoy them, and to dominate them.*"

- Oscar Wilde

Lana

I WOULD'VE FOUND it amusing how predictable they were if a detective's job wasn't to keep the general public safe. So rather, I found it pitiful.

"You have the right to remain silent…" The detective, a woman about ten years my senior, tugged on my arm a little too harshly as she guided me to the car.

I knew she was trying to show dominance, but truly, it was kind of funny.

"Anything you say can and will be used against you in the court of law…" she rambled on.

As I walked with my hands cuffed behind my back, I wondered if they knew that I could get out of them if I wanted to. Or, at the very least, I was flexible enough to bring my arms around so my hands were in front rather than behind. It was one of the many things I learned growing up, and the flexibility of my shoulder joints was one of the many things I practiced daily in case of moments like these. It kind of made me sad that even after all this time, after everything I'd done to leave, I'd always subconsciously known something like this would happen.

I wondered what these detectives would do if they knew of my abilities. Or how they'd feel if I told them. Narrow their eyes? I liked cops normally, appreciated the danger they put themselves in to help civilians, but I couldn't lie that I would've loved to see the big, bad detective's face if I'd told her that piece of info.

I wasn't listening because I truly was worried about their thought process here. What reason would I have had to commit this murder they were attempting to pin on me? Had I done it, I wouldn't have been so easily tracked to that cafe, that was for sure.

Or maybe I would've. I like to believe if I was a murderer, I'd be a fun one. So maybe I would stick around and allow myself to get caught simply in order to play with them. It would have been quite entertaining, especially with the knowledge that they didn't have any evidence on me.

Mrs. Tough Guy here was trying to scare me into slipping up my words, but she should've known better. From what I'd heard, this was a brutal murder they were trying to solve, and if I knew anything about murder, it was that the crime was normally committed by men. Especially the brutal ones. Which meant I had to be in the very slim bit of women who committed gruesome murders. It was actually quite flattering that Mrs. Tough Guy thought so highly of me.

But it brought me back to the point—if I was the cold-hearted killer, her mean detective act wouldn't have slipped me up in the slightest.

That's not to say I was Mrs. Squeaky Clean, but I certainly was a good—enough—person.

I was so lost in the memories of those not-so-squeaky-clean

acts when Mrs. Tough Guy tugged hard on my arm. "*Do you* understand your rights as I've read them to you?"

I realized then that she'd probably asked that question multiple times. I couldn't help that I hadn't been listening. She was kind of pompous.

I quirked a brow at her and made a mockery of my tone, not because it was innate in me to do so but because Father had always said not to show our true selves. "Yes, Mrs. Tough Guy."

She ground her teeth and pushed me into the back seat of her car. She was pretty, her black straight shoulder-length hair angling her face impeccably. Too bad she was an ass.

I made myself comfortable as she and her colleague got in the front and began the drive. It wasn't a cop car, so there was no cover between my seat and theirs. I wondered if they felt safe with me behind them. Mostly because they kept glancing up at the rearview mirror as if I was going to jump them at any moment. Especially the colleague—Detective Langly, I thought I caught Tough Guy saying. He was kind of cute.

But that worried glance he kept throwing my way killed it. I was honored he thought so highly of my abilities, but it wasn't very attractive if a man was afraid of a little killer. I needed a man who, even if I were a crazy gruesome killer, could take control. Was that crazy? Maybe. But it wasn't fantastical. I knew many men who would fit the bill. They simply weren't *for me*.

But I definitely didn't want someone who threw worried glances even while I was cuffed. Even Goody Two-shoes me knew that wasn't an attractive quality.

Though maybe that crazy fantasy I desired was the reason he was scared. *He* was smart enough to know that if I wanted to, I would be out of these cuffs, and if I had the ability to do that, who knew what else I could do to him.

Or maybe they both knew it and lady cop was simply too prideful to admit it. For that, I wouldn't fault her.

We were stopped in front of their building in almost no time, and while I waited to be escorted out of my carriage, I glanced over to the bushes surrounding the building. The flowers were so beautiful, full of color and distracting in plain view.

I wore a small smile as I stepped out of the back seat and stopped before Detective Langly. "You know, you have no proof of my guilt. I understand cuffing me for your safety, but it's honestly not needed. I promise I won't run."

He eyed me with narrowed eyes.

"That's a lifetime promise, Detective."

"Promise not to be a pain?"

I gave a twinkling, wide smile. "Now, where's the fun in that?"

He rolled his eyes but turned to uncuff me. It was a good thing too. Not that it mattered all that much since we were another minute or two from being inside where they would've done it anyway. But the sooner, the better. The cuffs were beginning to aggravate my skin.

He took my arm when the cuffs were off and led me into the building. His grip was strong but nothing like Mrs. Tough Guy's. He wasn't trying to show dominance. He was simply leading someone he didn't trust. I liked Langly.

The elevator ride was quiet, and I could feel the tension with both detectives behind me. It made me want to giggle. I was not a scary person. In fact, I was a pretty soft one, but sometimes, it was nice to be made to look a little daunting.

When the doors opened, I was led through the hall to the open set of double doors into a room with desks everywhere. There were a few small groups of people talking between themselves, but my little friends seemed most interested in one—the two men by the desks on the right.

The older of the two wore a suit that looked to cost a pretty penny, which told me he valued his clothing, and though he couldn't afford too many of them, he'd rather buy a few of the best than dozens of shit quality. That made me like him instantly.

His partner, one at least twenty years his junior, was dressed in the same type of suit, making me like his decision-making skills instantly as well, but it did for him what only fantasies should've been allowed to do. He was beautiful in a clean-cut way rather than a rugged one.

Eyeing him slowly, I realized the persona that was the opposite to me—the one Father insisted be used in times like these—would begin flirting. I wasn't nervous about it, but it was always a mindset I had to put myself into.

But that persona would've decided he was the one I'd be giving any answers to. I hadn't promised Langly I would behave, so... why shouldn't I have fun while I was here?

We stopped before Hottie and who I presumed was his boss simply based on age difference. "You're so... wow."

I wasn't even trying to be annoying in the way I had been with Tough Guy. The words were just so true I lost the persona for a moment, and they tumbled out. Softer and less cocky than they should've been.

"Miss... Lana, I suppose." His voice was deep but soft, like he didn't want to intimidate me.

"That's what your partner tells me." I let a little sparkle I hadn't felt in a long time fill my eyes, and I swore I saw it reciprocated in both his and his boss's returning stares.

He took the following moment to take me in from head to toe, more like he was scrutinizing than checking me out.

I stood straighter. I didn't care if we were on opposing sides at the moment; I wanted to present my best to those beautiful browns. And the persona part I was meant to be taking on stuck my chest out a little bit, and I had to fight off the recoil to such an act.

I smirked. "Do you find me attractive?" His hotness made me feel like I should trust him the least. Did he think the same thing about me?

He didn't have a chance to answer—though I knew he wasn't going to—as Mrs. Tough Guy shoved me toward the small hall of doors off to the side. She opened one and pushed me a little too harshly into it.

I held that smirk in place as I made my way around the interrogation table and took my seat. "Do you like him? Is that why you're so upset with me? Think he wants me too?"

Should I be baiting the mean one? Probably not.

Was I going to? The persona said, "Abso-fucking-lutely!"

There was death in her eyes as she stood by the door. "Your interrogation will begin shortly, murderer."

"I thought I was innocent until proven guilty?"

She glared. Grr, mean little detective.

I smiled as my head tipped back like I didn't have a care in the world. "As long as that delicious specimen of a man is the one doing the interrogating."

She visibly kept herself from saying any more as she turned and slammed the door shut. She definitely had a crush on Hottie. Another thing I wouldn't fault her for.

I laughed. She was far too easy to rile up. My persona could have fun with her. I, on the other hand, might get my feelings a little hurt if she threw my faults in my face.

THEY'D BEEN AT IT FOR HOURS, AND IN THAT TIME, I'd learned that Mrs. Tough Guy's name was Ava Porter. She wasn't the one with me at the moment, but I knew without a doubt she was standing on the other side of that one-way mirror, seething at my ease. To be fair, neither I nor my persona were worried about being in here, so there was no faking going on in that regard.

Their boss was taking his turn with me. I tilted my head at him—Axel Finnegan. He was trying to analyze me, and I knew he wasn't getting far. Not because I was cocky but because there was a twinge of frustration in the back of his deep brown eyes as they met mine once more.

I gave a warm smile, but it was a shame that he would read that as the persona rather than the cocky bitch I was making myself out to be.

But, alas, if cocky bitch was what he wanted, she'd come out and play for a little while. So I turned my smile into a smirk and leaned back in my chair. "Considering you only have twenty-four hours to hold me and you've wasted a few of those already, don't you think you should send in the attractive one? Not that the rest of you aren't attractive." My persona winked.

Since when could I wink? This persona needed to teach me how it did some of these things.

Mr. Boss Man narrowed his eyes at me.

The smile was back, but there was nothing honestly sweet about it. "Then I'd be distracted and could give you what you want."

He was silent for a while before heading out the door.

I sighed, leaning back in my chair. From what I could tell, it'd been closer to five hours since I'd been brought in, and they were wasting precious minutes leaving me alone in the interrogation room.

Actually, they were wasting precious minutes speaking

with me at all when they should have been looking for this killer, but hey, who was I to tell them how to do their job?

I wondered if they were working the "make me restless which would make me anxious and lead to blab-a-babble-blab" ploy?

A small smile lifted my lips at the thought. I liked silence. One of my favorite things to do at night was to sit on the ground and look out of the large window of my room, getting hypnotized by the moon with no distractions. Just me and my thoughts. And unlike most people, I liked my thoughts. They came up with cute stories of a life I would never have, made me happy to at least vicariously live through them.

I wondered, as I waited, if it was making me an even bigger suspect that I wasn't showing any real concern? Innocents went berserk in moments like these, right?

That made it sound like I wasn't innocent. I was. If certain people in my life were to be asked, I was possibly a little too good.

Too bad detectives wouldn't put any faith in such people.

It was another ten minutes before the door finally opened and Hottie walked in.

I sat straight up with a genuine smile on my face. I didn't think they'd actually send him in. "Hi." My voice came out soft, so my persona quickly took over with a teasing "I missed you."

He didn't react, and I wasn't sure if it was only my attraction to him that made me think so, but he was the best detective out of the lot.

Yeah, definitely my attraction.

Maybe Finnegan knew what he was doing by indulging my joke. This one was distractingly good-looking. Something that was hard to prepare for when you never really found many people attractive.

He stood before the closed door, not moving for the seat across from mine. He looked so domineering yet still so welcoming as he stood there, and it made that imaginative part of my mind wander.

"Do you find me attractive, Detective?" My persona broke the silence in order to stop my mind from the romantic productions it liked to put on.

"No," he answered bluntly.

A grin grew on my lips, and I didn't know where it was coming from, but it felt right. "If you want me to be honest here, you need to start, Detective. Now, let's try that again. Are you attracted to me?"

He ground his jaw, and darkness filled those cognac eyes. "Yes."

I sighed softly, relaxing a little. Not because he'd given me the answer I wanted to hear but because it was the truth. He didn't like me—as a suspect, that wasn't surprising—but he was into me. That must've been so very frustrating. It was quite frustrating on my part.

But maybe that also had to do with the fact that I didn't so easily find anyone attractive, so I wasn't used to these... what? Butterflies?

I eyed the seat across from me. "Why don't you take a seat, Detective..."

He didn't answer my unasked question. "Can I offer you some water? You've been here a while, and I wouldn't want you dehydrated."

I allowed softness into my features. "That'd be lovely. But only if I get gloves as well."

He narrowed his eyes.

"My hands are freezing."

Into slits then, completely not trusting me.

My smile was more sad as I stood. He stiffened as I drew closer, but he didn't back away.

When I was standing before him, I took only his hands. The way he stiffened told me he could feel just how cold my hands were. Or maybe he really didn't want me touching him.

He gave a single nod, looked behind me as if telling me to go back and sit, then turned for the door.

I followed his wordless command.

I was curious if he'd actually bring the gloves. My hands truly were freezing, and there wasn't much sitting on them could do. Once I lifted them away from my body heat, they'd freeze back up.

It wasn't a medical condition. Wasn't even an all-the-time condition. It simply was. Sometimes my hands froze. It kept the rest of my body warm though, so I didn't mind it all too much most of the time. It did suck when I was working on computers though. Having to sit on my hands or stuff them under my arms every other minute when I didn't have gloves was a hassle.

I sighed as the minutes ticked by and fell back into the chair. I threw my feet on the table so I could easily fall into my daydreams as I waited for whoever was next.

I'd thought this was a waste of my time—which it was—but not as much as it could've been. At least now I could picture Detective Hottie in my fantasies. At least for a couple of weeks, and then I would forget all about him.

I **MOVED** for Finnegan when I left the room. He was out by the desks with Porter and Lansly, all of them having come out when I'd left the interrogation room.

"She's smart enough to not want to leave prints," Finnegan started.

"Which means she would've been smart enough not to leave them at the scene too, don't you think?" Lansly defended.

I shrugged. "Her hands *are* freezing. If that's a biological abnormality, she would've gotten lucky with it. It would've forced her to wear gloves, and she wouldn't have left prints."

Lansly looked in thought. "Maybe."

I moved for my desk, where I always kept a little kit for days it got cold.

Porter scoffed. "You're actually going to give her gloves?"

"I need her to trust me. At least more than she does you lot, or else we definitely won't get anywhere."

"That isn't a problem," Lansly said. "If she takes the water, we can still get DNA, which would be way better than prints anyway. She could've left prints when she was in there earlier.

DNA is what'll really catch her. We match it, bing-bang, case closed."

A grin fought to escape me. "You think it'd be so simple?"

He shrugged. "We deserve a simple one every now and again."

I chuckled as I found the gloves hidden behind three beanies. I then moved for the water cooler and filled one of the nicer cups for her. "Let's see what she gives me."

I returned to the room to find her lounging back like she didn't have a care in the world, her legs propped up like she was bored.

She was either great at keeping her composure, or she truly believed she would get out of this unscathed. But we knew it was her. We had a witness putting her there. Now we needed evidence to tie her there without a defense arguing it was her job at the hotel that put them in contact in any way.

She dropped her feet and sat straight up in her chair as I placed the cup of water before her, hoping she'd forget herself and reach for it first. She eyed it, then traced those striking eyes up my arm to meet mine. She quirked a brow as if waiting for me to sit but didn't move.

I sat and handed her my gloves. "Your hands."

There was shock in her eyes, though she tried to hide any reaction. She hadn't been expecting me to deliver on such a request. Understandably so.

To be honest, had I not felt how cold her hands truly were, I wouldn't have brought them. But I couldn't, in good conscience, leave her to freeze like that. I knew I shouldn't feel compassion toward a cold-blooded murderer, but I couldn't help it.

She didn't move for the gloves immediately, and I tried to be patient, see what her next move would be. In the silence that followed us, she slowly used a fingernail to turn a glove around and maneuver her hand within it without touching the tops. When she had one on, she grabbed for the other and easily slipped it on.

She was smart. Not that it was likely we could've gotten any conclusive fingerprints off the leather of the gloves, but it would've been something to check out, maybe enough for a search warrant. Or a warrant for her DNA. Having the only witness be hysterical apparently wasn't good enough.

The crime scene unit was still digging through all the blood in that room, all the glasses and anything that could've gotten prints or DNA on it. They didn't know yet if all the blood belonged to our victim—which, given he was a man, it was likely he'd fought back and got skin or blood or something off the killer—but I had hope they'd find something to tie an outsider into the crime scene.

Lana had been smart enough to think of leaving prints on the leather, which meant she either knew far more about law enforcement than she was leading on, or she was one of those paranoid who thought the police were out to get them.

Or maybe she was simply a woman. They tended to be the ones obsessed with crime documentaries.

"Why don't we start with something simple?" I leaned forward to make sure her attention was on me as I finally broke the silence. "Your name, for instance."

We already knew her first name, but that and the fact that Shriberton staff had seen her go to that coffee shop right before our arrest were about it. Had they not known that, it would've been damn near impossible to bring her in for questioning at all.

She quirked a brow, amusement lining her eyes. "Oh, c'mon, I have faith in you. Your colleagues may not have your looks to try to play with, but even they got my name out of me."

I imagined Porter scowling at that comment. "Humor me."

"Lana."

"Humor me with a full name, Lana."

That DNA could help us with more than just tying her to this murder. We could also learn of her background because so far, we had zilch. And someone this secretive usually had a very illegal reason to be so.

"Isn't that your job, Detective? To find the facts yourself?"

She was confident. That either meant she truly wasn't at fault here—which then brought on the question of why avoid prints and DNA collection—or, more likely, she'd covered her tracks.

"Interrogation is part of how we do that, Lana," I responded coolly. The last thing I needed was for her to get under my skin.

She gave a close-lipped smile that was on the edge of condescending. "Then perhaps some more lessons on how exactly to do that?"

I gritted my jaw but kept cool. Her little games only made her look more guilty.

Then, to my relief and excitement, which I didn't let show, she reached for her water. And a good thing I kept the feelings hidden, too, because the girl tipped her head back and let the water fall from the cup and into her mouth. Not a trace of DNA to be found.

She'd been smart enough not to touch the gloves. I should've figured she'd be more than smart enough to waterfall her drink.

She only winked at me when she put the glass down.

It'd been hours.

Hours and nothing.

We'd taken turns with Lana once more, but her time was drawing to a close, and Finnegan wanted to take one more chance with me. He hoped even her slight attraction for me coupled with how tired she must've been, would make her slip up. I was beginning to see she wouldn't. She was trained. Why, I couldn't fathom, but whatever the reason, she hadn't broken a sweat once in all the time we'd held her.

Porter scowled every time the attraction factor was brought up, and I couldn't tell why. She didn't like me—I hoped—so it shouldn't have been such a big deal.

When I returned to the room, Lana was sitting at the table in a ladylike manner, far different from the first time I walked in. Her hands were gracefully resting over one another on the table, and her head tilted to look me over.

"I was hoping I'd see you again. You keep leaving so abruptly," she said with only the slightest hint of a tease in her tone.

It was so odd having watched her all this time. It was almost like she had two personalities warring, and she didn't know which to stick to. Porter wanted to believe she was psychotic—it made a stronger case—but I didn't think so. One of those personalities was an act. The tough part was figuring out which one.

I took my seat and leaned forward. "I must confess, I'm intrigued. You've been here close to twenty-four hours, and you hardly look tired."

"Upset I haven't let anything slip, Detective?"

"It is quite frustrating." Hopefully, my honesty would open her up.

She smiled, and I knew I was right to do so. "You still haven't revealed your name either. At least you know mine."

"Shipman," I answered without hesitation. Then to one-up her, I added, "Dorian Shipman."

"Ah." She leaned forward like she was going to share a secret, but her voice didn't drop. "So much to unpack there, Detective *Shipman*."

"What is it you'd like to unpack?"

Her hand lifted so her face fell into it as she took me in. I hated to admit it, but she was so beautiful in this moment. I wouldn't fault a single soul for walking straight into her traps when even I was liable to fall for it.

"You're a detective looking for a murderer, yet you hold the name of an infamous serial killer yourself, for starters." Her free hand reached over, and the too-big-for-her-hands glove brushed my bottom lip. "I wonder... was Dorian a family name or based off fiction?"

It was nearly hypnotizing, this soft way she took me in, spoke to me. This had to be the act.

"My mother was a great fan of Oscar Wilde's. I have a sister named Gwendolen. As for the surname, I'm afraid that is not something we had much control over. I am impressed to see you know of him though."

Her hand dropped and she leaned back a little. "You'd be surprised by the odd facts any average person may know."

Her fingers began tapping on the table, light but melodic.

"I'm rather more interested in your knowledge about murder," I said, glad my name had somehow gotten her talking about the topic.

She smiled like she knew what I was doing but played along, those gloved fingers still tapping away. "I know a great many things about murder, Dorian. Most women have that fascination."

Her use of my first name sent shock waves straight down to my dick, and I had to remind myself she was the suspect here.

"You do not seem upset with the crime."

"I will not pretend to hold the same morals as you, Dorian. Some people deserve death."

I narrowed my eyes. She was telling a lot without saying a thing. What could Mann have done to so abhorrently deserve his death?

"And what may some of those reasons be?" Preferably ones that put you with Mann four nights prior.

"Your moral high ground doesn't fool me, Dorian. You recognize the reasons as clearly as I do."

She was right. I could come up with a few reasons to kill a man. Most of them having to do with hurting children. But she didn't have to know that. "So you do not believe life is precious, then?"

"I think you're precious, Dorian." There was that switch of personas again.

And her constant use of my name. I couldn't tell if she was playing a reversal game and trying to get me to drop my guard and trust her—which her beauty and seduction made me believe was very possible—or if she was doing it for herself. If the latter, I wanted to know why for more reasons than this investigation.

I dropped my gaze to take her in when she said nothing more. She was relaxed, and I couldn't tell if that was highly honed acting skills that kept her so or if, like before, she truly was innocent, so she found herself with nothing to worry about.

But if it were the latter and she were a normal citizen, her innocence, coupled with the possibility of prison, would not leave her so calm.

"What is it you're tapping away at?" I asked because she wouldn't answer any real questions, so I figured I could get other facts about her. Plus, she hadn't stopped, and it was nagging at my brain, the familiarity of it not sticking.

She glanced down to her fingers but didn't stop. "Do you recognize the song, Dorian?"

I did, yet I couldn't place it. I was more impressed with how well she kept the melody and held this conversation. "It's a song?" I could look back at the footage of this interrogation and find it later if she held back on talking now, but I had a feeling she wasn't going to.

"I believe life is like any one of those pretty stanzas in sad songs," she returned to my earlier conversation on the preciousness of life. "Waiting for the inevitable."

"Death?"

She shrugged. "Everyone dies."

"So life is a ballad?"

She smiled wide. "Just waiting for the finale."

"Are the finales of ballads their most striking?"

"Personally." She winked as she rose to her feet. "Think of it, Dorian. Death is a person's most striking time. An artist's work sells for thousands, if not millions, more after so. Tell me, do you truly not believe it the most striking?"

Did Mann have something of value that she wanted? Was that the reason behind this? She so much as said he was better off dead.

I fell back in my seat but didn't stop her movement. She knew she still had a little bit longer here, and as she'd been smart enough not to push it thus far, I knew she would wait it out.

Instead, I traced her as she slowly began walking, felt her presence behind me as she circled the table before she was back in my periphery. In that time where she passed from my right to my left, she changed. Her breasts were a little more protruded now, and there was a wickedness in her eyes.

Was she bipolar? Multiple personalitied? Simply a great actress?

"You know what my favorite finale to a ballad is, Dorian?"

"What's that, Lana?"

She peeked over at me as her lips tipped up, and she began peeling the gloves off. "Kutless, 'Promise of a Lifetime.' Think of me when you listen to it."

"As you wish," I responded as she passed behind me once more.

Instead of continuing her track this time, she settled the gloves on the table and surprised me by sitting on the edge of the metal thing. She slithered her leg around before I had time to react, and I was caged between her legs, propped up on my chair.

She leaned forward.

I watched her like I was unperturbed, but my dick was throwing a party down below. Man was damn near ready to rip straight through my trousers and take her right here on this table. Maybe it had been a little *too* long since I'd been with a woman.

But this went to show—if I was fighting my attraction, a civilian would have no chances against her. She was the ultimate weapon. Especially this vixen I'd decided must've been her true character.

She continued forward, and I noticed a little too late that she was doing it so her hair would cage our faces in. I didn't know what she planned since even not hearing this conversation, my team would know of it, but I was very curious about where her mind was taking her at the moment. As I waited to see what she'd do, I knew with absolute certainty—absolutely no man would be a fool to fall for her.

Or, more accurately, we were all fat, fat fools.

Her hands slowly rested over my shoulders, fully caging me now, and I was assaulted by her scent. My cock jumped at the smell, at how badly I needed to be inside her. I bit the inside of my mouth to keep the humorless laugh in. She was good.

Her gaze jumped from mine to my lips and back again, over and over.

"You plan on kissing me?" I narrowed my eyes because I couldn't quite figure this girl out.

She laughed as one of her hands fell to the back of my neck, fingertips grazing my skin and sending thrilled nerves down south. Then that hand slithered further up until she was playing with my hair. I wanted to close my eyes and let my head fall back it felt so heavenly.

"No, baby. When we kiss, it'll be you making the first move. I need to know you want to take my firsts as much as I want to give them to you."

Some of the fog cleared with that news. "Your firsts? You've never been kissed?" A beauty like her? I found that hard to believe.

"Never even sent myself to orgasm," she said nonchalantly, fingers still distractingly in my hair, and my eyes bulged at her openness, especially as she continued. "Tried. But I could never get a clear enough picture or sound in mind to get there. Rest assured though, Dorian, with you filling every ounce of my thoughts, I'll be experiencing one tonight." She said that last bit with a teasing twinkle in her eyes, which made it difficult to tell if she was flirting or joking.

In any case, I didn't know what she was playing at telling me all this. I simultaneously needed her to stop and never wanted her to. Even if that made me one of her victims too.

Long minutes passed.

"Your time's up."

Her lips twitched up, and I wondered if she knew I was only saying that to get her away from me.

"Imagine getting head only to have your shaft ripped off."

My brows furrowed because what the actual fuck. "What?"

Her beautiful browns dipped down to my pants. "Don't want the boss seeing how affected you are when you stand, do we?"

My eyes widened as I glanced down to see the imprint in my trousers that, rest assured, was now dropping due to her delightful little imagination. More suspicion grew in me then. What the hell was she playing at?

She bit her bottom lip—which did nothing in helping the erection go down—and pushed away, throwing her leg back around and moving for the door. She stood there and waited for me, her gaze softening before glinting once more.

I huffed. At this rate, it had to be multiple personalities. As I moved for the door, I wondered if she wasn't reaching for it so she didn't leave prints behind or if she was waiting for me, waiting for something more.

I didn't let myself ponder the thought as I grabbed the gloves she'd left on the table and led us out of the interrogation room. Finnegan, Porter, and Lansly were already waiting for us by our desks.

Finnegan stopped Lana as I dropped my gloves back in their drawer. I'd wanted to tell her to keep them, but a large nagging feeling in me told me that'd be inappropriate. She'd barely touched me after taking them off, and I'd still felt a bit of the chill.

"Miss Lana," Finnegan started, looking down at her like she was already guilty. "We'll be seeing each other soon."

Lana didn't react as she tilted her head like she was analyzing him. "Surely."

Then she came for me. I didn't move as she reached around me for a pen from my desk, and I internally jumped with joy. The metal would definitely hold her prints.

She didn't say a word as she took my arm, pushed the sleeve to my button-up higher, and began writing on my arm.

"Please don't share this with your friends," she whispered, not because she didn't want them to hear but in a way that was almost vulnerable. "It'll be our space. Use it whenever you want me."

I didn't give her a reaction, didn't even nod. Her thumb played with my arm like she didn't want to let go before she finally did.

She was moving for the double doors that would lead to the elevators before she turned to walk backward, propping up the pen still in her hand. "I think I'll keep this. It will be my name soon anyway."

She gave me a final wink before disappearing.

So she'd seen my name imprinted on the side of the pen. She'd been more observant than I'd thought. I should've figured, though, that she wouldn't leave the pen.

We stood in silence as the elevator pinged as it dropped to the ground floor. Then I knocked myself out of my trance and pulled my phone out, taking a picture of my arm in case I needed the number in the future. Then I dialed it with the phone propped on my desk. "Let's see if she has anyone helping her."

I pressed the button to put it on speaker so my team could listen in and was shocked when three rings in, Lana picked up. She didn't have a phone on her, hadn't had anything on her. How did she get to a phone so quickly? Was her accomplice waiting outside for her?

"Miss me already?" she purred, and it did exactly to my dick what I suspected she'd hoped it would.

"How do you already have a phone?"

"I don't know." By the way she said the phrase in a sarcastic lilt, I knew she was going to begin teasing again. "Maybe you should do a more thorough job searching me. Though, I'll admit, with your hands on me, all you'd find is wet—"

I growled to let her know her antics weren't funny, and the softest and most beautiful of chuckles reached me through the phone. "Remember, Dorian..." She made hard, biting sounds to remind me of teeth ripping at my...

"Lana."

"I've gotta go. I'll talk to you soon, Dorian."

She hung up before I had a chance to say anything more, and I turned to the others, glad she'd reminded me of that distracting little tidbit that did a great job at squashing erections.

Thankfully, the others didn't comment on her flirtations before Finnegan asked, "What did she say in there? When she leaned into you?"

I shook my head, trying not to remember that specific encounter.

Porter quirked a brow. "Don't want to talk about it now? Little Miss Sunshine didn't give up any info?"

I rolled my eyes because Porter was a little more harsh on the females, and I didn't understand why. "It's not that she didn't give info. It's that it wasn't very useful to this case."

Finnegan squared his shoulders. "What did she say?"

"That she'd never done anything. Never even been kissed."

Lansly shrugged. "You're right. Not very useful."

Thankfully, they backed off and headed to their desks to see if they could find anything else for this case as I looked down at my arm. A weird part of me jumped with excitement at her name written there, marking me.

I pushed the thought aside and sat, hoping I could find something useful for any one of our cases because it scared me how very easy it was to fall victim to Miss Lana No-Surname.

Lana

I GAVE A TEASING smirk to Elliot, the elderly security guard at the Hollis Hotel. He was breathing hard but looking at me with that twinkle in his eyes like he could take more ass kicking.

I really liked Elliot. He was old and didn't have much family, so the security position at the hotel got him most of the interactions he needed, but even the loneliness that settled when he went home didn't deter his great moods. He always wore a smile on that wrinkled face for me. Even when I was kicking his ass.

"That all you got, pretty girl?" he poked fun as he brought both fists back up to shield himself.

"Aw, Elliot, sweetheart, I can't hurt you." My fists came back up, and I started circling the mat we were training on. "Then who would pretend to like me?"

He laughed as he moved around the mat with me, then defended as I attacked. He wasn't the best of fighters, but at least I could rest easy knowing he could defend himself if needed. The other, younger security at the hotel could handle defending their guests. Elliot could only really defend himself, but he was my favorite. He only kept this job for all the interactions anyway, so it wasn't like he was hellbound to protect citizens.

The man was sweet on me, but that wasn't why I loved him. It was because he didn't hold back when I was training him. The others always held back as if they were the ones training me, as if they could injure me.

Not that their hits wouldn't hurt, but it definitely wasn't anything I couldn't handle. Plus, I liked taking hits. It kept my body primed for future real attacks. Elliot wasn't as strong as the others, but he always actually hit me.

I darted away as he tried to strike and got him in the gut. *I* held back my strength. *I* was the teacher.

We moved again, defending and attacking, and I was reminded why I loved this job so much. It was just the right pump of adrenaline I needed, and it came with its own surprises. Like when Elliot's fist met my jaw before I saw it coming. It reminded me that no one was ever undefeatable.

Elliot stepped back as I flexed my jaw, smiling as I eyed him. "I'm so proud of you."

The twinkle in his eyes said he knew it and would continue making me so.

It was another half hour before he was wiping his sweat, and I reached for my phone, hating that subconscious part of me that was looking for a missed call.

I must've looked disappointed because Elliot asked, "Who's the boy?"

I quirked a brow as I brought my water to my lips. "Excuse me?"

"You're like those little teenagers, *cara mia*, the way you look at your phone with hope."

I rolled my eyes but couldn't help the little grin that came up with that nickname he liked to call me. "I'm not waiting for anyone's call, and I'm most certainly not like those annoying lovestruck teenagers." *How very offensive, Elliot.*

He only smirked as I gathered my things and walked beside him on the way to the small locker rooms the men in the security team were given. "I'd like to see you with a man, *cara mia.*"

"And I'd like to see you with a woman."

He paused in the middle of the hallway and lifted his hand. "Deal. You find a man, I'll find a woman."

I laughed and took his hand. There was no way he was going to find anyone.

He must've known I was thinking that because he leaned down to whisper in my ear, "To make sure you find a man, I'll come out of my hermit ways, *cara mia.*"

I pushed away with a big smile on my face. "I never should've shown you that movie, old man." I was glad he cared that much about me though.

When we stopped before the locker rooms and my not-in-the-job-description-but-I-felt-the-need-to-with-Elliot job of walking him was over, I turned to leave. Before I made it far, he called out with that nickname, and when I turned, he only winked before heading into the locker rooms.

I shook my head and giggled as my back pocket vibrated. I hated how fast my heart started to race with anticipation.

Especially since it wasn't the phone number I'd given him. This was my work phone.

It was the Shriberton Hotel.

A quick talk with them told me my work for the day wasn't over. It was simply switching industries—from physical trainer to computer skills.

I was sure whatever they were having trouble with would be a quick fix, so I ignored my growling stomach and headed over to deal with it first.

I was there in no time and taken to the room with the entire computer setup, then left alone. I'd been working here long enough for them to completely trust me, even with this new investigation up my ass. And really, they should trust me. I didn't want anything from them, and if I did, someone being in the room with me wouldn't have stopped me from taking it. They'd simply go night-night for a couple of hours while I took what I wished for.

But as I clicked away, looking for their problem and the inevitable easy fix, my mind wandered up to room 46P, the suite Mann had been in when he was murdered.

I remembered walking out of that room only an hour before the estimated time of death after fixing a computer problem they were having—one that apparently required *my* special attention.

I scoffed as I thought back to it. Mann hadn't been in the room at the time, only one of his lousy security guards—who mysteriously disappeared not long after I left the room—and he'd learned rather quickly not to try and touch me.

I'd been sure not to touch anything more than the computer while there—which was also gone—though no part of me had thought he'd end up dead. I'd simply wanted to avoid problems with the rich fucker trying to blame me for something.

But once I'd heard he was dead and I got security to tell me what they'd estimated the time of death to be, I knew the cops would be coming for me. It wasn't unreasonable—if I had been there earlier, I could've easily swiped a key card or found a way to let myself in and killed him. I could've found money to try to rob or seen his accounts on his computer and tried to take more. All of it was plausible, but none of it required death. I could've done all that without killing him. And if I had done any of that, trust you me, I would not have been seen walking out of that room. In fact, there'd be no record of me ever walking into that room. That was like Criminal 101.

But the detectives wouldn't have known that about me, so I'd sat at the cafe I knew the security would tell them I frequented—not because they were snitching but because they assumed the cops simply wanted to ask questions—and waited. I hadn't expected them to come with claims of a witness. That was still an interesting predicament I needed to check out.

I had the hotel's systems cleared quickly, and then I was on my way out. I needed to stop at a diner and grab a bite before heading home. I wanted to go to Toni's, but I wasn't sure if Lukov would be there. He had an annoying way of always visiting when I was around. And right now, I really didn't want to see him.

So instead, I went to Ted's. At least Ted's had amazing coffee, though nothing compared to the cups Nairi made, and I really shouldn't be drinking any at this time.

IT WASN'T DARK, BUT THE SUN WAS DIPPING LOW. IT was right about this time every day that I chose to stay in. It felt almost like being imprisoned, but that was the life of women. We had to be careful, vigilant. All of the time.

Me especially, considering I had actual threats from men who'd like to perform every sicko's fantasy. It was another reason I wanted the guys at Hollis to actually hit me. If I could take their hits, my body would grow numb to any perverts tried to throw my way.

I was on my way home a little later than normal, but I didn't have my headphones in, so I was sure I'd be fine. I never walked with headphones in. That was probably my paranoia from how I grew up because during the day with tons of people around didn't seem like the type of time I'd need to worry about music distracting me, but I remained vigilant. Music was only for moments I was safe in a space, even in this nicer part of town.

I was passing by an alley that I'd been hit at one too many times when I caught a glimpse from the corner of my eye. A woman was pressed against the brick wall, a well-dressed man's hand covering her mouth as the other worked at her clothes. She was struggling, turning her head from side to side like she wanted to scream. I paused to watch a moment. It looked like a scene I should stop, but I'd had this problem before—a couple roughing it in an alley and growing annoyed when I interrupted.

The sinking feeling in my stomach told me this wasn't a rendezvous.

And if it was, oh fucking well.

I moved for them, and the woman caught my eyes, hers widening as if begging for help.

I took a large breath, then swiftly kicked the man in the balls from behind. He immediately released her, crouching for his dick, and I helped the girl get out from under his weight.

"Go. Wait up front for the cops or leave, I don't care."

"What-wha-what about you?" she stuttered.

I winked. "I'll be fine."

When she ran, I didn't wait to see which she chose. The ass was already recovering, and there was a savage glare aimed at me for ruining his fun. "You? Aren't you that European bitch?"

That European bitch. How eloquently put.

"That's an interesting description considering you are also European." I didn't know who he was, but I could tell that much. Honestly, I was kinda surprised he recognized me.

He growled and ran for me. "She got away. You won't."

I danced out of his way with a smirk. "You're right. I won't get away."

I punched him as he turned for me, and he hit the brick wall beside us. It gave me the moment to shake off my hand because fuck, that hurt.

He was prepared for me when he ran at me this time. I tried to dance out, but he bulldozed over me, dropping us both to the gravel ground and knocking the wind right out of me.

Instead of reaching for my clothes like I'd suspected, he went for my head, grabbing both sides to lift and bash straight back down. Before he got the chance, I rocked my hips and whipped my elbow around, knocking his face into the pointy bone.

He growled, but his heavy load was still on me. It took all the strength I could muster to thrust him off. It didn't entirely work. I got him partly off me, giving me enough leverage to swing a leg around, but I was still stuck.

I kicked him away three times, gasping as his fist hit my gut in the middle there before I got him off me enough to roll away from.

I was quick on my feet, so I was standing before he could get up. I brought one foot up and bashed it into his nose. And though he was out immediately, I brought my foot up another time and stomped down on his dick. He didn't deserve to have a working one.

Standing over him and admiring my handiwork, I breathed out, wincing at the sting of my ribs, and turned to see if the woman had stuck around.

Nope.

It wasn't surprising. She wanted to get away from the danger as fast as possible. Fight or flight. In this case, she was smart enough to know she needed the latter.

I only hoped she would head to the cops and tell them of the ordeal so there was cold hard evidence to put this fucker away.

Turning back for the unconscious shit, I pulled out the burner phone I had on me and called the cops.

Part Two

"Man is many things, but he is not rational."

- Oscar Wilde

Dorian

IT HAD BEEN five days since Lana walked out of those doors, and every single one of them, I'd spent at least an hour staring at her number. I never allowed myself to call it, but I couldn't help but feel the need to, if only to hear her voice.

That hour also ended up being passed with constant replays of that song she'd mentioned. That last part she said she liked so much made me sad. What storm was in her past?

It was a dangerous situation I'd found myself in. If she was our murderer, she'd done a splendid job messing with my mind in only the few short hours I'd been with her. I couldn't even imagine what she could've done if given real time.

Thankfully, the office had a distraction today. Though I definitely shouldn't have been thankful for this one.

Sydney Walters was here.

She was the one who'd given us the insight about Lana's involvement with this case. Had been the one to insist she'd seen Lana move in and out of that hotel almost every day since Mann had shown up and, multiple times, left with some blood on her.

When asked why she hadn't thought to say anything before, Miss Walters argued that she hadn't thought anything of it because she'd had a little sister who'd get major nosebleeds, and that's what she'd assumed Lana had.

After the murder, Walters had thrown up talking to one of the detectives as everything began puzzling together in her head.

Though that part of the equation had quickly been cleared when the hotel mentioned Lana as part of their security detail—both technologically and physically. Plus, the woman was too smart to leave simple evidence like that if she were guilty.

But now Walters was here, and she was hysterical.

I hated when women cried. Even more so when it was out of fear. I came into this career to try and help them feel safer, so it gutted me every time I saw tears.

"Why-why-why…" she stuttered through the tears. "Is she out? I saw her again. Why, how is she… she killed him!"

Finnegan definitely had more patience with hysteria than I did, so I was glad he was the one beside her and the one leading this team.

He softly grazed her arm to let her know he was there for her, then pushed aside some of that blonde hair that was beginning to soak with her tears as he got her to face him. "I understand this is a scary situation, Miss Walters, but please answer me this—are you sure it was her?"

The fact that she'd seen Lana at the hotel multiple times, and with blood, was definitely something, but it was insufficient. Any halfwit in law school could argue us out of getting a warrant. Hell, Lana could argue her way out. She seemed talented enough to do so. We at least needed something that put Lana with Mann that night rather than simply in his suite before he was there.

My stomach roiled at the thought of Lana with that old fuck. At the thought of any woman in her twenties with him.

Walters nodded vigorously. "I know it! I know it was her! I saw them!"

I perked at the mention. Was I happy to have something against the psychologically manipulating beauty? Probably not as much as I should've been.

Walters hadn't mentioned anything about Lana and Mann being together before. "Together! I saw them making out. Tongues straight down each other's throats. I know she did this! Out of vengeance or jealousy, I don't know, but I know it was her!"

What would Lana need to seek vengeance for? Be jealous of?

I would've wondered why Walters was so affected by this kill if I didn't know she lived in the area, and had seen firsthand the amount of people who got hysterical when they thought a murderer was on the loose.

But I was more curious about what she'd just said. And the rest of my team seemed to have the same idea as I met their gazes.

I hardly listened as Finnegan calmed Walters down and promised to search twice as hard before calling for someone to sit beside her as he came for us.

We moved for the interrogation room hallway but stopped so Walters was still in our line of sight.

"She told you she's never been kissed?" Finnegan opened the second we were far enough away.

I nodded, remembering the exact distance Lana's lips had been from mine when she'd said it.

Finnegan eyed where Walters was sitting. "So which of our girls here is lying?"

"Lana has a lot stacked against her," Porter answered. "On

top of not giving her DNA or prints, she won't even give a full name. That's a girl with something to hide. If I had to guess, she has quite the record that would tie all these pieces together. Plus, let's face it, she was smart to plant that random 'fact' before evidence could be brought against her."

"It does come to reason why she'd tell Shipman that," Finnegan added. "With how smart she likely is, she was playing us from the beginning. Probably realized she could play the love-struck girl who happens to let that little piece of information out while flirting that would eliminate her from the suspect pool."

"Damn, she's good." Lansly looked lovestruck himself. "I need to get a look at her history. I bet she has some good stuff there."

I looked over to Sydney. She wasn't paying attention to us. Her leg jittered as she spoke with the cop at her side, trying to calm her down. I had no reason not to trust her, but if I did, what would it be? Why would she lie?

Porter smirked. "Jealous she's flirting with Shipman and not you?"

"Nah." Lansly came back to us. "I don't need that kind of mindfuck."

I turned back for my team. "It could be neither of them is lying. Walters's fear of what happened could be causing new realities in her head. Things she thought she saw. Or maybe she saw exactly what she said and didn't recognize the woman and needed someone to blame, and since she'd seen Lana walking out of there with blood before..."

Or maybe Lana was playing us. Playing me.

Lansly nodded. "It wouldn't be the first case with an unreliable witness."

"Or the last, unfortunately," Finnegan muttered, looking back at Walters.

Porter was asking what next when I realized my phone was dialed and at my ear.

The others stopped talking, and I could see the judgment in Porter's eyes. Could she tell I was Lana's latest victim?

"One can always be kind to people about whom one cares nothing," she answered the phone on the second ring.

"What?"

Her laugh had my mind turning to mush. "Come now, Dorian. I'm sure your mother made you read the book."

I rolled my eyes, choosing to analyze the quote she'd chosen at a later date, but couldn't help that little smile that wanted to tip my lips. Otherwise, I kept myself cool because I had three sets of eyes on me. All the same, the vision of how beautiful she might look at that moment with the smile on her face had my heart doing wild performances.

The ultimate thrill of getting to hear her voice again didn't help.

This was all absolutely ridiculous. I'd had all of two conversations with the girl, and I knowingly was foolhardy enough to fall for her tricks.

"What can your suspect do for you now, Detective?" She saved me by turning the conversation back to the matter at hand.

"Take a lie detector test." I hadn't known that would be my request until the words came out. It was a stupid plan. If she was trained enough to calmly sit through twenty-four hours of being questioned, then she was definitely trained enough to pass a polygraph test.

I hoped I could fix that part.

Unless she'd been playing me this whole time. Then not only would I be a fool, but her "passed polygraph" would be more evidence of how she wasn't our killer.

"You want me to come in for a lie detector test?" she reiterated my request.

"Yes." No. This was stupid. Stupid, stupid, stu—

"Okay. On two conditions. One, you do all the questioning."

"Done. Next." There hadn't been a moment's hesitation in my mind that I'd be the one doing the asking. Stupid, oh so fucking stupid.

"I'm allowed to refuse any questions I want to."

I thought it over. That could be counterproductive to the point, but the main purpose here was to find out if she lied about never having done anything. If she truly hadn't been kissed, then she'd immediately be taken off the suspect pool—for now—and the other questions wouldn't be important.

"Deal."

I knew she was smiling as she said, "I'll be there in half an hour, my picture of gray."

She was almost exactly on time.

When she walked through the double doors, she was in a black minidress and a cropped leather jacket that fell to her hands and gloved her fingers but not her palms.

I allowed myself the moment to roam over the black army boots, black tights, then the dress and jacket with the excuse that I was assessing her. But she knew as well as I did that I was checking her out, not that she was naive enough to fall for any flirtations on my part. That was her trick to master.

"Nice outfit," I opened when she was only a few feet from me.

She gave me a twirl, and that smile was as radiant as ever. "You like?"

I didn't answer as I nodded back toward the interrogation room. Surprisingly, she didn't tease or distract me as she turned to the hall of rooms and waited for me to lead. I moved for the same room she'd been in last time she was here. The lie detector test was already sitting on the table, and the chairs had been moved to the side so we could sit with barely any space between us.

I eyed that cropped jacket. "You know I'll need access to your arm, right?"

She gave a small smile. "I'm aware."

The way she said it made me pause a moment. She sounded vulnerable again.

I knocked myself back out. I needed to focus, stop falling for her traps, *this* persona. This wasn't the real her. But damn, if I was a crime lord, I'd do anything to have her on my side. She was perfect at messing with heads.

She didn't utter another word as she turned away from me and removed the jacket. When it was set aside, she took her seat and waited for me to strap her up to the machine.

I knew she was aware of every time my fingers brushed her skin by the way her chest heaved each time.

When we were set, I turned the detector so I could see her answers, and in turn, the camera in the corner behind me would pick them up. The mirrored wall behind me would also give my team access to her honesty or lack thereof.

Our knees touched when I sat, almost distracting me.

"Is your name Lana?" I tested.

"Yes," she answered, and I saw the way the scan picked up her answer.

"Is your full name Lana?"

She narrowed her gaze. "Pass."

Hey, at least I tried. "Are you fifty-three years old?"

Her lips twitched up. "Yes."

I glanced down at the scan to see how the lie was picked up. When my eyes were on her again, she was wearing a close-lipped smile as she winked.

"What is x in the equation eight-x plus thirteen equals fifty-three?"

She smirked, working the equation quickly but still giving the machine the time to pick up on the effort her mind took to do the work. We needed to know what her mind looked like puzzling a problem in her mind so she couldn't use that same skill to come up with lies. "Five."

Satisfied with her answers thus far, I knew the next question would throw her, but I needed to ask it to know what the pulses on the test would look like when she was *affected*.

If she was affected.

"Do you want me to kiss you?" I wasn't anxious for the answer. Absolutely not.

Yeah, I needed to call a therapist.

Her brown orbs, which had the power to hypnotize me, widened. "Yes," she whispered.

I turned it up a notch with the excuse this was for the case. I was an asshole. I knew this had nothing to do with the case. "Do you want me to get on my knees for you right now?"

Her breathing accelerated only slightly as she tried to control herself, but I also picked up when she figured out what I was doing. That spark in her eyes made me happy. I didn't know when I decided it, but I'd been waiting for that spark. I loved knowing she'd figured it out.

Even though this was bad because she could now go back to manipulating the test.

"No," she lied, but it gave me a read on what truth and lies looked like with her nerves in a blunder.

I WANTED SO BADLY for him to get on his knees and lick away the desire pooling in my panties. Saying no, even though he knew it was a lie, was just about the hardest thing I'd ever had to do. And I'd had to do a lot of hard shit in my life.

I had no idea what facts the detector was for, but I definitely would've never guessed this line of questions. I knew he was doing it to unnerve me, make it impossible for me to manipulate the machine. With the get-out-of-jail-free card of refusing any question I wished to, I hadn't planned on lying, but it was a genius plan in any case.

"Good girl," he praised, and I had to wiggle in my seat. I wasn't familiar with this feeling, this pressure building and the emptiness inside me.

"Now the real questions?" I asked breathlessly.

There was hunger in his cognac orbs as he leaned forward over his knees, and I knew even if he didn't like me, he was enjoying the show. Even more so since his back was to his team and he didn't have to hide his reactions.

"Now the real questions," he answered.

I swallowed to ready myself but forgot all about interrogation nerves when his gaze dipped to my legs pressed together.

I wondered if he'd be able to smell my desire if my legs opened even the slightest bit. That was a little mortifying, if not as equally thrilling. I hadn't yet thought about how I'd be leaving this room, but for now, I'd much rather he didn't detect just how much of an effect he had on me.

This was stupid. Flirting with him was supposed to be my fun way to pass the time, not his fun way to arrest me.

His eyes were dark, almost completely black, as his gaze met mine once more. "Did you have your first orgasm to thoughts of me?"

I couldn't even imagine what his team was picking up on the machine behind him. The lines must've been a mess of sporadic jumps. I thought he would start asking about the murder or my background now that we were past the test questions. Never would I have guessed *that* to be a *real* one.

"I thought we were doing real questions now?" I stuttered.

He swallowed, jaw gritting, before he answered, "It is a real question. Did you have your first orgasm to thoughts of me?"

"No."

His eyes narrowed. "Did you not touch yourself?"

"No." Did he hear my answer? I hardly heard me.

"Why not?"

"I—how is this a real question?" I licked my lips, staring at the ground. This was torture.

When I glanced back up, his stare was focused on my mouth like he didn't want to miss another movement. "Why not, Lana?"

"I... just haven't."

"You said all your firsts would be mine."

"Yes," I whispered. Had I been serious about that in the

moment? No, but subconsciously probably. Okay, yes. I never would've said that to a man I didn't mean it toward.

It'd been such a bold, ridiculous statement, but it'd been true in the moment.

"So if I were to kiss those lips right now"—the way his stare wouldn't break from my lips almost made me whimper—"I'd be the only one to know the taste?"

I nodded. Aggressively. They were small but telling him a million and one times that I'd be all his. Fucking stupid.

Did I even want to kiss him? To truly give *him* my firsts? He was trying to arrest me.

"I need words, Lana." There was a hint of restraint in his voice, and I was glad he was at least a little affected by my presence.

"Yes," I gasped, even though I was pretty sure I'd decided he shouldn't be taking my firsts.

He eyed the machine, then narrowed his stare my way. "You're passing."

I had no idea how this was passing. "These aren't exactly things I felt the need to lie about."

Translation: Inexperience didn't mean naive innocence. My simply never having done any of the things we were speaking of didn't mean I was afraid or shy to speak of them. I was sure he'd be more shocked to find out the filth I had up in my noggin.

Or maybe he wouldn't be.

Maybe he had those same desires.

He watched me in the stifling silence for a long time, like he was trying to figure something out. Maybe whatever had made him ask these questions was being puzzled together in his mind. I couldn't lie, I was curious. What could've possibly led to this?

I was going berserk in this quietude, under the watchful gaze of the handsome detective. I needed out of here.

After long moments of being his muse, I leaned forward. "May I ask you my own question?"

He eyed the wires connected to me.

"I'll trust your answer, Detective. No wires."

His gaze narrowed, but he nodded immediately. Just a single one letting me know to go ahead with what I wanted to know.

I dipped my head, indicating for him to come closer so we were only a couple of inches apart and my hair was blocking the camera from reading my lips. "Do you trust me?"

His breath caught in a deliciously distracting manner. He was quiet for so long after I asked I didn't think he was going to answer it until he finally whispered, so low I barely heard him. "Yes."

My lips twitched up without my permission. I actually hadn't been expecting that answer. At least, not sounding so sincere. "You can tell them I asked if I may go home now" was all I said before leaning back once more.

He didn't move for a couple of minutes—which the irrationally hopeful part of me decided was because he was trying to ease an erection—then sat up and held his hand up toward the one-way mirror before beginning to remove my wires.

Not a minute later, Detective Langly came in and took the machine out of the room. He didn't say anything, but he watched the two of us like he was figuring something out.

When Dorian and I were alone once more, I stood and took my jacket. I tried to hide my face as a wince slipped past my lips, but Dorian noticed anyway.

His brows furrowed on that gorgeous face. "What happened?"

I gave a weak smile, one that I knew showed my vulnerable

side. A side I tried to keep hidden for far too much of my life. "You guys aren't the only ones after me. It is simply unfortunate that you happen to be overlapping at the moment."

His frown was so much deeper than I would've expected as he took my jacket and helped me into it, slowly easing one arm, then the other. I was thankful for his softness in the moment. I craved that in my life. That kindness. I was grateful for his, especially considering it wouldn't get him favors with the others on his team to be buddy-buddy with the suspect.

When my jacket was on, he took my hands and slipped the fingers individually into their rightful spots. Every single time he touched a finger, I grew more needy to feel more of his touches. This entire day had been a delicious form of torture I didn't want to give up.

I didn't want to keep thinking like this—it would only make me sadder when I left—but I couldn't help it when that concentrated furrow between his brows deepened. It was too cute to think of anything else.

The gloved fingers of the hand he'd already finished moved to smooth that furrow. "Don't frown, Detective. You're too wholesome. Nothing should upset you."

He didn't say anything but finished with those final two fingers before those light brown orbs met mine. Then his fingers reached for my breasts, and I was left speechless.

Until I realized he was a gentleman and wouldn't have groped me with his team watching. He was only buttoning up the few pieces on the cropped jacket like I'd had before. He'd been attentive enough to know the top two around my neck and the bottom one hadn't been done up.

It must've been wishful thinking, but in my head, he had to force himself to step away from me and turn for the door.

He walked me out, past the desks, and through the double doors to the elevators. He stood to wait for my ride with me.

As we waited, I stared up at his handsome face and imagined it smiling as he hefted a baby into the air, catching it before throwing it back up. As he kissed the chubby spots on a chunky baby. As he softly held a newborn. As he whispered to a swollen belly.

It was always a bother to me—the fact that I'd probably never trust anyone enough, have them fall for me hard enough, to have a family of my own—but never so much as this moment.

"What is it?" His tone was harsh, needing to know what was bothering me like it was another one of his cases.

I shouldn't have let my guard down around him, let him read any of my thoughts. "Nothing," I answered as the elevator doors opened for me.

Dorian grabbed my arm before I stepped inside. "Lana, what—"

I hissed at the pain that shot up my arm, and he immediately released me, hand moving instead to my waist. "I'm sorry."

I met his gaze and imagined the tears brinking at finding out he was going to be a father. At hearing the words "I do" at his wedding. At hearing the "yes" at his proposal. It was all so beautiful.

"What is it?" he whispered this time.

I shook my head. "Nothing."

Before I could suppress the need to, I rose to the tips of my toes and kissed his cheek. It was too long of a kiss, but I didn't want to pull away.

When I did, our lips were so close I almost felt his on mine.

Then I pulled back enough to meet his darkened orbs and smiled, knowing it was fake. "Guess you have my DNA now."

"I told you," he argued, those brows still enticingly furrowed. "I trust you."

Do you? Or are you lovestruck. I scoffed internally. *Lust-struck was more like it.*

I pulled away and stepped into the elevator, letting the doors close without another word. I already missed the sight of him.

I DIDN'T KNOW how it happened, but I did—I trusted her.

I didn't want to turn away from the elevators. I wanted to peel them open and step inside with her. Or rush down the stairs so I was waiting when they opened for her.

I wouldn't do any of it, but I was shocked by how much I wanted to.

I also didn't want to turn around because I knew that though I'd somehow come to trust Lana, the others hadn't. If Sydney's testimony, coupled with the truth of Lana's lie detector, were enough, she wasn't our murderer.

But I also had a feeling Porter had followed us out here and seen her kiss me. She'd want that DNA.

And I hated to admit it after I'd just told her I trusted her, but I wanted it to0. Not to run it through any of the evidence in Mann's room but to see what Lana was hiding.

When I turned back toward my team, Porter was waiting for me with a swab in hand and a large grin. "Good job, Shipman. I guess her liking you was a good thing after all."

I didn't stop her as she swabbed my cheek, then placed it in its tube for safekeeping, winked at me, then turned for the forensics lab to put a rush order on the results. She'd been watching the interrogation, so she was as aware as I was that Lana was telling the truth about never having been kissed, but that didn't mean she wasn't still out to get her.

Lansly turned to me at his desk beside mine when Porter was gone. "You miss her, don't you, Shipman?"

I quirked a brow. "Porter? I could spend a while without her."

Lansly gave me the smirk that said he was onto something. "Miss Lana No-Name. If everything adds up with Sydney's insistence the girl Mann was making out with was the one who got him upstairs and Lana's insistence that she's never done that, she's a free girl. An innocent one."

"I think that DNA is what's really going to make her a free girl. Walters's testimony can only mean so much. She has no way of knowing for certain Mann went up to his suite with the girl he was kissing."

"But you don't need that DNA, do you, *Dorian*?" He was teasing me now, and I wondered when I became everyone's little target. "You already know Lana's not it."

I shrugged. "Call it a gut feeling."

"Or a cock feeling."

A growl passed through me. "Lansly, get the fuck back to work."

He laughed but left me alone.

As I flipped through the paperwork on my desk, I wondered if Lansly was the only one to pick up on it. I knew Porter was likely too blinded by her desire to lock Lana up to think I could ever want a suspect, but Finnegan wasn't. I only hoped he was as focused on the case as Porter and wouldn't pick up on my attraction to our only suspect.

A GLASS OF SCOTCH AND A QUIET NIGHT overlooking the city out of the floor-to-ceiling windows in my condo was the perfect way to end the night and forget about the mess that had become of my mind.

My armchair was turned to face the city, and I lounged back as the sparkling city lights lulled me into a peaceful state. All of those lights represented all of the people in the city who were living their normal day-to-day lives. People who might've called for my help in the past, those who I'd worked with and those who'd I'd failed. The justice system wasn't always so just, and I made it a point to remember the ones I'd failed, to see if there was a way I could right those wrongs at a later date.

I tried to forget about it now though. Mother had always insisted I not bring my work home so I could get a clearer head for the next day, and though it felt like a waste of time, it actually helped more often than not.

So I relaxed back and thought of my mother, of my entire family.

My father had been nearly two decades older than my mother and had passed away a few years back. He'd stayed around long enough to teach Gwendolen and me a few things, to tease us and raise us to know what a man's role in the world was and what a woman's was. He always said I took my responsibilities to an extreme, and it was the reason I felt the need to protect everyone.

My sight blurred with the memory of finding out a detective was what I was meant to be.

"Momma," I called as I slammed the town map on the breakfast table. "I got it! She was here, but they don't know where

she went. I think if we go over here and search those spaces, then we can find her!"

Momma scrunched my chin. "Oh, darling, you're so precious. But you're eight!"

"So?" I exclaimed. "We can find her."

"What's going on in here?" Father asked as he came into the kitchen.

Momma gave him that look she always gave when she was worried about us. "He saw that report on the Ashley girl and has decided he's going to find her."

Father laughed. "Is that so?"

"Yes!" I furrowed my brows, determined.

Bailee Ashely was a seventeen-year-old girl who had gone missing in the town half an hour out, and in the week since she'd been gone, nothing had been found.

"What's your plan, bud?" Father sat down at the breakfast table beside me.

I turned the map for him. "The news said they looked here and here, but that's so dumb. Why would she be in the forest?"

Father gave Momma an amused look, then turned back for me. "And where do you think she might be?"

"The news said she likes to hang out here at the shops with her friends, but why would she only be at the shops! My friends and I go to the shops for candy and drinks, then we go to other places to have fun. I think Bailee and her friends do the same!"

"And what would you know of seventeen-year-old girls?"

I crossed my arms over my chest, narrowing my eyes at him. "I'm very advanced."

He chuckled, ruffling my hair. "Oh yeah, stud?"

"I can find her! I'm just not allowed to drive there by myself."

He cackled then. "By yourself? You wanna take the wheel while I nap in the passenger, then?"

I stuck out my hand, and as Father went to drop his keys, Momma smacked him. "Stop it!"

Father brought Momma in for a hard kiss, then smacked her butt. "Leave us be, my love. We have a girl to find."

Momma shook her head as she left the room. "I can't with you two."

Father turned back for me. "So where are we going, Dor?"

My eyes widened. "Really?"

He nodded. "Oh yeah. Let's go find this girl."

I jumped down and ran for my shoes before he could change his mind, the map of the town flying behind me as I dragged it along. "Mani said his brother likes to take girls to the school on weekends because nobody's there."

"You think she's at the school?" Father waited for me at the door as I tied my shoes. "But they haven't canceled. Kids have been on campus all week, Dor. And especially to all those places people like to shack up."

I stood up, determined, then paused. "What's shack up?"

He gave an airy laugh. "Nothing, kid. So, the school? You sure?"

I nodded, running before him to the car.

The ride there took nearly forty-five minutes, and the entire time, Father and I spoke of cases and solving problems and anything else he thought might interest me. He was really good at that—finding the things that we liked and making sure he encouraged it.

The school was empty since it was a Saturday, but Father helped me jump the fence, and we made it in. Then he gave me a smirk. "Don't tell your mother we did that."

We didn't know the layout of this school, so we spent most of the time walking around until we could find what I'd been looking for—the auditorium closets. The ones in the back that held props and clothes from plays that hadn't been on in years.

The ones that were so stuffed, both inside and in front of, that nobody bothered with them. The ones that held so much stuff that no one would wonder about an odor for a long time.

"There!" I pointed.

Father amused me by moving things out of the way for us to get to the door, and he allowed me to open it.

I'd never forget the look of Bailee Ashley's eyes frozen in time as she hung there.

Father blocked me from it immediately, but I'd been the one to open that door. I'd seen her.

Momma brought Gwen, and we all spent the rest of the day in town, answering questions and helping the cops in any way we could.

They ended up finding Bailee's murderer. He'd been one of the teachers she'd been in a relationship with. I hadn't understood why that was a bad thing, but my parents told me that made the teacher a bad man. He'd killed Bailee to stop her from telling anyone.

At the end of the case, Momma had turned to me when the news came out. "I'm so proud of you."

"He's a hero!" Gwen had exclaimed.

Father's pride was the best of all. "He's our little detective."

I'd forever be their little detective.

It took two days for the DNA results to come back. Porter had insisted they get it done right away, so it wasn't shocking that it'd come in so quickly. Porter was kind of scary, so when she insisted on something, it normally got done.

Lana's DNA didn't match a single part of the evidence. Something told me her fingerprints would only match the keys on Mann's laptop we'd found with the security who'd tried to run away with it since we knew she'd been in there with him fixing it an hour before the murder.

I—or maybe only my cock—had known she had nothing to do with this, but the results gave me a chance to breathe easy because this meant she wasn't being framed either.

Porter didn't look all too happy, and Lansly and Finnegan both wore furrowed brows as we leaned around our desks and went over the case once more.

"Base knowledge. Donovan Mann walked into the Shriberton Hotel on the evening of May the nineteenth at five thirty-six in the evening after a day of meetings, and instead of heading straight up, he stuck around at the lounge downstairs for a few hours. In the interim, his security called for Lana to fix a bug in their computers. What happened in the middle isn't known, but Mann was then killed around eleven fourteen," Lansly stated. "We got the call the next morning at nine twenty-three; the body was found only minutes before. That gave our murderer about ten hours to do as he or she liked."

"He walked into the Shriberton's lounge with a dark-haired female, though not a single person could give details to what she looked like," Porter continued. "Except Sydney, and that could very well have been her mind conjuring up past sightings of Lana to fill in the blanks."

"Somehow," I continued, "Walters still saw them dry humping and making out in the dark corner they took. She stated they were doing so when she went into the lounge for a drink of water during her break. The hotel agrees Mann was there, but not a single person remembers the female enough. Nor are there cameras to pick them apart in the route they walked or the spot they chose to sit. Fucking blind spots."

"Though every one of the staff remembers Lana," Finnegan added. "She goes there multiple times a week, so they all know what she looks like and would recognize her instantly if she were the one on Mann's arm. Even if they didn't get a clear view of her face. Which adds to the hypothesis that Sydney's mind was filling in the blanks of not knowing who that woman was out of fear."

"According to Shriberton's management," Lansly continued, "Lana goes in to aid with security. It's how she makes her money. She aids them in trainings and helps them with their technology—cameras, computers, protocols."

"Security training also means she knew every way out of this situation," Porter argued. "She knew where the cameras wouldn't be pointed and what protocol the hotel would use once he was found dead."

"But the hotel insists the cameras had been moved prior to Mann's appearance that evening," I add, stupidly jumping to our only suspect's defense.

But I understood the need to keep bringing up how she may be involved. The more we did so, the more reasons we could find that it wasn't her, completely erasing any involvement she may've had with Mann and wiping the bias that she was guilty therefore blinding us to the real culprit.

"It could've been a team," Lansly suggested. "A man to mess with the cameras and do the killing and a woman to distract Mann."

"What makes you think the woman wasn't the killer?" Finnegan asked.

Lansly shrugged. "She definitely could be. But the kill was a lot. Savage. That's normally a man's playground."

"Okay," Finnegan accepted. "Let's turn to that. What do we know of the killing?"

"Overkill," Porter opened. "Mann had twenty-four stab wounds, but he would've bled out from only three of those, and by fourteen, he was dead."

"The first few were in less serious locations, which made it possible for Mann to live through them before the bleeding out was too much. He would've been able to crawl to and reach for a phone and call for help," I continued. "But they became erratic afterwards. More serious locations right before his death that ensured blood squirted out everywhere. It definitely would've gotten our killer soaked."

"Neck, chest, lungs, dick." Lansly winced as he read out that last location, flipping through Mann's file once more.

"Which means the cameras would've had to remain off of their room for the killer to shower away the evidence," Finnegan added. "We already know from forensics that the shower was used to wash away some of the mess and DNA left behind, but most of it can be attributed to the hotel staff."

"Problem is," Lansly added, "hotel staff could very well be behind this."

"So why Mann?" I went back to our most original question.

"He's filthy rich," Porter answered. "Could've pissed off the wrong investors or partners or lovers."

"He's an old fuck, but money made him desirable," Finnegan added, only slightly amused at himself for calling Mann an old fuck when they were nearly the same age. "Jealous boyfriends of girls that wanted to be his sugar babies?"

"Anything not to do with his money?" I asked.

Porter shrugged. "That's really all he had going for him."

"So back to Lana," Finnegan said, and I had to physically stop myself from reacting. "Walters saw her multiple times with blood. Knowing she's part of training security could very well have been the reason for every one of those times. I spoke with the hotel, and they said multiple times people bled, but no one really paid attention to who they stained. If every single one of those was from trainings, Lana's good. But it could very well be possible that she had an altercation with Mann or someone close to Mann before May nineteenth."

"The entire hotel also knew she stopped by that coffee shop when she was in a rush for the closest spot," Lansly added. "It's all a bit public for someone planning a brutal murder."

"Or the perfect alibi," Porter suggested.

Finnegan was lost in thought, but when he came out of it, he had a decisive look to him. "All evidence points her out, so for now, we're sticking to it. Lana's not our killer. Who's next?"

I inwardly sighed. Lana was cleared for now, and I was unreasonably thankful for it. I didn't even know this girl, yet I wanted nothing to happen to her. That sad way she'd looked up at me in front of the elevator made the feeling stronger— she needed someone to protect her, care for her.

And I foolishly wanted to be that someone.

NAIRI WASN'T WORKING TODAY, so I didn't have the coffee I'd been so excited for this morning. Toni's served the best, but mostly because Nairi made the best. Today's pot was still good, but nothing I had to come all the way over here for when I could've simply hit Ted's.

But it was bright and early in the morning, and I had my cup of mostly black coffee brewed with a butter pecan flavoring to make me feel warm inside.

None of the hotels had scheduled me in, so I didn't have work today. Days like these made me even happier to have gone with contract work for all of the spots. My bank accounts were beginning to look hefty enough to finally move away from the mess my family had left here. I wasn't sure what'd been stopping me before, but the excuse for now was that running would make me look far more suspicious in the Mann murder.

So I sat at the booth I frequented often with my laptop open. I didn't know who this witness was they'd referred to when speaking of my involvement with the case, but I wanted to do some research.

Hacking into their systems wasn't hard when my family had already encrypted their way into the systems years ago with the help of a dirty cop. The rather difficult part came with the details of the case—not everything had been submitted electronically yet.

Matter of fact, there were far fewer in the systems than I'd been expecting to find.

I scoffed. I didn't know whether to find Finnegan and his team genius for not having posted them yet, therefore eliminating chances of this specific crime I was committing from happening, or incompetent at doing this simple, yet time-consuming, part of their jobs.

I couldn't fault them with the time-consuming area though. As protectors of civilians, it was definitely more important for them to get through this case than to submit documentation into their systems. I'd hope any law enforcement would consider it so.

I huffed, staring out the window at the beautiful sun that'd risen about a half hour ago. The leaves softly brushing along evidenced the breeze, and I smiled. Images of children going for walks with their parents, of children going exploring on their bikes with their friends, of teenagers taking strolls with their first loves bombarded me.

I'd had these images my entire life, but most especially these past few years. I wanted, quite ardently, to have a family of my own. To take my children on walks where they ran ahead as I snuggled into my husband's side; to laugh as my children walked into the house dirt-ridden from the time they'd spent with their friends; to tease my teenagers for the dates they'd been on.

I turned back to my laptop, erasing those images immediately. It did me no use losing myself to such fantasies. I couldn't see a man taking on the baggage that was my family, lest they were also in that life, and I most certainly didn't want that.

Going back into the precinct's sites, I brought up everything they had on Axel Finnegan, Guy Lansly—which I now realized wasn't Langly—Ava Porter, and Dorian Shipman.

Finnegan had gone into the military immediately after turning eighteen. Had served for eight years, then applied into the precinct. He'd worked his way up to detective, sergeant, lieutenant, and now captain of his team. According to his files, he'd been offered chief position and had declined, wanting to stay on with his team. He was married and had one son, who lived an hour away with his wife and two kids. They had a pretty serene life from the looks of it.

Lansly was a thirty-four-year-old bachelor who'd been on this team for three years. He was originally from Chicago and didn't have much else about him.

It'd be something to look into later.

Ava Porter, the woman who watched me like I was a terrorist, was a thirty-two-year-old she-devil who'd been on the team for nearing six years and had a track record for putting away some of the worst of the worst.

And finally, Detective Dorian Shipman. He was only thirty-one, which for some reason felt younger to me than I'd thought, and had only joined this team last year. He was from the area and the only other member of the team who'd been in the military at eighteen, though he'd only served four years.

There wasn't much else on him, but a file of his father showed that the man had served for nearly forty years. I read over the quick description on him and sighed when I saw the date of death.

I closed my laptop after asking Leni, the barista working today, to get me another cup and decided I'd do more research on the team at a later date. I didn't have any worry they'd actually get me for this murder, but it felt better, right, to do my own research on them. They'd be going into everything about me soon enough, if not already.

When my new coffee hit my table and I handed Leni a ten-dollar bill, I rose from my spot with my to-go cup, laptop in the bag over my shoulder. It was a nice day, meaning the streets would be crowded enough and I could enjoy a leisurely walk without having to worry about an ambush.

I smiled to myself at the thought, knowing I needed to make that decision on moving soon so I could walk without worry more often, as I moved for the exit.

I was looking at the little bits of coffee that had spilled to the top of the cup's cover when I slammed into a chest, thankfully soft enough not to spill any more of my drink.

"Lana?"

My brows furrowed at that voice. Glancing up, I found beautiful cognac eyes staring down at me. "Detective Shipman." I allowed a moment of silence between us before a bit of a smirk lifted my lips, more amused than cocky. "Are you stalking me, Dorian?"

"I feel like that might be less embarrassing than admitting I ran out of coffee at my place and needed some ASAP."

My eyes narrowed, but they held the same amusement. "Why would running out of coffee be embarrassing?"

His lips tipped up in a sheepish manner as he shrugged. "I guess I forgot to mention that I'm also out of bread and eggs and sausage and potatoes and bagels and just about anything that could be made for breakfast. Even cereal."

I bit my lip to stop myself from laughing. "That is quite embarrassing, Detective. I'll give you a C in Adulting."

"Why, thank you. Quite generous."

A soft laugh left me and I was surprised by how much I was enjoying this conversation. "Well, you chose the perfect spot. Nairi's not here for the best coffee of your life, but you'll still get a kick-ass coffee and some great breakfast."

His grin was still there, beautiful under the perfect rays the sun cast on him. "What did you have this morning?"

"No food today."

His brows furrowed. "I think that also gives you a C in Adulting, Miss…"

I smirked. "Nice try, Mr. Already-Have-My-DNA."

He probably hadn't checked my name against any records yet, but soon they'd match me through my brothers, my father, hell, maybe even my mother.

He chuckled, and it was a heavenly sound. "Fine, but you still have a C."

"Hmm." My finger played at my lip. "I think B minus. I have food. I simply haven't eaten."

He tsked. "I'll stand with my grading."

I shrugged. "C's get degrees, Detective Shipman."

His grin was large now. "Have breakfast with me, Lana."

I narrowed my eyes.

"I promise no case talk. No interrogations. I'm simply trying to raise both of our grades this morning."

I laughed. "Fine. I guess you need expert help on what to order."

He held the door open for me. "That I do."

I WAS A LUCKY BASTARD.

Not because she'd actually agreed to have breakfast with me but because this meant I could finally begin figuring her out. Without the tension of being in the precinct, I hoped I'd be able to pick out definitively which of the two personas I'd seen earlier was the true her.

I expected her to take one of the tables or wait for me to choose one and pull out a chair, but instead, she led us to the back.

"This is my spot, Detective." She tucked her bag into the booth and took a seat.

I followed right across from her. "No Detectives, Lana. I told you, nothing about the case or your background."

"Mm. We're supposed to have a conversation without bringing up my background?"

With any normal person, maybe, but she wasn't stupid enough to give anything away she didn't wish to. "We'll manage."

Before she said any more, the waitress stopped at our table.

"Lana! You're back already."

"I bumped into a *friend,* and I couldn't let him come in without my secret menu tips."

The waitress, whose name tag read Leni, laughed. "Don't go telling others of the secret menu, Lan. That was made for you."

"He won't tell anyone," she whispered, then turned to me with her pointer finger at her lips. "Shh."

I chuckled, unable to stifle my laugh, then met Leni's eyes. "I won't tell anyone."

Lana sat up like she'd been presented the stage and it was her moment to shine. "He'll have the honey roasted full breakfast, make his eggs scrambled, bread wheat with no butter and a little bit of jam with the honey, sausages only, and tater tots instead of the hash. And... let's wrap it with a full honey. The honey coffee. I'll have 'The Lana.' It's been a while, and I miss it."

Watching her like this, I didn't pick up cocky at all. She was pleasant, kind, almost demure. Captivating in her quietude and smallness because though it hid who she might be on the inside, it gave away enough to prove she wasn't inherently bad.

Her beauty helped in that department, but I didn't think it had anything to do with this initial hypothesis of her. Neither my cock nor my heart were speaking right now. This was purely based on logic, and logic was telling me there wasn't a hint of the cocky persona I'd gotten at the precinct. I had a feeling being in this spot she was comfortable in, around people she had to know well enough in order to have her own secret menu, she didn't have a reason to change personalities, to hide herself. I couldn't fathom this being the persona she was faking.

So it gave to question whether this hypothesis was a correct one, and if so, how she'd known to jump personas so much to throw us off and what kind of acting she'd undergone to do it so well?

"'The Lana'? You have a whole meal named after you?"

She scrunched her nose in an adorable way a cocky, prideful person wouldn't. "I'm kind of a big deal, Dorian."

"Oh? And how is it, then, that I hadn't heard of you until recently?"

She narrowed her eyes, but there was a small lift to her lips. "I thought no talk of the case."

I quirked a brow. "Did I say anything about a case?"

She laughed, throwing her head back and eyes shining. "You're funny, Detective Hottie. I think I like you a little more now."

"So you gonna answer my question?"

She tsked. "You need a little mystery in your life."

I grumbled as Leni placed my coffee before me and walked off. "You sound like my father."

"Oh?" She smiled.

"He used to constantly tell me that everything doesn't need to be solved. He said he loved that I had a detective mind, but allowing some mystery was part of the beauty of life."

She gave a fake gasp. "What a wise man."

"You have any family advice you live by, *Lana*?" Anything that would give me a hint to who you are, who the real you is?

It only took her a few seconds to think about it, but it was time enough for me to take her in. She was so open, so light and free. She was the complete opposite of the woman I'd met at the precinct. She flirted less now and smiled more. Genuine smiles.

I simply couldn't tell which was the real her.

To close this case sooner, I'd need it to be the first.

But as me and not a detective, I hoped it was the latter. We needed more truly good people in this life, and I didn't care what she may be hiding; if this was the real her, she was good. Maybe too good. Maybe that's what she needed to hide.

"Mama used to constantly tell me that fairy tales were all real," she answered, bringing me out of my thoughts. "That every story was real, and like the telephone game, the story was simply altered with each rendition. But she said all stories, no matter how fantastical, were based in truth. I like to believe that's true."

I didn't know what I was expecting as an answer, but that surely wasn't it. What that was, on the other hand, was more evidence that this girl sitting across from me was in her soul a kind person, a giving one, a nurturing one. Maybe too much on all accounts.

"That's a very romantic way of thought."

She shrugged. "We're all romantics at heart."

"Us as humans or as your family?" *Who is your family?*

She didn't answer as Leni placed our meals before us. Mine smelled amazing with all the honey, and I had a feeling I was going to become addicted to this place and require knowledge of my own secret menu.

Lana's meal had a little bit of everything on it—veggie omelette, mini pancakes, mini waffles, hash browns, sausages soaked in syrup, and a muffin on the side.

I quirked a brow. "You're going to eat all of that?"

She grinned, eyes glimmering. "A challenge like that was what got this named 'The Lana' to begin with, Detective."

"Oh. Now I *have* to challenge you to it."

Her features were so serene as she asked, "What do I get if I win?"

"What do you want?" *Please nothing about the case.*

"I want to know a secret you've never shared with anyone else."

"Okay. And if I win..." I couldn't ask about her background. We'd established that at the beginning. Which meant no family background questions either. "You tell me..." How you learned your tech skills. How you learned to fight. How... No background. "Your plans for the future. Everything you've thought of so far."

Her lips tipped up. "Deal."

I smirked as I cut into my meal, hoping learning something of her future would give me more about her past.

"All humans."

I quirked a brow at her.

"Your question earlier. I think all humans are romantics at heart. When society isn't trying to corrupt them, all everyone wants is someone by their side, to love them. But I think my family takes that to a slight extreme."

As I bit into my honey breakfast, I barely stopped the moan from how good it tasted before responding, "I agree."

"You admit to being a romantic?"

"I think men show it differently, but when we need to take care of our woman, it jumps up. We need to be needed."

"Now I know I like you, Dorian."

I smirked. "Why's that?"

"You're a romantic."

"I thought you said all humans are."

"Inherently. But most won't admit to it because of the weakness it provides. I like that you're not afraid to admit it to your suspect."

"You're not my suspect anymore, Lana."

"For now." She smirked.

I stole a piece of her muffin. "Are you done? Have I won already?"

She scoffed. "You know your taking my food doesn't count against me. You're only helping."

I rolled my eyes as I took another piece of her muffin.

I ROLLED MY EYES. Lukov was here again.

I couldn't be too mad. I knew he had a way of finding me when I was at Toni's. A glance in Nairi's direction—my favorite barista behind the counter who had the hots for Lukov—told me she was the one who'd called him like she had so many times before. I knew there'd been a reason my pancakes had taken longer to come out. Fucking Nairi had been buying Lukov time.

Poor thing. If only she could see Lukov wasn't into her. But apparently, those small smiles he gave her continued to have their desired effects because he got these calls damn near every time Nairi saw me here. Thank the lords she hadn't been working when Dorian had caught me leaving the other day. The very last thing I needed was that bit of information getting out.

The man in question popped down into the bench seat across from me in my booth, reserved for me the way the secret menu was. I tried to ignore him, cutting into my pancakes for another bite, but I could feel his wide grin aimed at me.

"C'mon, Lani-Bunny, you know I don't like being ignored."

"And I don't like being stalked, yet here we are."

"I'm not stalking you." At the quirk of my brow, his grin grew. "I heard you were here. I could use your computer help."

"Don't you have people for that?"

"But no one's better than you," he teased, scrunching his nose like he was talking to a one-year-old as he took the fork from my hand and cut himself a large piece of my pancake.

"Asshole," I muttered as I sat back and crossed my arms before my chest.

He gave me a wink as he pulled out his computer and handed it over. "Just a little virus that I can't clear out on my own. I don't need any of the guys at home seeing it."

"What could you possibly have to hide from Ilya? He's just as skilled as I am."

"There're some things I don't need even him knowing."

I quirked a brow. He was so full of shit. "Yet you don't mind me knowing of the pornos that got you that virus?"

He switched out my stack of pancakes for his computer and went to work clearing my plate as I finally rolled my eyes and opened his computer.

Just perfect.

Exactly what I wanted to see was the screen frozen as a redhead with a short bobbed haircut was getting dicked down.

I quirked a brow at the man across from me, took a sip of my coffee, and got to work.

But, of course, we both knew he wasn't only here for computer help.

"How're you doing, Lan?" All that humor that made up Lukov was gone.

"Mighty dandy, Luk."

"I know you're going to give me that die now look, but you

know it's not safe for you to be alone. With all those investigations no less."

I rolled my eyes but focused on my task of getting that porno out of my sight.

"Serg is especially worried," he continued. "And you know when he's worried, things don't look pretty."

"Tell Serg to find someone else to worry about."

"Or I can tell him you're coming back."

"Don't waste your time, Lukov." I sighed and pushed his computer away as I finally got the thing to work again, only to be bombarded by six pop-up videos all with the same type of girl. "You've got to be fucking kidding me."

As I pulled the thing back to completely clear his computer, I couldn't help but glance toward Nairi to make sure she couldn't see because if the girl saw that she apparently was, in fact, Lukov's exact type, it'd be even more impossible for her to move on. At least now she was working with the theory that he didn't really see her.

He gave a cheeky grin at my curse and continued to gobble up my food. "How about you tell me what's going on with you? Any boyfriends?"

"Yes. Tons."

I saw his smirk from my periphery and tried to ignore the way it made me want to giggle.

"Don't be a smart-ass, Lyubov."

"Don't be annoying, Aleksandr."

He sighed but finally shut up and finished my food while I got the rest of his computer sorted.

In the silence that followed, I saw his hand shoot up to call Nairi, and I wanted to beat him for keeping the girl on a peg, constantly giving her those winning smiles and twinkling eyes only for things to never go anywhere. Good thing too. The poor girl didn't need this life.

As she came over, I turned his laptop so she wouldn't see she was the literal embodiment of the woman Lukov wanted to screw and finished up with this as the asshole across from me leaned back in his side of the booth. "Two coffees to go, please, *kyanks*. And a sandwich for Lan."

My brows furrowed because whatever he'd just called her wasn't in a language I understood. The blush on Nairi's face told me she really liked the sound of it though, so when she walked away, I kicked Lukov under the table.

He shot up in his seat, eyes snapping away from watching her walk away from him. "What?"

"Don't be an ass! You know that girl is basically in love with you!" I pushed his finally cleared computer away from me.

He rolled his eyes. "She's not. She thinks I'm cute. She's cute too."

I scoffed. "From your little searches, I'd think you find her more than cute."

He gave a devilish smirk.

"Don't even think about doing something stupid, Lukov. Leave that poor girl alone."

He stopped himself from whatever he was about to say as Nairi came back with the two coffees and my favorite sandwich. She'd gotten that ready surprisingly fast. She winked when I met her gaze, and I knew she'd already been preparing it when she saw Lukov steal my food. Yeah, she was way too good for the ass.

Lukov plopped down a hundred-dollar bill that was plenty to cover the meal and way overtip her—though she deserved it after having to deal with him—as he got out of the booth, laptop in hand. He was an inch from Nairi as he whispered, "Thank you, *kyank*."

I needed to find out what that word meant, but until then,

I pushed Lukov away from her blushing form and toward the doors. "What part of 'leave the poor girl be' don't you understand?"

"Like you said"—his smirk was teasing as he opened the diner door for me—"she's my type."

AS ANNOYING AS LUKOV WAS, I COULDN'T LIE TO myself that I loved seeing him. I lied to him all the time about it but never to myself.

Like seeing him during brunch set up the rest of my day, I was walking with ease from such a beautiful and uneventful— which was a very good thing—day.

Because I'd been enjoying myself so far, I took the long way to get back to my place. It was the most scenic and secluded way as it put me straight through a beautiful garden with high hedges, but it was worth it. I'd gone to this garden a few times in the past to think and never seen anyone else about, which for me presented positives and negatives.

I didn't necessarily need to think like I had before, but I missed the place. A stroll through it felt like the perfect wrap to the day before I locked myself home and enjoyed spending the night painting on one of my little canvases while watching a sitcom.

My hands were brushing the leaves on the hedges as I made my way through the little maze, smiling to myself, when a sudden slam hit my back.

I fell to my hands and knees, catching myself and glancing behind me at a moment's notice.

There was a man only a few years older than me getting closer. He wore all black, and the stubble on his jaw was unkempt. He licked his lips and moved to grab me, but I was already on my feet, stepping back.

"Manvel Uzbekki? What the hell do you want?"

He took a large step for me, eyeing my body like I was the first drop of water to a man in the desert. "Your pussy. Or your ass. Or both. I want both."

"You've got to be kidding me," I muttered.

He shrugged, coming in closer and softly brushing a length of my hair behind my ear. "Your brothers annoyed me."

"So go bother them."

He smirked. "Nothing would bother them more than knowing you weren't a purity any longer."

That wasn't necessarily true as long as I was a consenting participant. It would bother them because they still saw me as the little girl—unsurprisingly, considering the closest in age with me was still nearly a decade older.

"What makes you think I'm pure at all?"

His grin turned sinister. "Even better. I want that whore mouth to do things a virgin would be too afraid of."

I stepped away from his touch. "This mouth isn't going to do anything to you."

"No?" He followed me deeper into the hedges.

"Why would I want to fuck the man who just kicked me to the ground? If you wanted something, I'd consider wooing the woman."

His hand reached for his heart as he got closer still. "My apologies. Had I known you were whore enough to offer yourself, I never would've done it. Let me make it up to you." He grabbed my arm before I could make a run for it.

Not that I was going to. I didn't need him following me home or, worse, following me to my family. They'd take care of him no problem, but it'd be impossible to keep my father and brothers from forcing me to stay with them then.

I kicked at his knee, so he knew I was willing to fight and enjoyed the way he buckled. His grip on my arm tightened, but it was worth it.

"Bitch." He seethed as he shoved me into the hedges, which were thick enough to hold like a wall, and tried to rip my shirt.

My knee hiked up, but he was smart enough to cover before I could get his dick, but his distraction did allow me to slip out from his cage. When he turned for me, he was cracking his knuckles, and he looked more excited to fuck me than he had before.

I attacked and got in two hits before he had my legs out from under me. The air was knocked out of me as I hit the ground, and he was smart enough not to wait around as his foot swiftly rounded into my stomach.

I was coughing, trying to breathe again, when his foot moved for another hit. I was barely able to roll out of the way before he could completely attack me.

Manvel moved with a cocky gait to him and fisted my hair, pulling me up to my feet. "You said you were a whore. Time to suck my cock like one."

I smiled as the thought that he actually believed he could dominate me took root in my mind, then quickly punched up into his jaw. The cracking sound was satisfying even though I was almost certain nothing broke and my hand hurt like a bitch now.

Because he still had a hold of my hair, I turned as much as I could, then thrust my arm up so my elbow rocked against his nose. I did it again in swift succession until he released me, holding on to his face.

"You bitch!" His hands were covered in blood when he pulled them away, and his nose was slightly askew. Barely broken. Damn.

"You wanted me to be your whore, you should learn how to handle me."

He grimaced, throwing out every curse word in existence as he moved for me again. My leg moved quickly then, foot kicking out high so it could slam into his face.

Because of the suddenness of the hit, he couldn't block, and he stumbled back until he slid down the hedges. He was still conscious, but it looked like he could succumb to going under any minute.

I strolled up to him, taking his jaw roughly into my hand and forcing him to meet my stare. "If you pass out now, I can make you my whore."

I was sure I could find a branch just the right size to stick up his...

"I'm gonna get you, bitch."

I smirked and squeezed his nose, reveling in his whimpers at the pain. "Okay." I stepped back and took in the mess that was his face, nose crooked and bleeding, and tried to ignore the pain shooting up my abdomen from where he'd hit me, hoping above all else there was no internal damage. I needed to find out what my family had done this time to get this fucker to come after me.

Until then, I sighed, wincing at the sting running through my body, then kicked out a final time and put him to sleep. "Fucker."

Part Three

> *"Whenever a man does a thoroughly stupid thing, it is always from the noblest motives."*

> \- Oscar Wilde

Dorian

⸎

"**YOUR GIRL WAS** smart to conceal her name from us." Lansly walked into the room and dropped a file on my desk. "We definitely would've subconsciously judged her as guilty, even if for a moment. I think Porter thinks her extra guilty now."

My brows furrowed as I opened the file.

Finnegan stopped behind me at my desk to read over my shoulder, and I was shocked to be met with a picture of Lana, though she was much younger in it.

"Porter traced DNA for an actual name. It's everything I could pull so far," Lansly added.

Svetlana Lyubov Romanov.

"She's the only daughter of Ivan Romanov, head of the Russian mafia, and only sister to three older brothers who followed in daddy's footsteps," Lansly summarized. "From what I could find, she pulled away from the life years ago."

"Least now we know why she was so calm," Finnegan said. "She was probably trained for moments like these since she could talk."

My heart raced, looking down at the list of crimes her family was involved in.

She was a mafia daughter. Which meant she very well could have been framed for Mann's murder. And if she pulled away from her family, they could've been the ones behind it. Loyalty was extra important in crime syndicates.

I needed to talk to her, find out how things were left off with her father and brothers.

I calmed myself before jumping ahead. I could be creating narratives where there weren't any. This could've entirely been coincidental that the murder happened at the same hotel Lana worked.

Could be fate in a way. Forcing us to meet.

My stomach roiled at the thought. What romantic bullshit was I spewing? This wasn't fate, and nothing was going to happen between me and Lana.

Me and Svetlana.

Romanov.

Mafia princess.

But I needed to talk to her.

But first. "Where's Porter?"

Lansly shrugged. "She saw Lana's name, then said she needed a drink. Guess she clocked out for the day."

My brows furrowed. So what if Lana was a mafia princess? Why would that bother Porter enough to step away for the day?

"Also traced Mann with the mafia," Lansly added. "Nothing. If I had to guess, they're not connected to this. She's not connected to this."

The way he met my gaze told me he knew that was what I wanted to hear.

"Nice findings." Finnegan smacked Lansly on the shoulder. "Now that we can rule her out as much as possible, we need a new lead. It's been over two weeks since he was killed."

And three torturous days since I'd left her at that diner.

Every single one of those days, I'd spent the entire night staring at her number, trying to come up with a reason to call her and never finding one. I'd stopped listening to that song she suggested because after I'd determined the vulnerable girl was the real Lana, it'd been driving me crazy knowing she was hurting in any way. I'd known it'd probably make her at least a little happy if I called just to talk to her—or maybe that was my delusion—but I hadn't let myself do so. As if that would stop any feelings foolishly growing inside me.

Now I had a reason.

I didn't care if it showed that I cared for her; I needed to find out more about her relationship with her family. Let her think I was only suspicious of her for all I cared.

When the others dispersed, I grabbed my jacket and Lana's file and headed out the double doors. "I'm gonna catch up with Porter."

I was waiting for the elevator when Lana picked up.

"I didn't expect to hear from you again after falling off the suspect charts," she opened with that beautiful voice of hers. "Or am I back on?"

"I need to see you."

"Livington Bar, bottom of the Artsoc Hotel. Eight p.m." She had that ready to go way too fast.

"Okay," I said and wanted to add more, but she'd already hung up. I didn't like how agitated I felt about that fact.

As I stepped into the elevator, I reopened the file and took a look at the quick rundown of her family and the crimes they were associated with.

One in particular stuck out.

Ronald AJ Howard, hereby referred to as 'the victim' states he was held by the Romanov crime syndicate for an estimated thirty-seven days. He states he cannot know for sure as he believes he lost days at a time, but he believes to remember the day he was taken.

The victim states that the don and his heirs were among the many men he saw, the four Romanovs delegating everyone's roles. Ilya and Lukov are the consiglieres. Sergei, the underboss, is the enforcer and said to be one of the most ruthless of men in position within the mafia. Ivan, the boss, is not far behind his eldest son.

The victim's claims are as follows:

"When I woke up, I wasn't chained to anything or locked anywhere. I didn't understand at first that that made my situation more dangerous. The Russians... they're vicious. They didn't tie me up because they fight with no rules. No gloves, no pads, nothing. They made me get up and fight them 'like a man.' The Underboss fought me. He hit so hard, I bled with the first punch, but that didn't stop him. He kept going, and all I could do was defend myself. I couldn't throw any punches. It hurt so much. I don't think I lasted more than a minute or two on my feet. When I fell to the ground, they were all yelling at me, but I don't remember it. I just remember the blood falling into my eyes. One of the brothers jumped into the fight then, and they beat each other. I don't know how much of the blood I was seeing was on them and how much had simply gotten into my eyes.

"They didn't fix me up after that. I don't think they cared whether I made it long enough, but I must've been left alone for a couple of days. I remember the sun streaming through the crack of a window in that basement every time I came out of unconsciousness. When they came back, the Underboss wasn't there, but the Boss and the other sons were. And a few more of them. The Boss wanted to fight too. I didn't want to get up, but there were so many guns around and... The Boss wasn't as brutal as the Underboss. It hurt a lot because I was already injured, but the

Underboss was worse. He was vicious. Came back to 'fight' me again a while later. Days started bleeding together at that point.

"I don't know what they wanted from me. When I asked, they made a joke of it. I don't think they had a reason."

No reason was found on behalf of the police department.

"One of the days, they brought in two more. I only got to speak with them a moment, hoping they could shine a light on why we'd been taken. I didn't get much. They made the two guys fight each other. The Underboss said they could fight each other or he could fight them one-on-one. When they saw what he'd done to me, they chose each other. The Underboss wasn't happy—none of them were, with how the fight was going—so one of his brothers stepped in and showed the guys what a real punch was like. I think one of them broke a nose from that. When he stepped back, he said they could fight each other or one of them. Then the guys really fought, the men calling out bets. It was to the death. They left the winner alone with me after that.

"I didn't get away. I don't know what they wanted from me, but they must've gotten it or gotten tired of beating on me because they dropped me off blindfolded in the middle of a park. I was so weak, so broken, I only made it to the edge of the park so passing cars could see me before falling over. Ambulance and police found me then."

The victim required three reconstructive surgeries to his face and one to his hip.

This case has been closed on retraction from the victim. With no other evidence, the case has been deemed closed.

I'd been leaning against the wall on the ground floor, finishing up the read, when I glanced up, sighing in contemplation. I'd have a lot to consider in regards to Lana later, but for now, I tried thinking up spots Porter could've hit up. She wasn't much of a drinker, so she didn't have a usual, which also made me guess she wasn't choosy about them.

I chose Hannigen's because it was the closest.

Half of me was surprised to find her there. Mostly because a large part of me thought she'd said she was going drinking so she'd be left alone while she went after Lana.

She was sitting at the bar, cup of brandy between her hands as she stared into the drink like she could turn it into a magic ball or something.

"I don't think the intensity of your stare changes how the drink affects you." I took the stool beside her and turned for the bartender. "Just water."

Porter side-eyed me. "What're you doing here, Shipman?"

"I'm here to ask you that same question. I heard you found out Lana was a mafia princess."

She snorted, then took another small sip. "Yup. Just making this case more exciting."

My water was placed before me, and I waited for the bartender to walk away before asking, "So what is it? Why're you here?"

"Just enjoying a little drink. We've been working hard cases. I thought I deserved it."

I shook my head. "C'mon, Ava. What is it? Finding out she's a mafia princess couldn't have upset you this much."

She gave me a displeased smirk. "Has it upset you at all? You still like her, don't you?"

I cleared my throat and took a drink of my water. "Who she's related to doesn't make her one of them, Ava."

"She's got computer skills. There're a few cases from years ago that were never fully figured out," she said. "I'd bet everything I own she was behind it."

I nodded because I was sure those were Lana's works too, but I didn't intend on judging the woman she was now for them. "But that's not what's bothering you. What was so bad about finding out who she was that you stopped working for the day?"

"Who said I was done for the day?"

I quirked a brow. "You're drinking. You're done."

"Yeah, well..." She took another sip.

"Porter."

She sighed and finished off her cup, slamming it on the bar top before turning to me. "I knew there was something about her I didn't like. I just couldn't put my finger on it. Just something familiar that was nagging at me."

"That's why you were extra bitchy to her?"

She rolled her eyes and raised her cup to the bartender for a refill. "You've heard the stories of that year I had to take off, right? I started back right when you were starting with us."

She'd been shot in the chest wearing no bulletproof vest—considering the job she'd been undercover for had her changing in front of others, she hadn't been able to wear one—and had still somehow survived. "Yeah, so?"

"Little Lana's big brother Sergei was the one to do it."

I almost dropped my water as I was placing it back down. "What?"

She took a sip from her new cup. "Yup. Found me out and shot me from across the living room we were in. Stared me in the eyes as he did it."

"How is he not locked up?"

"One of his men took the blame. Atop simple loyalty, he wanted to be locked up because he had vendettas to complete against people who had hurt his little sister. It was my woozy word against a confession."

"Ava..." What was I supposed to say to that?

She shrugged. "I know that part's not Lana's fault, Shipman. I don't blame *her*. I just... God, I hate her brother."

I was now staring down at my cup like I could make it change objects. "She left that life."

We didn't turn for each other as she said, "But did she leave that family? If her brother didn't mind doing that to a cop for a lousy undercover project, what would he do for her?"

Those were all questions I intended on learning the answers to when I saw Lana tonight. I fool-heartedly knew I could trust whatever answers she'd give me.

"You think Sergei had something to do with Mann's death?"

"No," she moaned. "I wish he did so I could lock his ass up for the rest of his worthless existence, but no, I don't think he did it."

I chuckled.

"What?"

"It's kinda crazy. How one man could possibly be the best brother for her and the worst piece of existence for you."

She actually chuckled, and I was proud of myself for getting it out of her.

Until I turned to look at her and realized the laugh was leaning toward hysterical over humorous.

"Tell your girlfriend I'm sorry."

My brows furrowed.

She smirked. "For when I kill her brother. My bad."

Now I was laughing. "Like you would kill him."

"Leave me alone with him, and trust you me."

I took another sip of my water, then got up to leave. I kissed her temple right before saying, "Take the day, Porter. We need your ass clearheaded and on the job tomorrow. Who knows, maybe you'll find something to stick it to Sergei."

She grinned. "Hopefully."

IT TOOK ABOUT HALF AN HOUR FOR ME TO GET TO the Artsoc Hotel. I was way too early, so I remained in the car and went over the file Lansly had given me about Lana's past again.

Svetlana Lyubov Romanov. It was a beautiful name.

October seventeenth nineteen-ninety-eight made her almost twenty-five years old. Only a few years younger than me.

She knew how to speak English, Russian, and Spanish. The desire to hear her whisper words in my ear in each language rushed through me with a force I'd never experienced before.

The part of the file that listed her combat and computer skills was newer information we knew because of her jobs at these hotels since all the other info had been based off her family, given she'd never been arrested before. Technically, she'd never even been part of the mafia's crime syndicate, so she'd never been researched heavily enough to have gotten that deep into her strengths.

There wasn't too much information about her in there, but as I flipped the page back to those on her brothers and father, I sighed. I'd only read that one account so far, but I didn't want to continue yet. I definitely would, but I wanted to hear her side before planting all those negativities into my mind.

My leg jittered at the fact that I was still waiting, but I was glad that the detour with Ava had eaten up some of that time.

At twenty before eight, I went into the bar in hopes she'd shown up early.

She hadn't.

As I stood to the side, hands in pockets, watching the door, I wondered where she was coming from, how she was getting here. I hadn't seen any cars in her records. Nor an address, which was a nagging thought I tried to push aside.

When the door finally opened and her beautiful dark hair flowed in, I felt a piece of me loosen in my chest. She searched the space for a moment before finding me, then those perfect, puffed lips broke into a small smile.

When she approached me, I pushed off the wall so we were barely a foot apart. "We're not talking here."

She quirked a brow. "Whyever not? This is a much nicer place to question me than the interrogation room. Though I must confess, of all our meetings, your stalking me to Toni's was my favorite."

"This has nothing to do with the case. And I wasn't stalking you. I live right by there." I ignored the way her eyes shined up at me. "In any case, we need to be alone so you feel comfortable talking." That was technically true. I didn't think she or her family really had anything to do with the case—unless she was in a bad place with said family and they were framing her—so this wasn't about getting her to slip up a confession or evidence.

She narrowed her eyes, but I saw that she trusted me enough not to trick her in this moment. "Fine. Take me to yours."

"Or yours?" I asked hopefully. We had information about Svetlana, but I wanted to know Lana.

She smirked. "Nice try."

"Lana, I mean it. Nothing to do with the case. I just need you to be comfortable." Something in the way she silently analyzed me instead of saying anything bothered me. "Do you trust me, Lana?"

"With my life, yes," she answered instantly. "With my freedom, not so much."

My gut felt like it'd taken a beating. "I deserve that, but I'll earn it. Just, we need to talk, and you need to be comfortable when we do."

She eyed me but didn't back down. "Then take me to yours, and let me wear one of your shirts."

I gave an airy laugh because I couldn't help it. But as I stared down at her, I needed to know if her flirtations were a genuine part of her personality or if they were a defense mechanism. "Okay."

My hand was at her waist then, needing to touch her, as I turned her back for the door and settled said hand on the small of her back to lead out.

I'd parked only a few doors down, and in no time, I was opening the door for her to get into the passenger seat. I was in my car and driving off quickly, feeling the need to get home as fast as possible. All in order to find out more about her but also to selfishly have her all to myself. I could already hear my entire team, but especially Porter, biting my head off for compromising this case.

I didn't realize my hand had fallen on her thigh, thumb subconsciously brushing her skin, until I heard her gasp beside me. I pulled away instantly, internally chastising myself. "I'm sorry. I didn't mean—"

She grabbed my hand and dropped it back to her thigh. "I liked it."

When we stopped at a red light, I brought her hand, still clasped to the one I had on her thigh, to my lips as I leaned over the console. "I'm not going to touch you tonight, Lana."

"But I want you to," she whispered, and I think even she was shocked the honesty came out so effortlessly because her eyes widened a little at the words.

A grin broke on my face, and I kissed her hand. "I know. But I'm already being a jackass. At least let me be a semi-gentleman and take you on a couple of dates first. And earn your full trust."

She nodded, but my focus was on the small bit of light that settled into her eyes, like she favored me more for that answer.

I was so distracted by her it was only when she said, "It's green," that I moved, dropping our hands back to her thigh and interlocking our fingers, Porter's voice chastising me the entire time.

I WAS ENRAPTURED with the view from the floor-to-ceiling windows on the other side of his apartment as he peeled my coat off. It was beautiful. I could imagine sitting wrapped in a blanket by that window on a rainy night and simply witnessing nature run its course. The view from here was even better than the one I'd scored.

He had a couch beside the window and a love chair directly in front of it. It was all placed above a beautiful rug with a coffee table between to tie it together.

And no TV.

That small fact probably shouldn't have shocked me as much as it did.

Dorian turned me around before I could assess much more. His hands were on the buttons of my cropped jacket and he wore a delicious-looking grin.

"What?" I couldn't help but smile back.

He lifted my hand. "I'm not going to take your fingerprints."

My smile turned down slightly. "It's not for fingerprints."

His brows furrowed before his gaze jumped to my hand. "Cold?"

I shrugged. "Not always, but just in case."

He didn't look pleased with the answer, and I wasn't sure why. He peeled the leather off my fingers and, to my shock, kissed each one before moving on to my other hand. It was frustrating, considering he'd already told me he didn't plan on touching me tonight.

But I let him do it anyway, took pleasure in this innocent intimacy.

When all my fingers were properly kissed, he peeled the jacket down my arms, and it took everything in me not to push forward and kiss him. His lips were so tantalizingly close, and the glimmer in his eyes said he knew it was affecting me.

When he turned to hang my jacket and his coat, his body blocked my sight, but I knew he was messing with the apartment's temperature too. I wanted to chastise him that I'd be okay, that my hands weren't cold at the moment, but it made my little heart sing that he would care enough to do so. I wanted to be taken care of. It felt nice.

Then he turned and interlocked our fingers, and though I loved the feeling, I was more than confused by it.

"The living space," he declared at the area I'd been assessing before, then pulled to the right to the open plan. There was a breakfast island cutting between the living room and the kitchen areas.

"The kitchen." He continued down the hall and pushed a door to the right open but didn't stop for it. "The bathroom." And further down to the end of the hall. "My room."

He didn't open it but stepped aside for me to do so.

My gaze narrowed on him, unsure of what was going on. Why show me his bedroom if he didn't plan on touching me tonight? Why bring me here at all? What did he want with me?

Would he still want those things when he found out my full name?

I tried to push the persistent questions aside and allow the night to progress however he had planned, but it wasn't in my nature to leave questions unanswered.

His room was masculine and exactly what I would've expected from Detective Dorian Shipman.

Dark colors accentuated the floor-to-ceiling windows that continued in here. A wooden headboard with matching night-stands and a high mattress with deep blue sheets that matched the rug decorated the space. The black walls with lights every-where to feed the ambiance finished the romanticism of the room. It was a perfect space.

But my attention continuously fell back to that bed. It was definitely big enough for the both of us, and I couldn't help wondering how comfortable it'd be—couldn't help wondering what positions he'd put me in on top of that mattress.

Then his chest hit my back and knocked me out of my fantasies. His breath at my ear was like a raging juxtaposition of an enticing flame tingling my nerves and a bucket of ice-cold water. This breath delightful, his words not so much. "Not for a couple of dates, Lana."

I turned for him, barely keeping myself from grumbling like a child.

He surprised me by cradling my face in between his hands as he smiled down at me. "And your full trust. That's far more important."

My stomach grumbled before I could argue that we were already there, even though I definitely didn't trust him yet, and the only two dates we'd been on had been in his interrogation room and his stalker breakfast.

He chuckled. "Hungry?"

"For something you're not offering," I muttered.

He fully broke out into laughter as he took my hand and led us back to the kitchen.

Back in the safety of the main space, his hands fell distractingly over my hips as he lifted me to sit on the counter. "I only have some leftover soup. Is that okay?"

"Perfect," I whispered, our faces so close I felt his words on me.

He took a deep breath, and I was glad to be having some kind of effect on him as well.

Then he pulled back, took the soup from the fridge and a pot from one of the cabinets, and placed it all over the stove. While he let the food warm up, he moved back to where our coats were hanging.

I fell back into the cabinets, wondering what file he was going to show me. I'd seen him hide the manilla folder inside his coat before and had tried to ignore the nagging feeling that this rendezvous was, in fact, about the case.

To my surprise, he handed me the folder, then backed up to stand by the warming soup. "I trust you. I didn't need to test your DNA."

"But your colleagues would want to, and it wasn't worth the fight to refuse them, especially when you were a little curious yourself?" I smirked but didn't open the file. "If I had anything to be nervous about, I wouldn't have left my DNA."

He sighed. "They didn't find anything connecting you to the case, but they still wanted to see who you were."

It's cute that he was saying *they* when he surely wanted to know who I was more than his team had.

I glanced down to the manilla file. "You found out about my family?"

He gave an apprehensive nod.

I gave a humorless laugh now. "Am I a suspect for something else now?" I could remember three, maybe four cases the cops were never able to place because they couldn't catch me as the computer wiz behind tasks for my brother and father.

"No." He looked like he wanted to move for me but stayed back. "And to me, you'll never be a suspect again. I just wanted to know if you would like to talk about it."

Should I trust that answer? My freedom would be on the line if I did.

So I tested him. "Never? I'm sure if you guys tried hard enough, you'd find a connection between me and an unsolved crime."

He swallowed, jaw clenching. "Never, Lana."

We remained silent then as he filled two bowls with soup and placed them on the breakfast bar, then broke two chunks of bread and filled two glasses to the brim with water.

When everything was ready, he turned back for me, and I allowed his hands to settle around my waist, then waited as he stood there.

"If you don't want to talk about th—"

"I do. I want you to know me, Dorian." I really did. I was only afraid of the outcome of knowing me.

His lips quirked into a pleased grin as he pulled me down from the counter and led me to the stool at the bar.

I took two spoonfuls of the delicious concoction before saying, "My dad and mom loved each other, and they loved us." He seemed shocked to hear that which wasn't surprising considering people always thought mafia men were cold. Correction: considering people thought mafia men were *only* cold. "But my mom chose that life, chose to be with a mafia man. My brothers grew up loving our father and wanting to be just like him. To them, nothing but the mafia life made sense. And honestly, I see their point sometimes. But that was the problem—sometimes. I was the black sheep. I wanted a normal life, not a mafia one. Now, I'm stuck in the middle, still trying to make my way to the other side."

"They were unhappy you left?" he asked around his spoonful.

I shrugged. "Understandably so. I was the baby and the only daughter. My mom died when I was ten, so I was the only girl left in the family, and my father and brothers loved me too much to want to let me go. But my mom had always told my dad that if any of us wanted an out, we'd have it. He'd promised her, and as much as he loves us, he loved my mom more. He'd never break a promise to her, so he let me go."

"How long ago was that?"

"Almost six years. I was nineteen and had enough money saved up, and I just wanted to be normal, boring." I finished my soup before saying, "My dad and brothers tried to give me money so I could buy a nice place and start my life, but I couldn't take it. It felt like they were trying to manipulate the mafia life back in since it'd be paying for my life. They tried for years to give me money but now stick with checking on me and offering a chance to go back."

"You always refuse?"

"I told you, I want a boring life. I wanna be the soccer mom, not the gangster's wife."

He tried to fight his smile, which made him more adorable. "And you teach security to the opposition whenever you can?"

I gave a sinister smile now. "Well, I have to make their lives a little more interesting. As it is, my family can walk in and out without a problem. What fun is that?"

His smile dropped. "You think they're angry with you for it?"

"Teaching the security teams?" My brows furrowed.

He nodded, assessing me, and it gave me the moment to realize what he was asking me.

"They didn't try to set me up, Dorian."

"Can we know that for sure?" His tone was hard-edged and it made me stupidly happy that he cared this much.

"Yes. I wasn't framed for this. Just a perfect match for what was needed. I don't have hard feelings for whoever thought I was responsible—I'm actually kinda honored so many people believed me capable. But I can assure you, my family had nothing to do with this."

"Lana…"

"Dorian, trust me." *Please.* "If my family was involved, they'd be the ones going in after the murder to make sure nothing of me was left behind, not the other way around. And if that were the case, best believe you'd never even know I was in that room an hour before—no computer, no footage, no witnesses."

"They still protect you?"

"They're just as irritating now as they were when I was living at home." And I still loved them dearly for it, even if it cost me that normal life I wished for.

He didn't look upset with the news. "They still protect you."

"I probably shouldn't have told any of that to the detective I'm trying to get into bed, huh?"

He laughed and pushed away with the two bowls in hand. He began the dishes as he turned his head to me. "Can I hear about them? Your family?"

An involuntary smile broke across my face. "My family. Ah, where to begin?"

"The head, I'd presume."

"Or the neck?" I counter. "You know, the neck can snap the head any which way she pleases."

He laughed, and those shining eyes met mine. "Is that what you are, Lana? My neck?"

I bit down on my lip to fight the even bigger smile that wanted out. "The head was my father, of course. Ivan Viktor Romanov. But the neck? The neck was my mother, Sveta Romanov. I was named after her. My father wanted Sveta exactly, but my mother wanted me to have individuality, so they met in the middle. She was the one who started calling me Lana because my father insisted on calling me Svet, and she wanted me to have that individuality. She was beautiful and demanding and could chop off my dad's balls in a second. He was probably only ever afraid of her."

I could talk about them all night.

Dorian

SHE SPOKE of her family the entire night.

Right up until her head drooped on the couch we'd moved to. She fell fast asleep with the tale of her brothers beating up stuffed animals to make her happy still on the tip of her tongue. She'd recounted a million stories of her brothers and father, and none of them presented as the Romanov men their crimes and victims knew them to be. They were completely different with her.

I enjoyed my time taking her in as she rested there. She was beautiful. Always had been. I'd noticed it the moment she'd walked into the precinct and had been annoyingly pleased when she took a liking to me but had denied myself the opportunity to appreciate her fully.

Now I did, and I was mesmerized.

But she had a tiredness to her. She hid it well, but when it was only the two of us, that mask dropped. Even at the beginning, when it was only her hair that curtained us away from the others, she'd allowed a form of vulnerability there. Maybe she recognized that, deep down, I wanted the same things as her.

There was less of that tiredness as the night progressed, as she settled into my home, a place she'd always be safe. As she spoke of her family, which I assumed she didn't get to do much, lightness filled her brow orbs, and I had to wonder if this was the first time she'd felt safe in years. Completely so, both in body and mind. Safe to speak of her family and know she wouldn't be hurt or judged for it.

I needed, more than before, to see where she lived now. Was it as safe as my place? Was it dingy so she could stay away from leaving a paper trail? Why didn't she have that quieter, white-picket-fence life away from the mafia she desired so much? Why stay in a business related to the field she was trying to leave?

I didn't let myself think too hard about any of the possible answers because, at least for now, she was where I could protect her.

I lifted her into my arms and moved for my bed, where she could sleep comfortably.

Placed in the middle of my bed, shoes long removed, I was annoyed that I couldn't change her into more appropriate sleepwear.

That was the wrong word. I certainly could change her. I simply wouldn't. The sick part of my brain had decided the first time I got her naked would be so I could make love to her. To cherish her body the way she desired, the way she'd held out in hopes for all these years.

And now was most certainly not that moment.

But her shirt did ride up as I was positioning her down, and I got a glimpse of something I really didn't like. I wouldn't invade her anymore after this, but I pulled her shirt a little higher because I needed to see what was marring her skin.

My teeth damn near ground out of my mouth as I took in her stomach. A large bruise against her ribs and three small cuts lower by her jeans told me this had something to do with the reason she couldn't fully get that "boring" life she desired. Her opposite side held another smaller bruise that was too low on her stomach, just peeking out of her pants, for me to properly see.

I eased her shirt back down and took large breaths in to remind myself to remain calm when all I wanted was to hunt down the fucker who'd done that to her and take my time with him.

But I had no way of knowing who he was, and Lana wasn't yet at that point in our relationship where she could trust me with that answer.

I also needed to ease away my anger at her. She hadn't told me because she didn't fully trust me, and I couldn't be mad about that. I needed to get her to a place where she knew I'd never hurt her in order to finally learn every little detail of her life, as Lana *and* Svetlana.

Eventually, I convinced myself to stop staring at her and go to bed, so I tucked her in and realized my room finally looked finished. It caused a little smile to rise on my lips as I leaned down to kiss her forehead.

I didn't want to move away, but I knew another second and I'd be wiggling in beside her. She didn't need that. She needed her privacy. To know she was here because I wanted her, not just her body.

I quickly changed into some pajama bottoms and headed to the couch. As I was preparing to end the night, my phone rang on the coffee table.

"Hi, Mom."

"Hi, sweetheart. I'm sorry for calling so late."

"Don't be. Another restless night?" She'd had a few too many of those since losing my dad. She said it was because she'd lost the ease of having a man at the house, and it made me want desperately to find her someone to spend the rest of her life with. She'd already refused my moving in with her.

"Yes," she answered solemnly. "I'm already in bed. I won't keep you long. I just wanted to hear my boy's voice."

"Keep me as long as you need, Mom."

"How're you? You sound happier? Am I delirious with sleep already?"

I laughed as my attention snagged to my bedroom door across the hallway. "I am happier, I think. It's new."

"It's safe to say it's a woman, then?"

"I'd call that a sound theory."

I knew she was trying to keep in her excitement in order to keep me talking. "Oh? And how'd you meet?"

"At work."

"Really? A new hero in your team?"

I laughed. "No. Not necessarily."

"Is she caring? Kind?"

My eyes glazed over as memories of all our encounters shot through. She'd played a persona at the precinct, and now I knew it was to keep us from seeing the real her. Because the real her was soft, too good to hold it together for a twenty-hour hold. "Too much for this world."

"Well, then she's lucky to have found you. Do everything in your power to keep her so."

"Yes, ma'am."

She laughed. "I love you, darling."

"I love you too, Mom. Everything good on your end? Lulu good?"

"Yes, yes. Everything's the same. Lulu's a spoiled princess, but she's very good."

"Okay. I'll come by soon."

She yawned. "I know. See you then. Good night, Dorian. Dream of your girl."

I laughed. "Good night, Mom."

When the phone cut off, I stared at it with a wide smile. She was the purest woman alive. I had no doubts she and Lana would hit it off right away.

I dropped the phone and lay back, a blanket thrown over me and a hand behind my head, sighing as thoughts of all that had happened in the last few weeks invaded me.

That's how long I'd known Lana—a few weeks. And of those, I'd only spoken to her a few times. Not even a handful. Yet I knew with everything in me that I trusted her and that I'd protect her if and when the need came. For now, I was glad she had the unconditional protection from her family, even if that meant the mafia employed some very illegal methods.

Finnegan and Lansly would say I was thinking with my dick.

Porter would call me a naive boy.

But I didn't care. They weren't the ones feeling this immense need to be beside her.

I fell asleep to thoughts of her safe in my bed and considering what I'd like to make her for breakfast.

I WAS AWAKE EARLY, AS PER USUAL, BUT I DIDN'T immediately get up like I normally would. Instead, I stared up at the ceiling for what felt like forever, reminiscing on the dream I wish I hadn't awoken from.

My father was alive in it, leading the route to the top of the volcano. He'd always loved those types of vacations—ones that consisted of adventure over sightseeing.

He led with my mother following right behind. My sister, Gwendolen, and her husband were also there, but the best part was that Lana was part of the group that I closed off.

Lana and Gwen were laughing, speaking of something I couldn't remember, but it had to do with my father. I knew that much because the memory of his wide grin as he turned for the girls, mouth moving in conversation that was lost to me, was so strong it was like it'd actually happened.

We did as we had in all our vacations growing up and hiked the trek with a picnic in the middle, my father teasing us as my mother chastised him, my brother-in-law and me chatting as the girls whispered to one another.

When we reached the top of the volcano, we were all excited about exploring it, taking a look inside. My father stood by my side at the edge of the hole, and his words were so clear I could still hear his voice.

"She's a good one, Dorian."

"Thank you." I'd beamed.

"She'll raise great kids. Like your mother did for me."

"She has a dangerous past."

He shrugged. "Trust your heart, son. Logic can always explain away the things we feel, but your heart never lies to you. Make her happy."

I nodded, staring off at the skies that looked a pristine blue with clouds bringing the heavens down. "Mom's happy. Not as much anymore though."

His voice was solemn. "I know. But she will be again. Soon."

"I love you, Dad."

"I love you too, son."

Lana's acceptance into the family wasn't the only message I got from that dream. It let me know my father was watching over my mother still, following her with his heart and not his head.

"I love you, Dad," I whispered into the morning before finally starting my day.

I remained silent as I readied the coffeepot for brewing because I didn't want to wake Lana.

While the coffee readied, I headed to the bathroom to wash up and pondered whether Lana would be okay using my toothbrush. I was confounded by how much I wanted her to be okay with it.

If not, I had a few extras in the drawers for when it was time to switch mine out, but I wouldn't be mentioning that until she turned mine down.

When I finished, I wanted to keep quiet and let her continue sleeping, but the desire to get a glimpse of those beautiful eyes of hers won out. Then maybe I could get a shower in.

When I reached my room, the bed was completely made and Lana not in it.

My brows furrowed as I made my way through the room, the closet, back out to the open living space. "Lana," I called out to no response. "Lana."

I went back to my room to find a note on the nightstand.

Detective Hottie,

Thank you for last night. I don't think I've ever slept so well in all my life, but definitely not since leaving my family. I owe you for that.

I stole one of your shirts so I can wear it while I touch myself since you decided to leave me hanging last night. :(bad detective.

xo Lana

P.S. I used your toothbrush ;)

I was annoyed she wasn't here, but I couldn't say I wasn't pleased with that last line. Actually, I was pleased with the whole letter, though I tried not to think of her wearing one of my shirts as she touched herself. I definitely didn't think my poor dick could take the visual.

I grumbled the entire way to the shower. I made it freezing cold to wipe away my erection, then shrieked as I got in.

Man down south wasn't very happy with me, but he started going down, which was what I needed. I'd allow him to get all worked up when Lana was mine, but until then, I needed to convince myself to get back to work.

Lana

I **WAS** in an alley far enough out of the city that I didn't need to worry about anyone trying to attack me unless they'd followed me here, and I knew I hadn't been followed.

I was in an abandoned area of a smaller town, so I also knew that I wouldn't be bothered. I'd been here enough times to gather that much.

Though an alley, the space was closed off enough to feel safe to pull out my weapons. Weapons I probably shouldn't have access to or knowledge of how to use if I wanted to have that quiet, white-picket-fence life, but oh well. For the time being, I was still part of the life, even if by only a little bit, so I needed to maintain my trainings. I preferred to do that out here in my private space, and given all of this newfound attention on me, it was my safest bet.

I dropped my duffle bag and took my time setting up the targets at the deadend, stacking throwaway crates and boxes with cans in order to select the perfect aim. I tried to make it contained so the clean-up process of picking up all of the bullets and clips was easy. Neither I nor anyone associated with my family had their names attached to these weapons, so there was no way for them to be traced back to us, but I still liked to clean up. The further I could keep trouble, the better.

Then I was back at my duffle, shuffling through my guns to pick out which one I wanted to start with today. I settled on an HK 45 pistol, then pulled out my suppressor to attach. The very last thing I needed was for anyone to hear gunshots and call the cops.

This gun was perfect for what I needed. It only carried ten rounds, so it made sure I took care with every bullet used and gave me the time to work on my skill and technique.

I stood as far away from the targets as I could without being detected by anyone who may pass on the streets—the ivy growing on the two buildings and coming together by the entrance of the alley helped in keeping me hidden. When I was ready, I held the gun with both hands—because one-handed practice always came at the end as something that would be used as more of a last resort—and prepared my breathing. These sessions were more for my own peace of mind than because I *needed* the training. I'd been practicing using a gun since I was eleven years old; I certainly didn't need training. It was more of a cautionary practice to make sure I never lost any of my skill and patience and targeting.

As one round shot, I thought of my family and how happy they'd be knowing I was still in this life. That they would see it as both a way to keep up practice but also as a way to keep me prepared in case I needed to be called in to their crap.

As the second flew, I thought of what Dorian might think if he saw me like this.

As the third went, I imagined Elliot watching me fire. Would he be excited to see me kick ass the way he normally was in our combat trainings, or would he be mortified that I was so good at it?

As the fourth soared, I pictured that white-picket-fence life I always wanted with my kids running around in the back, getting dirtier than it seemed possible to be while I baked cookies for them.

As the fifth hit its mark, I pictured that same white-picket-fence life except this time with moments where the children would also have trainings the way I had growing up. Maybe not as complex, but ones that taught them how to use weapons, from guns to knives to bats to anything else.

As the sixth shot fired, I thought of my parents standing together as they watched me practice. They'd done such a good job raising us that it was my life's mission to emulate it. Maybe not in exactly the same ways since I had no intentions of staying in the mafia, but with the same care as they had.

As the seventh flew, I tried to figure out what kind of man would want a woman like me. Was there one not in this crooked lifestyle who wouldn't be afraid of me?

"I'm sure you're aware silencers are illegal out here." A voice came from behind me.

I jumped, turning with the gun raised.

Until I saw Detective Dorian Shipman leaning against the brick building enclosing us into the alley. He didn't reach for his gun to defend himself or try to shelter himself away from my aim.

I dropped the weapon, taking in his form. His hands were lazily dropped into the pockets of his trousers, legs crossed, and body at ease. His eyes, though, showed a bit of mistrust. I knew at that moment that he'd been giving me his trust from the beginning because I hadn't seen that look so clearly pointed at me.

"And target practice out in the open like this endangers the well-being of the public."

"How'd you find me?"

"I may not have your computer skills, but I know how to track a phone."

I sighed. I still didn't know why I'd given him that number. That one specifically was for my family alone, and the reason I kept it on me, knowing I could be tracked—though it still took some skill since I had the tracking devices disabled—was because I didn't always mind if my family tracked me. Why, why, why had I given it to a detective?

"You have SWAT back there?" I nodded to the opening he'd just come from, my body readying itself. I didn't know for what, but I had the sudden need to protect myself.

"I had no reason to believe I'd need SWAT with me."

I tilted my head. "But a quick speed dial to your team can send them?"

"You're not a threat, Lana."

"Do they know that? They see your search, they may think so. Or maybe just use that as an excuse to arrest me again."

He huffed. "I did the search on my personal laptop. They don't know we're here."

"So I can kill you and completely wipe the evidence?"

He narrowed his eyes. "On top of the fact that I don't believe you'd do that, you'd become top suspect."

I shrugged, defenses wrapping around my heart against the man across from me. "My brothers could clean out your place, take care of your body, give me an alibi. I'd be fine."

I was a mafia princess and out here with my weapons, there was no denying it. He would no longer be able to fool himself into the picture of who he thought I was, and I needed to be ready when he decided I wasn't what he wanted.

He finally pushed off the building and moved to stand

before me, his eyes narrowed and his voice roughened. "You'd do that?"

No. I couldn't hurt you.

But I needed to protect myself, and I didn't even know why. But this felt the safest way to do that. To make sure he hated me. "Maybe."

Dorian

"YOU'RE LYING," I growled.

"Says who? Your soft little heart?"

"Lana!" I growled. "Stop it. You're bringing up that persona you use to protect yourself. Stop it! You don't need protection from me!"

"Says who?" she yelled.

"Says me!" I roared back, eyes widening when she stepped away from me. The very last thing I wanted was to scare her. I was breathing hard, but my voice softened as I said, "Lana, please. What—"

"Do not worry yourself with me, Detective. You have cases to work on—go do that. If you want to arrest me, get it over with."

"You're shutting down on me, Lan."

"That puts you under the assumption that I'd been open with you from the beginning. Maybe this is me, Dorian. Maybe the woman you thought you liked, the one who only put pretty pictures of her family in your head, was the lie."

My initial instinct was to argue with her, but I paused. Was she finally being a hundred percent honest with me and I was the one having trouble accepting it? Was I the one who'd created a fantasy in my head that I refused to allow reality to alter?

She was so plainly telling me. The vulnerability—it could've been a way to make me trust her. So much so that when she told me stories of her family, I believed them. So she could alter the way my mind pictured the Romanovs—not the men who, on many occasions committed great violence for no other reason than because they could but the protective carers of the woman who deserved it.

She must've seen when I realized that all of this—her working for the hotels to being the one who got caught up in the arrests to the one who manipulated us in interrogations to catching my desires—was a ploy from the Romanovs, one that proved Lana had never left them after all.

She smirked, and it was so clear that it was the other persona I hadn't seen since her original interrogation, the one I was starting to believe must've been the real her all along. "Oh, poor, Detective. What's going on up there?"

"Svetlana—"

"Oo." She made a sizzling sound. "I'm Svetlana now?"

I don't know who the fuck you are!

"Why are you doing this?"

"Doing what, Detective? The gun or this conversation?"

"Either. Both."

"Well, Detective. Target practice is eternally important. Especially when you always have people after you. As for this conversation, you're right, there is no point to it."

I didn't stop her as she unarmed her pistol and dropped it into the duffle on the ground, zipped it up, and pulled the strap onto her shoulder. "Your family is lucky to have someone as good as you on their side."

She wouldn't look at me, caught up in fixing a knot in her strap, when she said, "I know."

I didn't stop her as she walked past me, but I was stuck with the sound of her voice as she'd said it. Was it softer because that vulnerable side was coming out? Or was she trying to fuck with my mind again by making me believe there was a vulnerable side? Was it simply softer because she was done with the conversation and wasn't paying much attention? What the *fuck* was going on?

My phone vibrated with a file attached and a message from Finnegan. *You're closer. Check this out.*

I'd told the team I was up here to follow a different lead, so I'd have to check up on both now. Both leads were only a few blocks from one another though, so things would hopefully run quickly. As I got back to my car and traveled toward the woman Finnegan wanted checked out for a smaller case we were working on, I thought back to the one lead who I found myself foolishly falling for.

I couldn't risk my entire career, my entire life, on this one woman, especially when she so adamantly told me she wasn't who I believed her to be. I couldn't even imagine the type of sick shit her family would try knowing she was a beautiful woman who would capture any man's attention. Her pure virtue wouldn't even have to be a lie because Lana had the power to capture attention without even a touch. She was, it turned out, probably the most dangerous Romanov.

And with Sergei's hatred for our precinct in particular but especially for Porter, I only had to allow my imagination to run wild for a few seconds before it was clear that a plan to get Lana into the doors—by making her a suspect—then make one of Porter's allies fall for her—by choosing me or Lansly—then learn more about her and a way to get into the systems and destroy Porter's life. Considering they had all sorts of help, help that would've come from dirty cops in the past, I had no idea what end such a plan would take.

If that were the case, and the more I thought about it, the realer it felt, the more I knew I'd need to warn Porter. Not that she would need it. From the moment she found out about Lana's background, she'd been looking for a connection she couldn't find.

As I parked in front of Finnegan's lead's house, I turned off the car and fell back in my seat. I didn't know what to believe.

Lana was a mafia princess, beloved by her father and brothers, likely honored by all the men that followed her family. She was trained in both interrogations and weapons. She knew how to fight and how to manipulate cameras and technology. She inserted herself perfectly into situations that made her look too obviously guilty so she could hide in plain view.

She was guilty.

But she was also a loyal customer at a diner where she had her own secret menu and a well-off enough reader to know quotes enough to recite to me. She valued promises, a guess I was making by her love of that one song, and she'd kept herself pure for nearly a quarter of a century. Her eyes were soft when it was only us, and I had a hard time believing anyone could fake that, even actors were not so talented as to do so. She'd left her family because she didn't want that same life.

She was innocent.

I couldn't fully trust her, I knew that, but I was tired of playing this back-and-forth game in my head. I needed to listen to my heart some more, remember that my gut was telling me I could trust her and it was probably time I listened to it and my heart over my head. I needed to get back to her, to make sure she wouldn't try to run from me again.

But first, I needed to get back to that alley.

Then I was going to find her.

I was surprised she hadn't gotten rid of the phone. She knew I could track her through it.

As I stopped in front of a ballet opera, I realized that she probably had gotten rid of it.

But I still got out of my car to check. She could be here playing a chance at another illegal thing and finalizing that I must be a moron for falling for the fantasy in my mind. But I stayed true to my beliefs—there was something off about her when she played that persona. It didn't feel like the real her.

I made myself believe that she was here trying to forget the night with the performance rather than anything that tied her to her family's behavior. There was so much I didn't know about her, so I wouldn't be shocked if one of those facts was that she was a lover of the ballet.

When I got to the front, the doors wouldn't budge.

I double-checked my phone, telling me her location was here, and tried the doors again. When they didn't budge and I couldn't hear noise of a performance coming from inside, my stomach dropped. This would be the final straw—if she wasn't that vulnerable girl I was falling for, I'd need to get my head out of my ass and take care of the problem.

But my stupid, annoying heart insisted I trust in the woman I knew, the one who spent the night with me telling me childhood stories.

So I pushed away from the building, looking for other doors. The side door I found was also locked, but when I finally reached the back of a dark alleyway, I sighed when the doorknob turned.

Though I wasn't sure that was exactly a good thing. I had

the excuse of my badge to allow myself in. She was simply trespassing if she was here.

I slowed the door behind me so it didn't alert to my presence, then slowly made my way through, my hand on my gun, though I hoped I wouldn't need it.

I was slowly making my way through the backstage when I heard a soft noise come from above. Covered by the darkness below, I was both relieved and stunned to find Lana walking out of a room and the sound of a toilet flushing following as she made her way to a set of pullout stairs leading to an attic area. I didn't even know places like these had those rooms.

I eased my hand from the gun and moved as quietly as possible to the ladder that would take me to the top floor, then to that staircase that was still left out.

A quick glance into the room she'd left showed a fully functioning bathroom with a small shower in the corner I guessed was for dancers in dire need between practices or performances.

My biggest problem now was that I couldn't see what was at the top of those stairs. Would it lead to another hall, or would it be a final room? Would Lana be alone up there, or was this a secret meeting spot for her family or whoever she might be working with?

I didn't want to aim my gun at her, but I eased the weapon from its holster in case there were others, then slowly made my way up the stairs.

There was the sound of some sitcom the closer I got to the opening, but nothing else. I took a deep breath in when I reached the top and quickly spun into the room, gun aimed.

Only to be met with the barrel of a gun between my eyes.

When my gaze met Lana's, her shoulders relaxed, and she dropped her weapon. "What the hell are you doing here?"

It only took a single glance around the space to show it

wasn't too big of a space and she was there alone, so I holstered my weapon and relaxed into the space, knowing she wouldn't hurt me. "I pose that question to you. You're trespassing."

She lounged into a chair at her small round table. "And you're what? Taking a walk in the park?"

"I can come in here."

She quirked an amused brow. "Do you own the place? That must be what you're saying because a badge doesn't give people the right to trespass."

The edge of my lips tipped up. "I heard a mysterious noise."

She tried to fight her grin, but it was evident. "Sure."

I met her at the table, where she'd paused the sitcom on her tablet. "You gonna tell me what you're doing here?"

"No."

I took a grape from the pile she had sitting on a plate before her and took my time chewing it, enjoying being under her scrutiny. "You know, there's no address listed for you."

She chewed on a grape slowly as well, capturing my attention. "You don't say."

I leaned back. "What in God's name made you decide to start living above a ballet opera, Lana?"

"So I'm no longer Svetlana?"

I shrugged. "You'll always be Svetlana. That's your name."

She smirked. "So it'll be what you use to throw in my face that I might be doing something illegal for my family?"

"No. It's what I'll use when I'm frustrated with you. No matter the circumstance."

She didn't say any more as she enjoyed her grapes, analyzing me.

I didn't find myself falling for the fact that this was her true residence, but I could see it as a place she stayed some nights, maybe nights she knew to be wary of being tracked. But I asked again, "Why above a ballet opera?"

She smirked. "Would you have thought to check here?"

"Never in a million years."

She gave me a satisfied nod. "Good job, Detective. You figured it out."

"Don't get snarky."

"Don't tell me what to do."

My lips tipped up, and I relaxed even further. "Don't run away from me, Lan."

"Tell me why I should trust you. Dor."

I cracked into a chuckle. "My father used to call me that."

She winked but waited patiently for my answer.

"I promise I'm not after you, Lan. I won't hurt you. I won't let it happen."

She chewed on another grape. "While I appreciate that, don't make promises you can't keep. I take them very seriously."

I let the silence take over rather than insisting I meant it because she was right. I wasn't entirely certain about what I'd stated. I couldn't be until I trusted in her, in us, completely. No more jumping to conclusions about her.

"Deal," I finally said because it was the strongest truth I could give her.

It was the right decision. She eased even more with my honesty.

DORIAN LEAVING last night left me up, unsure whether his tracking me down was because he truly believed we had something or if it was just some sick way of gathering more information on me and my family.

It was all my fault anyway. I shouldn't have given him my real number, given him the ability to track me down wherever, whenever. I still didn't know why I'd done so. I certainly hadn't trusted him when I'd done it. Still didn't entirely trust him.

I was still sad to see him go last night though.

He didn't have to know that. It would give him too much power over me, but it was the truth.

Plus, I'd needed him to go. The most obvious reason being that if this was his ploy to gather information—which, given his tactics with the lie detector test, I had no doubt he'd use my desires for him against me—then I couldn't stick around and actually fall for the detective. I might've left my family's life-style, but I would still protect them above all else.

The other reason being that his bed was far too comfortable, and I'd wanted more than anything to tell him to take me with him so I could lie in it again. If he'd stayed any longer, I feared I would've blurted just that.

This morning, I'd gotten up early in order to get back to that alley to pick up the bullets I'd had to leave behind because of Dorian. I was still shell-shocked after arriving at the alley that Dorian hadn't been kidding when he'd said he'd gone back to the alley after his assignment and picked up as much as he could find. He'd gotten all of the clips and half of the bullets, so I only had a bit more to pick up. While finishing the alley cleanup, I'd gotten a message from the Hollis Hotel. It wasn't from Elliot, so I wasn't looking forward to being there, but hopefully, I could find him after fixing their connections. For a hotel this massive, they had a great setup and actually kept the connections throughout the entire place running smoothly, but I'd been called a time or two before in order to fix things... and normally bright and buttfuck early in the mornings.

It was their way of making sure everything was running smoothly when guests awoke, so I couldn't fault them their impeccable hospitality.

Plus, they paid a very pretty penny for my time.

A pretty penny that accounted for more than enough money to leave this life behind.

The privacy of the computer room gave me the space to think of the last few days. Only two days ago, I spent the night at a man's house. That was kinda wild to think of. Before leaving my family, I'd never been allowed to sleepover anywhere, and after leaving, I hadn't found anyone I trusted enough to do so.

And I still hadn't technically. I didn't trust Dorian, not all the way, at least. I trusted him to keep me safe if something were to happen, but I wasn't yet sure how I felt about letting him learn about me and my past. Would his detective morals require he lock me up? My gut told me the answer wasn't a definitive no, so I'd fought him, tried to push him away.

But I think my gut understood now that it might've been wrong. Or maybe it'd been right, and Dorian was simply changing now.

At least he'd given me those two dates to see how things progressed. If that was still a thing. I wasn't entirely sure after he'd caught me "acting like my family."

If it was still up for grabs though, I was excited to go on dates with him, to be normal. And honestly, I was kinda happy about the two-date rule before touching me. And I knew if I said I wanted to change it to six or fourteen, he'd be okay with it. He was a gentleman, a stand-up proper man—it was what made him such a great detective. He was simply a good person looking to help people. And good men would never force a woman to do anything she didn't want to.

The memory of stealing his shirt made me smile as the looming threat of never actually getting those dates because he truly didn't trust me sat over my head. I hadn't touched myself in it as I'd told him I would, but I'd had a feeling being in it would make me feel close to how safe I felt in his bed.

I'd been right. Wearing it last night after he left made me feel almost as good as being in his apartment.

It was odd. I knew I could protect myself, but I desired to be around a man to do it for me anyway. It was probably the best part about living at home—I had four men ready to put their lives down for me. And dozens of others who would follow their commands and thus also put their lives down for me. It was the safest place imaginable.

Being at Dorian's almost felt like being back home, except... less lonely somehow. There were far more people at

Romanov estate, but I felt connected for the first time ever when I was sitting on that couch with Detective Hottie asking about my past. I didn't want to lose that.

Yesterday, so much had been in the air. After last night though, I felt better about us. It didn't mean I would completely throw caution to the wind, but my gut told me it'd changed its mind about him, that he would never hurt me, even if his morals demanded I be put away.

At least, it made my heart believe that. My mind was still on the fence.

ELLIOT WAS WAITING FOR ME BY THE LOCKER ROOMS. He sat on the bench right outside like he'd known I'd come looking for him after finishing my tasks.

"What pretty flowers." I sat beside him, a small bouquet of tulips and lilies on his other side.

He gave a satisfied grin. "There's a pretty little lady who walks her dog by my place every afternoon. I figured I get off work early enough today, I could stop and talk to her. But I wanted to see you first."

I gasped. "You actually found someone! Elliot, your annoyance with the societal force for constant human interaction was the reason I liked you to begin with!"

He laughed. "I don't mind human interaction. Why else would I keep this job?"

I pushed at his shoulder, pouting. "You know what I mean. You take us in small bursts, then have the rest of the day to yourself. I like that. I'm like that. How will I relate when you have a lady at home with you?"

He laughed. "By having a man at home with you."

"Oh god," I grumbled.

"You made the deal, *cara mia*. I found my lady—"

"She hasn't said yes yet," I whispered.

He ignored me. "Have you found yourself a gentleman?"

I almost snorted. Dorian quite literally was a gentleman. He led me when we walked even a short distance, opened doors for me—whether buildings or cars—and carried me to bed, leaving me alone rather than taking the opportunity to jump in beside me. Hell, he was even gentleman enough to not rat me out to his team for my silencer and had pushed in chairs at my place. "No. I don't want one."

"You're not a very good liar, Lan."

"Contrarily, I'm an extraordinary liar."

"Then you hide the guise for me? I feel honored." He touched his heart.

I couldn't help but laugh, pushing him again. "Shut up."

"You going to tell me who he is?"

I shrugged. Talking about it made it real, but wasn't that what I wanted, for this thing with Dorian to become real? "You know that investigation at Shriberton, the one I was taken in for?"

He snorted now, brows furrowing and mouth snickering down. "Lousy good-for-nothings. How they could ever think it was you."

Maybe one day I'd tell Elliot about my past, then maybe he'd have a different opinion of me. "And here you were calling him a gentleman."

Elliot watched me closely before realizing it. "You fell for your detective?"

"What can I say? He's hot."

He took my answer, then laughed loud and full. "That makes so much sense, *cara mia*. Your attention was glued to your phone only that one time, and it was after your investigation. Whew. He must've made quite the impression on you, Lan-Ban."

"Okay, I think I'm done with this conversation."

He grabbed my arm as I rose and dropped me back to my ass. "Sit back down.You're not done. I said tell me about your gentleman."

"That's quite demanding, considering you've told me nothing about your woman."

He brought me into his side and hugged me there. "I don't know much about my woman, to be honest. Not even her name." His gaze was far-off, like he was imagining her walking past us at this very moment. "She's probably a decade my junior, so I don't even know if she'll want an old fart like me, but I can't help but desire for her attention to be the one I hold. She's about your height, lighter brunette hair, beautiful hazel eyes. She always has her nails painted red and smiles the whole time she walks her dog, even if it's pouring down rain."

My lip jutted as I listened to him. "Aw, Elliot! You're not that old. She'd be a fool not to want you."

He smiled. "You just say that because you're sweet on me."

I laughed. Elliot was sixty-eight years old, so he was definitely up there in age, but he wasn't that old. And he had the sweetest heart. He'd be nothing but good to this woman. "Promise to tell me how things go?"

"Always." He hugged me in tighter to his side. "Now, you tell me about yours."

I took a large breath in to think about it. "His name is Dorian. Dorian Shipman, if you'd like to look him up later." He laughed, but we both knew he was going to. "He's gorgeous, a few years older, a complete sweetheart. Kinda reminds me of you—opens doors, listens to me talk, is gentle with me."

"He has to listen to you talk. It's called an interrogation," he muttered.

I sputtered, mouth agape. "That's not what I meant!" My smile was wide as I shook my head. "You are such an ass sometimes."

He kissed my temple. "What did you mean, then?"

"I'm no longer a suspect. We were together last night. And the one before. Just talking. He wasn't simply hearing my words, but he was listening. I could see the emotion, whether good or bad, as I spoke, which only made me want to speak some more. He's sweet yet powerful and confident and... good. He's super moral. Which, I mean, he *is* a detective."

"So what's the problem?"

"I haven't really trusted anyone like that in a long time. I'm just... making sure I'm not being stupid, is all."

"Falling for the detective investigating the murder you're a suspect for? Whyever should you be cautious?" He took in my glare, then added, "You're a great judge of character, Lan. Always have been. And if you're feeling like this about him, then I know he's a good guy."

"Yeah. Too good though?"

He kissed me again. "Let's not ponder on it. You try your luck with him as I will my lady, and we'll report back."

I laughed. "Deal."

"Ah, another deal. My girl is a gambler."

I pushed away from him. "I hate you so much."

"I love you too, *cara mia*."

Lukov was waiting for me when I finally left Elliot, choosing to take the back exit rather than the front one he was taking. He was simply lucky I'd gone my usual route today, but I found myself wishing to have gone in Elliot's direction.

My brother was leaning against the tanned brick of the hotel with two coffees in hand—suspiciously from Toni's, even though Ted's coffee was a little bit closer, no matter the direction—and a conceited smirk on his handsome face.

"Lukov." My brows furrowed into an irritated bow as I realized the stupid task Hollis had me fixing earlier would've been my brothers' making. All to get me out here.

"You figured that out faster than you had years back. You're getting real good, *sestra*."

Imagine how impressed he'd be if he knew I'd stopped to talk to Elliot too.

I didn't take the compliment as I stuck my hand out, waiting to see which of the drinks was mine. "What did the poor hotel do to you that you had to fuck with their systems like that?"

"They took my sister." He handed me a coffee and poked my nose. "Now, why don't I walk you home."

Because even though my residence was a secret to all, my brothers and father knew exactly where I lived. And they all hated it. I think Dorian had joined them in that department last night, though he hadn't mentioned it.

I didn't move as I opened the lid to my coffee and took in the beautiful aroma that only one person at Toni's got so right for me. "What did I tell you about leaving that poor girl alone?"

He gave a teasing smirk, but I'd always been the best at reading his eyes, and they were entirely serious—and a little too sad—as he said, "I am leaving her alone. Stopping by for a coffee isn't doing anything to her. She's too much like you. Too good. She wouldn't want it."

But you would? More than flirtations? Really?

I dropped the line of thought because if there was one thing I knew about my brothers, it was that they didn't talk about their feelings. Typical annoying males.

"So, your reason for stalking me this time?" I turned for my place.

"None. I just miss you. It's weird not having you around."

"You act like I just left a month ago rather than years ago."

He shrugged. "I don't think I'll ever get over it. You're my best friend, Lan."

I frowned. "I know. You're my best friend too."

"And... I wanted to check in about your boy situation. I know you were joking the other day about a ton of boyfriends, but *do* you have anyone?"

Technically I didn't have anyone. Yet. "No."

"And Carrini? He leaving you alone?"

I sighed. "Has since my last birthday." It was another reason to live in an untraceable location, though I wasn't stupid enough to think Carrini couldn't simply find me at work and follow me home.

"Good. You still promise to let me know if he shows back up?"

"My promises are gold, Alek, you know that."

"Lyubov, my love"—he ignored the snort I always gave at the double endearment—"there is nothing I am more sure of. Which is why I like constantly hearing it."

I sipped my coffee. "Then I promise, *brat*"—I used the Russian word for "brother"—"that I will call you if Carrini contacts me again."

"Thank you."

I winked. "It's the only way to keep your stalking at bay. I don't need you putting twenty-four-hour surveillance on my ass."

He laughed. "Don't go giving me ideas."

"Oh please, like Sergei hasn't tried already."

"You're lucky *Otets*'s promise to *Mama* makes it so he won't allow it."

"And that *Otets* is still head instead of Sergei," I added, then sighed softly as another thought came to me. "Serg have Ilya put an electronic track on me?"

Lukov laughed into his cup. "It was Ilya's idea, not Sergei's. And it's your fault for teaching Ilya everything before you left."

What was I supposed to do? Trust someone other than family to protect them? I didn't care how loyal their men were; I wanted my brothers to protect one another, and my brother closest in age to me was the most willing and eager when it came to technology. I'd already been teaching him for years before I'd officially decided to leave.

I rolled my eyes. "Whatever. I had no delusions that my psychotic brothers would actually leave me be. Neither did *Otets*, by the way. That's why he acts so cool with me gone. Because he knows you guys are crazy enough to make up for it."

He tucked me into his side as we walked. "That's what you get for being the only girl."

I relaxed into him and enjoyed the rest of the walk. My brothers truly were my best friends, which made it far more difficult to fully leave this world behind. I could've easily moved cross-country and started over, really had that normal life I dreamed of, before any of this mess happened, but I couldn't imagine ever actually leaving them.

When we reached my building, he kissed my temple. "Don't work too hard. You're too pretty for that."

I kissed his cheek. "Love you."

"Hate you too."

It was still early as I said bye to Lukov and headed in. He stayed out there until I was safely inside, and even though it was still morning and nothing would happen, I was thankful for his protection. As I made my way up, I smiled to myself, remembering Elliot's words from earlier. As I reached my place at the top and looked through the large window to wave bye to my brother, the thoughts made me wonder how Dorian's day was going today. I hoped it went well, even if I possibly still was a suspect.

Part Four

"The only way to get rid of temptation is to yield to it."

\- Oscar Wilde

THERE WAS STILL a lot racing through my head when I got out of my car and headed into the precinct. From having such a nice night to her leaving me to finding her doing illegal activity—no matter how light a case simple possession of a silencer would be compared to her family's actions—to figuring out, once and for all, which the real Lana was.

Leaving her place—if you could call it that—was a war. I wanted to take her with me but knew she wouldn't be up for it. On top of being one of the detectives investigating a murder that she could become a suspect in again, I'd shown her only a few hours earlier that I didn't trust her. She had absolutely no reason to put any faith in me.

But I couldn't help wanting to take her with me, wanting to hear her voice before going to bed and the first thing waking up. A fact I hadn't even realized until I awoke this morning and she wasn't there to tease me.

Heading into the building, I decided just because she wasn't with me didn't mean hers couldn't be the first voice I heard this morning. I needed this. I already felt too distracted to be of any use today, so before I talked myself out of it, my phone was at my ear.

She picked up on the second ring as per usual. "Hey, Det—"

"If I wake up and find you gone next time," I barked because it was the only thing holding my annoyance in, "we're going to have a problem."

"What?" she muttered.

"You left the other night. Do that again and we're having a problem."

"That's under the assumption I ever stay over again, Detective," she teased.

I breathed a sigh of relief at hearing that beautiful sound that was so uniquely her. "It's a promise, Lana."

"Don't make promises you don't intend to keep, Detective," she sang.

"You're not leaving next time, Lan," I insisted, my voice growing rough.

Her laugh filled the space around me as I waited for the elevator. "Oh, really? What're you gonna do if I do? Spank me? Because I can definitely get on board with that."

"Stop playing, Lana." As she laughed some more, I interrupted before the elevator could open for me. "Be ready tonight. I'm taking you on date one after work."

"Eager to get into my panties, Detective?"

A growl left me as I put my foot out to hold the elevator doors from closing, the kid inside running out at hearing it. "Desperate."

She giggled, making my dick hard as a rock. "And who said I want you there any longer?"

"Lana, please!"

She gasped. "A begging detective? I like this."

"Don't play with me, Svetlana."

"Ooo, full name again. I must be in a lot of trouble."

"Lana," I begged.

She laughed. "Okay. I'll stop. But only if you remember to spank me later."

"Dear *fucking* lord," I muttered.

"Remember, Detective." She interrupted me, making hard biting sounds. "It'd be a bloody mess."

An airy laugh finally left me as the vision of my dick bleeding out came to mind. "I don't even think that could help me today."

"I'm sorry." She sounded quite the opposite. "Next time, I'll give you a blowjob before we leave each other's presence."

That most certainly wasn't helping my erection. "You're not leaving next time, Lana."

"Whatever you say, Detective."

I huffed out. "I have to go."

"Okay. Have fun at work, baby."

"Thank you. I'll see you tonight."

"Mhm." She hung up, and I was glad because I felt like a teen who'd stay stuck on the phone with the "you hang up, no you hang up" nonsense.

With my phone safely put away, I finally stepped into the privacy of the elevator and rode it up, adjusting my dick so it wasn't so obvious and hoping it'd die down soon.

When I stepped into the office, Lansly and Finnegan were talking between themselves by our desks.

Lansly looked hesitant as he turned for me, but Finnegan didn't seem to catch it as he answered whatever they'd been talking about. "We got three men in here."

"For the murder?" I interrupted, causing Finnegan to turn to me. Three suspects? Or partners? That was great work.

"No," Finnegan answered. "For a different case."

"Which one?"

"Apparently, these three have been after our dear friend Lana." I froze, but he didn't process it—probably thinking I only had the hots for her rather than any real feelings. "I've been waiting for you and Porter to begin interrogations. Rundown of findings so far—it took a few days, but word ended up traveling down from some homeless that saw some of what happened and ran in fear. Once Shriberton's staff heard of it, they called, and we picked them up. Fuckers weren't even trying to hide."

My blood ran cold. I was terrified for what may come next, the memory of those bruises covering Lana's stomach flooding me.

Lansly kept watch like he felt for me, which made me fear for the possibilities of what we were about to learn in there.

"Apparently," Finnegan continued, "a few homeless men saw these men, on separate occasions, and once as a unified front, have their way with her."

I was going to be sick.

"Shriberton staff don't know how accurate that is since Lana's a fighter, not to mention her Romanov background, so we gotta see what really happened. Then maybe we can talk to Lana too. All this time, she could've been a victim, and we've been treating her like the guilty."

I wanted more than anything to tear into those interrogation rooms and rip the fuckers limb from limb, even if all they were guilty of was looking at Lana the wrong way, but I needed to remain calm if I was going to get any sort of justice for my girl.

I scoffed. She wasn't my girl. Not yet. But soon.

Porter showed up ten minutes later.

It was the longest ten minutes of my life.

I STOOD ON THE OTHER SIDE OF THE INTERROGATION window so I could watch Porter and Lansly speak to suspect number one.

"Look," Lansly began as he lounged back in his chair, playing "good cop." Men already had a predisposition to set women as "bad cop," so it was really a no-brainer for Porter to play that role. "We already know you attacked Lana, so there's no point denying it."

The man quirked a brow and spoke with an accent. "I do not know a Lana."

"Svetlana better suit your memory?" Porter spit out as she walked laps around the table.

Now the fucker was giving a cocky smirk. "What did the bitch say?"

I ground my teeth, more for my own sanity than to hide from Finnegan how affected I was by this case. Though that second point was equally as important. I didn't need him taking me off because of "personal bias."

"Why don't you give us your side and we'll tell you if it corroborates?" Lansly suggested.

"That bitch broke my nose." He pointed to the bandage on his face. "Why is she not here so I can lock her ass up?"

"I think you should be more worried about what would happen to your ass when you're locked up," Porter responded.

Lev, the slimy suspect, grimaced at her, then turned to Lansly. "Why's the bitch here?"

"Protocol," Lansly answered nonchalantly before pretending like Porter wasn't there at all. "Now, why don't you tell me, man to man, what you did to her?"

Lev ignored him and followed Porter with his gaze, a vile

grin spreading across his face. "You want to know the plan, princess? Maybe you're jealous. Want me to rip that ass up too?"

I had to hold my breath to keep from doing something stupid—like killing the fucker—and leaned into the window, grabbing for the edges to hold myself up.

"Is that what happened?" Porter paused her strut for a moment, leaning over the table. "You tear her ass up?"

"The plan, sweetheart. You're not locking me up for something that didn't happen."

"So what was the plan?" Lansly asked.

Lev sat back like he thought we weren't going to lock him up for this. "Manny had his turn first. Came back with a broken nose. He wanted to shove her to her knees and break the bitch's throat with his dick, then fuck that whore until she was bleeding more than virgin blood."

Bile traveled up my throat, and I barely held it back. We still had to interview Manny and Park for their stories, and I had no idea how I was going to sit through all of it. But I had to. If Lana had to live any of this, the least I could do was hear it.

"Then Park went. Same plan, but he came back with bruises, no breaks. We knew not to underestimate that bitch then." His smiled wickedly. "I am the biggest, so I was last. I was happy, actually, that the others couldn't get to her. It meant that tight cunt would be mine and that ass wouldn't be broken into. Her cries of pain would be fresh."

My nails were scraping against the window's edges as I barely restricted myself from shattering through the glass and ending him. I ignored Finnegan's worried glances my way.

"She was fast though. She got away. So no harm."

"And big tough guy got a broken nose?" Porter mocked.

Lev looked like he wanted to show Porter a lesson right

there, but he was smart enough not to try it. "The bitch gave me this a few days ago."

I completely froze now.

A few days ago, I'd known Lana. In all that mess, she'd come in for the lie detector test, told me childhood stories at my place, then tried to run away from me.

"And how'd she do that, Big Scary Man." Porter continued her role, though I knew it wasn't a hard one. This was actually how she felt, whereas Lansly held the more difficult role.

"Once she's no longer a virgin, she's worthless. We needed to break the bitch. But, apparently, princess was taught to fight. All three of us went to her. Manny and Park held her down while I pulled a syringe to stop the bitch from moving." He leaned in. "Now, if you want a psycho, find her. She stopped moving after the sting. Made the clothes easy to rip off..."

A deep and long growl left me as I clung to the window so hard I was seconds from breaking it. I wanted to too badly. Wanted to shove my gun up this fucker's ass and pull the trigger until the clip emptied.

"But then the bitch started moving!" Lev exclaimed. "The last thing we'd expected was for the princess to get herself immune to a fucking relaxant. She kicked up so fucking hard my nose broke. Then she broke Manny's arm and Park's knee." He held up his wrapped hand. "Bitch broke three of my fingers. And don't get me started on all of our stitches."

"Please do." Porter grinned. "Svetlana has become my superhero."

Lev was now throwing insults at Porter, but Finnegan was speaking to me, so I stopped listening to his vile voice.

"You wanna get in there? See if you can get more?"

I was still gripping at the edges of the window. We still needed to know why the men had done all of this, but I had to trust my team to get that information. "Boss, if I go in there, only one man is coming out alive."

Finnegan eyed me, but my focus was on what I'd tell the prisoners in whatever prison he was sent to. I already knew I was gonna pass some gossip that he was a kiddy lover, so the men went hard on him.

"Okay," Lansly finally broke through Lev's insults. "How about you inform us as to why you had this special little plan for little virgin Svetlana?"

"The Romanovs are only so powerful when they're all protected and sane. Let those brothers of hers find out she's not a virgin, that it was ripped from her and she'll have the trauma of it all her worthless life and"—he exploded his hands —"chaos."

"Svetlana's not part of the mafia," Lansly argued.

"You're always part of the mafia!" Lev shouted, slamming his fists on the table. "But who cares about Svetlana? The bitch is a tool. We're getting at her daddy and brothers."

"Yet you couldn't even get the tool," Porter mocked.

Lansly interrupted before Lev could throw another round of insults her way. "Why not go after her again? It's been quite the break."

Lev smirked. "Let her think she's safe. Or fear she's not. That's half the fun."

"So, anticipation?" Lansly asked.

Lev shrugged. "And waiting for my injuries to heal. I'm gonna get that bitch for hurting me. See how she likes being locked up."

"You do that." Lansly was hardly paying attention any longer as he and Porter left the room.

It took a moment for them to fill our room, but then they were behind me. It took all my willpower to break away from Lev's relaxed state in that room and face them.

"He gave a full summary," Lansly said as he watched me with a softness about him. "I'll continue with the others. Make sure all the stories match but not too closely. If any of this was rehearsed, Lana could've actually been... hurt."

Porter tsked. "I don't think this story's a lie. The fucker really thinks he won't be busted because the rape didn't happen. He's too proud to not be stupid."

Finnegan nodded. "Let's see what the others have to say."

I pushed away, ready to hold on to another interrogation window as Lansly and Porter got the information out of Manny and Park.

By the end of the day, I'd listened to all three talk about trying to rape Lana, and though I was proud of the way she was able to protect herself, it all made me sick.

And in a more desperate need to hold her. To have her. To never let her go again.

I headed out of the office without acknowledging the others. They knew the spew of my emotions at the moment, so none of them tried stopping me.

With the way my nerves were thrumming, I couldn't wait for the elevator to slowly descend, so I headed for the stairs and took them as fast as the adrenaline pumping inside me allowed.

I was fuming as I headed to my car and was so glad I'd told Lana I was seeing her tonight because I didn't know if I could handle not being with her from this moment on.

As I turned the corner toward my car, lightness shattered through the horrors pulsing in my chest because there she was, leaning against my car.

MY SMILED, faltered when I saw how very angrily he was headed straight for me. What could I have possibly done now?

"Doria—" I didn't get to finish as he ripped my arms apart from where they were crossed over my chest and threw them over his shoulders.

He had me lifted into his arms, holding so tight my air supply cut for a moment, and I sighed into him, realizing he wasn't angry with me. But it only slightly relieved my anxieties.

His face was in the crook of my shoulder, and I knew he was breathing me in, the imprint of his lips pressed against my skin.

"Baby." I tried to pull away just enough to look into his eyes, but he wouldn't let me budge. "Dorian, what happened?"

He moved until he placed me on the hood of his car, arms slipping from around my waist to cradle my face. "You're in my arms. That's all that matters."

"Wha—"

His lips pressed to mine, cutting off any thoughts.

I was frozen for all of half a second before I was kissing him back. This was what I'd wanted since that moment in the precinct when he'd asked if I was going to kiss him. This was what I'd dreamed of as a little girl imagining my future husband, though I never would've guessed he'd be a detective.

My legs pulled him, and I played with his hair, tugging, needing him closer.

He groaned into my mouth when our centers touched, and I followed right behind him with a moan, whimpering his name as he pulled away only enough for breath.

Our foreheads rested together as he groaned against my lips, "A first. All mine."

I smiled. "All of them. Always."

That was a pretty hefty promise. But was it a promise? Was I actually ready to make such a large promise?

With his mouth back on my lips and his tongue tangling with mine, I didn't let myself overthink it. I was ready. I must've been because nothing about this, about giving Dorian any of my firsts, felt wrong.

This wasn't fair though. He couldn't kiss me like this, then refuse to touch me when we got back to his place.

When he pulled away this time, he quickly pulled me off the hood and walked me to the passenger side, opening the door for me. "Get in."

His tone was demanding and turned me on so much that when I got in, I rejoiced in the moment I had alone to pull myself together. I needed to behave because as unfair as it felt not to be able to touch him tonight, I liked being able to simply spend time with him, date him.

His hand fell on my thigh when he sat down, and it was a habit of his I adored.

In the silence that followed as he drove us, I got to really take in his profile. He was angry again, the tension radiating off him and suffocating me in this enclosed space.

"Dorian, what happened?"

He swallowed, darkness flashing in his eyes a moment before wiping away as he turned for me. "We have three men in custody."

"With the Mann case? Isn't that a good thing?"

His jaw ground as he turned to watch where he was driving. "Not to do with the Mann case."

"Dorian..."

"Why didn't you tell me you'd been attacked?"

"What?"

"Why didn't you tell me you were attacked? That these men tried to ra—" He breathed out, and his hand on my thigh squeezed like he needed the reassurance that I was beside him. "Lana..."

My heart broke as I realized what was happening. "I'm fine, Dorian."

He swiveled the car into an alleyway and parked it, then turned entirely toward me. "Lana, you didn't tell me. I could'v—"

"Technically, I did tell you. That you weren't the only ones after me, remember?"

"Lana."

I sighed. "Why would I tell you? Up until yesterday, you weren't exactly on my friends list. Hell, you were hardly an acquaintance, trying to lock me up and all."

I didn't say it to hurt him; I was simply stating facts.

But it did hurt him.

His gaze softened. "Lana... Lana, I would've protected you. I... from the first interrogation, I would've fucked all and protected you if I'd known you were in true danger."

"Dorian, come on. You would've thought I was trying to fake my wa—"

"Lana! I could've protected against the three of them

jumping you together!" His voice broke. "They almost got you. I can't live with... I should've been there."

"Dorian." I softened my tone. "You'd just met me. You can't be angry about not being there."

His thumb grazed my face, passing over my lips softly. "But I was thinking of you. Every single one of those days I didn't see you, I thought of you. I thought of calling you. I stared at your number, wanting an excuse to call you. I should'v—"

I took his hands slowly. "You don't understand how much I love that you wanted me then because I thought of you constantly, but that doesn't change that we didn't have a relationship I could trust enough. You cannot blame yourself for what happened. I'm fine. They didn't do anything."

He scoffed. "I should thank your father and brothers for that, I presume?"

My smile broadened. "They'd like a popcorn machine. They want one, but none of them wants to admit it."

He gave an amused roll of his eyes before taking me in. "I suspect you can kick my ass as well?"

I gave a cheeky grin. "The only thing I'll be doing to that ass is kissing it, Detective."

He laughed before the humor left him. He just stared into my eyes and let his thumb graze my skin. "I'm sorry I wasn't there for you, Lana. I'll never let that happen again."

I knew it was dumb to do, so considering we'd only met a few weeks ago and up until he found out about my family, we hadn't truly talked, but I trusted those words to be true too deeply. "I know."

DATE NUMBER ONE WAS THE PERFECT NIGHT OUT OF the traditional movie and dinner, and though it was cheesy and cliché, I liked it more because of how cheesy it was. We whispered to one another the entire movie, sitting in the back of the theater with no one else around us, and I'd had so much fun with him that it hadn't felt like a simple movie date.

He'd taken me to a taco truck afterward, which was the perfect wrap to the night. We'd sat on the hood of his car, eating and teasing one another, and I'd wanted to keep ordering simply to make sure the night never ended.

But it did, had to.

And though I didn't want to leave his side, I had a feeling Dorian was thinking the same thing, especially after learning about my recent encounters. The man had glued himself to my side like I would evaporate if he weren't touching me the whole night. Not that I was complaining.

But now he was insisting we head back to my place instead of his. I didn't understand why since he had an actual apartment, but I obliged him.

When we got to the ballet house and I took him the to the back, letting myself in with the key I'd had made, Dorian quietly followed behind me. He held on to my trouser belt loops so he didn't crash into anything as we made our way through the dark. I knew this place like the back of my hand, and though there were times things were left where they shouldn't be by the dancers or directors, I almost never had any issues making it across in the darkness.

We climbed up until we were in my living quarters.

It was a fairly large room with an enormous window on my right where the moon shined in and lit the space up.

The room was enough for a bed in the corner, a chest of possessions at the foot of the space, and a rack of clothes, all of which were brought up here by a group of men from the hardware store who I'd told the room would be used for any dancers staying late for rehearsals. They hadn't cared enough to question me since I'd had a key and easily let them in.

There was also a small table to my left, where I normally watched shows on my tablet while painting on the small canvases. It was really all I needed, and in case of bathroom needs, there was a small one at the bottom of these final stairs we'd just climbed. I tended to use Shriberton's showers when I needed or wanted something more extravagant, but the shower in this bathroom normally did me justice.

This space, in all its quirkiness was home.

Turning for Dorian, there was a darkness in his eyes. He wasn't happy about the space, that much was clear. He was so similar to my brothers and father where I was concerned.

"I can't believe you live here," he said in a monotone voice it was clear he was trying to keep cool.

I shrugged. "I like it."

And I did. It was a nice place, and I loved the access to the ballets. This was never going to be a long-term plan, but it'd been perfect for my needs in the time it'd housed me. But eventually, I wanted that normal life. Maybe a proper apartment like the one Dorian had, but really, I wanted a house with a yard and privacy.

Dorian stood in the middle of the room by the hole that led back down and took it all in as if it was his first time up here. His expression was a mix of all emotions, none of them giving each other the moment to settle.

Then his gaze landed on me, and one of those emotions won out over the others.

"*This* is where you actually live? Is this a joke? I told you you could trust me, Lana. This isn't funny."

"It isn't a joke. This is where I live."

"I thought I'd tracked you here last time because you knew

I could locate you and didn't want to give away your true home. How do you live here? What about food?"

"I have a minifridge by that chest. I eat most of my meals by six in the evening, so I don't *need* a kitchen."

"And your family allowed this!"

I shrugged. "They didn't really have a choice. And it's safe, and no one would think to look for me here. It's really a lot nicer than you're imagin—"

"Pack your things," he cut me off.

"What?"

"Pack. Your. Things," he bit out, turning for the rack and starting to pull clothes from it.

"To go where exactly?" I watched him throw my clothes on the bed.

"Home. With me."

I forced a smirk to turn my lips so he couldn't see what I was really thinking as I said, "One date and you're already asking me to move in with you?"

"Yes." There wasn't any amusement in his eyes. "I'll sleep on the couch until you're ready for more, but you're coming home. *This* isn't a home, Lana. And if you're not there in the morning, I'm tying you to my bed."

Heat pooled in my core. "Is that a promise?"

I could play cat and mouse. A good chase was always fun.

"I won't touch you, Lana."

I grumbled and finally moved for my bed, sitting back as he took my final piece of clothing off the hanger on the rack.

"Where's your luggage?"

"Thank you, Dorian. You've been amazing tonight, but I don't need you to feel the need to take me in. I'm fine here. Now, if you'll stop messing up my organization, it'd be much appreciated."

He finally turned back to me, eyes blazing. "I don't feel the need to take you in because of this, Lana. I want you by my side always. I was simply going to wait a bit longer so I didn't freak you out, but there's no way in hell I'm allowing you to live here any longer. Not even a tiny fucking kitchen or proper bathroom, are you fucking kidding me?"

I stopped listening after that one word. "Always?"

His anger evaporated, shoulders slumping as he crouched before me, taking my face into his hands. "Always, baby."

"Why?"

His lips twitched up slightly. "Because you're mine, Lana. And I want everything you're willing to give me when you're willing to give it to me. We can go as slow as you'd like."

"Dorian..." I didn't know what to say.

The small smile he gave me told me he understood anyway. "Pack your things. Let's go home."

My heart skipped a beat.

Home.

I was going home...

I WOKE up the next morning giddy.

Giddy.

I hadn't woken up giddy since I was a child on Christmas. I felt like a child on Christmas.

Then dread washed over me—what if she left? I'd made myself clear about her not going anywhere, but that didn't necessarily mean she'd listen. In fact, she was more likely to leave just to prove that I wasn't the boss of her.

I shot up on the couch as the panic that she actually had left filled me.

Then turned my head to catch her in one of my T-shirts, dancing around the kitchen to music so low I wasn't surprised I hadn't heard it when I first awoke.

She was so focused on beating whatever was in that bowl in her arms that she didn't realize I was awake yet, and I got the chance to watch her hips sway. I wished it wasn't Friday and I could sit around doing anything I wanted. Hell, actually, I wished I wasn't a detective so I could sit around doing nothing with her. My job meant I worked all sorts of days, but I didn't want that with Lana. I wanted to be around her. Constantly.

She looked so at ease, and I was glad my home was giving her that feeling. I hadn't been lying the night before—I intended for it to be her home. At least, for as long as she would have me.

When minutes passed and she still hadn't realized I was awake, I slowly rose from the couch and moved for her. She had her back to me, the shirt clinging to her as she danced.

As I adjusted my hard-on, I knew one thing—I really needed to get her on that second date. I was more certain about the trust, given she was still here, but that second date was part of the promise I'd made, and I intended on keeping it. Because taking in her body and not being able to do anything about it was torture. Gods help me if she needed more than two dates. I'd give it to her, give her a hundred before touching her if that's what she needed, but gods help me if that's the case.

I moved slowly and wrapped my arms around her waist, laughing as she yelped and jumped against me, the bowl tumbling to the counter. "Aren't you supposed to be good at knowing when someone is coming for you?"

She giggled as her head fell back on my chest. "You're breaking down my barriers, Detective."

Thank. Fucking. God.

I turned her in my arms to get lost in those captivating dark eyes. "Morning, beautiful."

Her smile was so wide I felt like the luckiest man in the world to bear witness to it. "Morning, baby."

I kissed her, butterflies shooting from my belly to every limb, every finger and toe, then settling because of how right this was.

She pulled away far too soon. "Go get cleaned up." Then

pushed me toward the hall when I tried to argue. "Go! Breakfast will be ready soon."

I bit my bottom lip, simply taking her in, taking in this moment. "How did I get so lucky with you?"

Her brows furrowed in mock fury. "You bring down the bad guys, Mr. Hero Man."

My mouth twitched as I moved to do as I was told when I remembered something. "Did you use my toothbrush again?"

A light blush filled her cheeks, but she didn't shy away as she said, "I threw mine out at the dance hall while you were packing last night. I used yours last night and this morning."

I was smirking, even though I shouldn't have been enjoying this as much as I did. "Good. From now on, we're sharing."

Her nose crinkled. "It's kinda gross, no?"

I growled because I knew she liked it. "I don't care."

She gasped, teasing me. "Well, look at my big tough gross guy."

I winked, loving her laugh as I moved for the shower. I was cleaned and dressed for work in no time, and when I made it back out, Lana had blueberry pancakes stacked on a plate as she slowly ripped one apart with her fingers and dipped it into the syrup she had poured onto a smaller plate.

"You know you're supposed to douse the pancakes, then eat them with a fork, right?" I wrapped my arms around her waist from behind.

She leaned into me. "Call me an anarchist."

I laughed, kissing the side of her neck. "They smell amazing."

When I moved for the stool and took a plate with two pancakes stacked on it, she watched me with a glimmer in her eyes as I doused my pancakes.

"What?"

"I'm not supposed to like you this much already, Detective."

My grin ripped open, but I changed the topic. "What do you have planned for the day, Suspect."

That glimmer turned seductive as she dipped a piece of her pancake into the syrup and brought it to her luscious lips. "I figured I could clean this place, even though it's immaculate already. Maybe go through your things."

I knew she was joking, but I couldn't help but smile wider. "Please do. Everything in here is as much yours as it is mine." Then I pulled out my wallet and handed her one of my cards. "Matter of fact, go buy yourself some stuff. Clothes especially."

Her gaze hardened. "Dorian, I don't need your charity."

I pushed out of my seat quickly and moved around the small peninsula until I was caging her into the counters. "This isn't charity, Lana. Whatever I have is yours. And don't get me started on the fact that you had all of two little fucking duffle bags to bring over last night. You need more clothes, and if anyone else pays for it, I'll kill them."

Her eyes were black, heated, as she took me in. "You wouldn't kill anyone, Mr. High Ground."

"I'll lock 'em up and spread some rumors."

She rolled her eyes, and it took everything in me not to bend her over this counter and smack her ass until she couldn't think of ever doing it again. Her pulling the card out of my hand brought me out of that fantasy, then she rose to her tiptoes and kissed me. "Fine. Thank you."

"They better be nice things too. Don't cheap out because you don't want to use my money."

She rolled her eyes again, and this time, I didn't stop myself from smacking her ass as I moved back to finish my breakfast. I'd never been so happy so early in the morning. I wasn't a morning person. I never thought I could be this happy in the morning. My little suspect was doing things to my life I hadn't thought possible.

When I finished eating, I moved to clean the kitchen, but she stopped me. "I'll clean. You, go to work." She gave me a soft kiss. "Have a great day, Detective."

I didn't fight her because I loved this. I had a woman at home. One who would be waiting for me when I got off.

So instead, I brought her close for a longer kiss, then moved for the door.

I missed her already, but I needed to push that aside. I had twenty minutes until I got to work to find a way to get her out of my head. If Lansly saw me like this, he'd have a fucking field day.

I WAS RIGHT. LANSLY'S GRIN WAS WIDE AS THE fucking Cheshire cat's. How the fuck did the man read it the moment I stepped into the office?

"What?" I asked, hoping he was simply having a cunning breakthrough on a case.

"Lana and Dorian sitting in a tree..."

"Oh, grow the fuck up," I mumbled.

"K.I.S.S.I.N—"

I threw the stress ball sitting on my desk at him, thankfully stopping the childish song just before Porter walked in.

"What're you so happy about?" She grimaced at Lansly.

"What're you so grouchy about?" he retorted.

She fell into her seat, dropping a file onto her desk. "I'm gonna go cross-eyed if I keep looking at these files."

Lansly met my gaze a moment before rolling his eyes at Porter. "Still trying to find something to see if you can put Sergei away this time?"

"Not an if," she corrected. "I will find something. Or I'll kill him. Right now, I'm trying to keep my job too, so we're looking into the former."

"Guys." Finnegan strolled into the room from his office. "We have any new information about the Mann case?"

"Nope," I answered.

"Then we can give it a break for the day. In the meantime, I have Silver Asher to pick up. Which of you would like that one?"

A prostitute who admitted to killing one of her clients? That sounded like a Porter job.

"Or we have brothers Julio and Arnaldo Sanchez. Or..." He flipped through the cards he had in hand. "Emma Suarez."

Did I want the drug-selling brothers or the hacker?

"I'll take the Sanchezes," I called before Porter could jump on it.

"I have Emma," Lansly called immediately, though it was no shock that the guy into research would want to pick up the hacker. He could probably learn a lot from her.

"Good." Finnegan stopped before my desk. "Make this an easy day. Shipman?"

"Sir."

"Anything from Lana that might help us?"

Would knowing I never wanted to stop kissing her help? Knowing she was now living with me? Knowing she was too good for me?

I definitely didn't think that second one would help in any case. Finnegan might take me off the Mann case altogether if he knew our original suspect now had access to the case files when at my home. Not that Lana would look, but they didn't know that, didn't know her the way I did.

"Nope."

"Anything about her brothers or father?"

"No," Porter grumbled.

Finnegan smirked. "You need to get past this vendetta, Porter. I need you of clear mind on the job."

"I am!" she exclaimed. "Trust me. If I weren't, he'd be locked up with nothing to back it up. I'm behaving."

I met Lansly's stare, and we both fought our smirks.

That's when a pen smacked Lansly on the side of the head and not a second later, me.

"Very mature," I mumbled right before Porter cussed us.

Lansly and Finnegan took the moment to make jokes, ones Porter always had rebuttals to. She always pretended she didn't like it, but she seemed to come alive when she was arguing with us.

I stopped paying attention as I flipped through the Romanov file we had, focus latching onto one thing in particular—their skills. The skill I was forever grateful for and that they required *everyone* associated with them to have—fighting.

"Okay, okay. That's enough!" Finnegan called. "You all have assignments for the day. Get to them."

Porter mimicked him as he moved for his office, then turned a wicked smile on us. "Twenty bucks says I'll get mine here before either one of you."

Hers was the furthest away, but the brothers were known to cause trouble and Emma would know of Lansly's visit and hide, so it was a fair bet.

I pulled a twenty from my wallet and threw it on the table. "Deal."

She smirked and turned for Lansly. He didn't look so sure but agreed anyway.

"Perfect! Let's go!"

I turned back for the file in my hands, and my focus latched onto the Romanov estate address.

"Shipman. You coming?" Porter called from the double doors, where both she and Lansly were waiting.

I could start ten minutes later and still win this bet.

Probably.

"You go ahead," I called back. "I have a call I have to make."

I'D INSISTED we stay in last night because I knew Dorian was tired from the full day at work, and though I knew he was thankful to be able to relax, he'd been grouchy with me. Because no date two meant he had to sleep on the couch again.

Clarification—he didn't have to; he chose to.

I had no problems sharing the bed with him, but a single glance in his direction told me he wouldn't be able to restrain himself if I was rubbing my ass against him all night. And we both knew I'd do that. Of course I would. Why would I ever pass up on that opportunity?

So he'd made sure his team knew not to bother him today —which, given it was a Saturday, they should've all been taking the time off—and declared we would be having our second date.

He was so sexy when he was like that.

I was dressed in a white sundress and low-top white Vans, deciding this was perfect for something more romantic or more casual since he hadn't told me what we were going to do.

As I placed his omelette before him, he groaned. "You're trying to kill me."

He was eyeing me up and down, gaze latching onto my breasts, then down to my legs, up the round of my butt, and back again.

He looked good in his jeans and dark T-shirt, but I knew the power my outfit had. Men had a weakness for sundresses. "I think it's called seduction, Detective. And men are easy, easy, easy when it comes to these." I held the bottoms of the skirt and twirled for him.

He was drooling the way he focused on my legs and ass before he snapped himself out of it and caught my eyes. "You're cruel."

I gave him a quick peck before hopping onto the stool beside him. "You're welcome."

He couldn't stop ogling me, but in the middle of it, he asked, "You have shorts on beneath that?"

"Yeah. Why?"

"If you didn't, I was gonna have you change."

I narrowed my gaze but didn't ask for him to elaborate. It made me guess some sort of physical activity though.

We ate and cleaned the kitchen in no time, then we were out of there. Dorian still hadn't told me where we were going, and I didn't ask. I liked the surprise aspect; I certainly didn't want to ruin it for myself.

We parked in a lot with tons of other cars, and when we got out, I heard laughter and music and life, and in the distance, I saw it—a fair.

I gasped, grinning from ear to ear. "We're going to the fair?"

"No." He was wearing a satisfied smirk as he took my hand and moved me toward the large building that was blocking the view of said fair.

I stomped after him, but my attention kept getting snagged toward all that noise. Doing anything with Dorian would be fun, but the fair would be a dream.

When we were inside, it was just as boisterous with laughter and yelling. My eyes widened as I took it all in. It was an indoor obstacle course. "Oh my…"

He looked proud of himself. "There're six courses, and I intend to beat you at all of them."

I quirked a brow.

"Okay. Majority of them."

"Really? You're not going to let me win?"

He pulled me toward the registration desk. "I'm not that kind of guy, sweetheart."

"Mm. Don't turn me on right now, Detective. I have some ass whooping to do."

"Two entries, please." He spoke to the teenage girl behind the counter but eyed me the entire time like he was accepting the challenge.

"To the courses only or the fair as well?"

I perked up at the mention. "You have tickets for the fair too?"

"Yes." The girl smiled warmly. "It's kinda like a fundraiser fair for this place. They wanna install another course and need the money."

"Ooo." I grabbed Dorian's arm and tugged, jumping in my spot. "We have to do them all. Please, please, please!"

He bit his lip but wasn't able to hide his amusement. "Damn, Lan. You like fairs that much?"

I gave him my best puppy dog eyes as I nodded.

He kissed my cheek, grinning from ear to ear as he turned back to the girl. "Both, please."

"Alrighty." The girl started ringing him up. "And have either one of you been here before?"

"No," Dorian answered.

"Okay. Well, the fair, as I'm sure you could tell by the fundraiser aspect, is temporary, so great timing. The obstacle courses come in six different variations. Your pass gives you access to all of the rooms, so you could complete all of them or stick to one. You can do them as many times as you'd like. Courses come with the normal races with obstacles in the way—pouf fighting over a ball pit, wrestling over a ball pit, swings, rope climbing, rock climbing, monkey bars, and more. We close at seven, but the fair is open until ten." She handed over the wristbands colored blue to indicate both, whereas green indicated the courses only and yellow the fair only. "Have a great time!"

Dorian gave her a genuine smile. "Thank you."

He moved us to the side and took my hand, slipping my wristband on before he handed his over for me to put on.

"It's almost like we're getting married," I joked up at him.

He smirked. "Good. Now you're stuck with me and for sure can't leave."

I laughed. "No. You're supposed to freak out."

He shrugged. "Tough luck."

"I'll just beat you so bad you'll feel too emasculated to want to be with me."

"Is that possible?"

"Very." I gave a fake I'm-gonna-kick-your-ass smile.

"You're really sexy when you threaten me, you know that?"

"I do."

"Tell you what. Since I know I'll win, I'll give you an incentive to try a little extra hard." He ignored my narrowed stare, enjoying himself too much. "If you beat me, I'll take you to that fair *and* win you an animal."

"And if you win, what? No fair?"

"If I win, I'll take you to that fair and win you *two* animals."

I pouted. "Well, now you have to win."

He smirked. "I know."

My eyes narrowed, and my competitiveness, which didn't normally shine, rose to the surface. "I'll be perfectly happy with one stuffed animal."

He leaned in close so our lips were brushing as he said, "May the best player win."

WE WERE REPEATING THE LAST COURSE SINCE WE'D ended in a tie at three against three. This was the tiebreaker, and since we'd both just done it, we had the advantage of trying to remember exactly what was coming next and exactly how to sabotage the other.

Given this was the most challenging of all the courses, it wasn't surprising that we were left alone with it. It started with a rope climb. Most people saw that and moved straight past this course.

The entire room was made of that jump house inflatable material, which made it both more exciting and more challenging to get across. We readied the self-timer on the side that would make a shooting sound when it was time to go and readied ourselves beside one another.

At twenty seconds, I jumped in place to ready my adrenaline.

At ten seconds, I got myself into a running stance.

At three seconds, Dorian jumped in his spot, his heavier body weight making my feet slip out from under me.

"Cheater!" I called as the shot rang and Dorian made a run for it.

He was already making his way up the rope as I slipped my way to my rope, socks not making it all that much easier.

"All's fair in love and war, beautiful," he responded when he got to the top, stopping for only a moment to throw me a wink.

I wasn't very far behind him when I got to the top, taking the swinging steps with all the precision years of ballet had taught me while I tried reaching for the unused ones to swing his way and throw him off-balance.

He almost slipped off one and cursed some naughty, beautiful words. "Who's the cheater now?" he called.

I made it to the other end and used a foamy bat to whack at a bunch of balls flying my way in order to get to the other side. "You asked for it," I called back.

When I made it to the end, I turned for only a moment in order to throw my bat at Dorian and saw he was right behind me. So I smacked him instead of throwing it, and he took no mercy in smacking me back with his bat.

I burst out laughing. "You look sexy. So professional."

He smacked me on the thigh, and I could tell he was using as little force as possible. "I played baseball until I was twenty-three."

I gasped. "Super sexy." As our eyes met, we were both hypnotized for seconds. Long, long seconds. Seconds that had us leaning forward until we were sharing breath. I broke it. "But if you're using your advantage, I must use mine." I made a reverse kick in order to smack his bat from his arms and enjoyed the look in his eyes when it went flying.

When our gazes met again, he licked his lips. "Who's the sexy one now?"

I winked, throwing my bat at him as I moved for the next course of balancing along a thin strip of foamy wood over a ball pit. The challenge here was the two opposing sides merging halfway through, so one of us would be left behind, and I refused to be that one.

My balance made it easier for me to move down, but Dorian's longer legs got him there just as quickly. I didn't want to risk pushing because though I was technically stronger than him, his maleness instantly meant he'd push me over, so I allowed him to overtake for only a moment before jumping on his back.

He lost his balance—and his cocky laugh—immediately, and we both went toppling into the ball pit.

We were hysterically laughing, and because we'd made up the rules here, we both followed them and made our way through the ball pit to the beginning once again to start over.

I jumped from his end to mine, sticking the landing beautifully before starting over. He was right beside me and this time, I didn't try to give him the space. I ran for it, far more graceful than his movements.

I made it in front by only a step and felt his hands on my waist the entire way down the single plank.

"You're turning me on, Shipman!"

"That's the plan, Romanov," he whispered into my ear, and a gush of wetness pooled in my panties.

We fought our way through balancing on a large ball to make it to the other side, more monkey swings of varying types, a rock climb, and more fighting one another before making it to the end.

And the most difficult part, especially in socks.

The final obstacle was to get to the top of a ramp and ring the bell. The problem was getting up a curved ramp was already difficult enough, but throw in that it was in that jump house material, and we bounced around with every attempt, and it became nearly impossible. Dorian cheated by bouncing high enough to knock me off my feet more than once.

But finally, I knew what to do.

As he was attempting his way up, I made a run for it and used the side of his rough body as leverage to jump off, barely grasping onto the top of the ramp as Dorian's hands wrapped around my ankles, and he tugged.

I kicked at him, then saw his arm land beside me and knew I was running out of time. I pushed off him some more and barely got to the little rope that rang the bell before his hand was there.

As the bell rang, I kicked at him again, and his arms wrapped around me as he went flying.

We were both laughing hysterically, laid out on the course, when he turned over and almost toppled me with all of his weight. "I think I won."

"Dorian Alexander, I will challenge you again if you try to cheat. I won!"

He bit my lip, eyes sparkling. "Svetlana Lyubov, I'm not sure if I should be more scared or turned on right now."

My brows furrowed as I leaned into his lips. "Turned on. Definitely turned on."

He kissed me with vigor before peeling away and tugging on my arms so I could stand with him. "C'mon. I have *a* stuffed animal to get you." As he moved for the area we'd left our shoes, he made sure to throw back, "If your pride wasn't so big, I could've gotten you two."

I smacked him, laughing all the way.

IT WAS ONLY A STUFFED ANIMAL, BUT EVERY ONE OF my childhood dreams consisted of a boy winning me a stuffed animal. With three big scary brothers, boys hadn't exactly lined up for the opportunity.

But this boy had won me a big stuffed elephant.

One big stuffed elephant.

I was giddy. Both from winning our bet and from now having Lloyd. Dorian didn't look too upset from his loss though. On the contrary, he couldn't seem to take his eyes off me the entire car ride back to his place and wouldn't stop laughing as I carried Lloyd—who was nearly my size—out of the car and onto my back.

When we were in the apartment, I placed Lloyd in the corner of Dorian's room, right by the floor-to-ceiling windows, then moved his two front legs to cover his eyes. Lloyd looked so cute like this. Like he was bashful.

"There you go, little guy," I said like I was talking to my child. "Cover up now. You don't want to see what Mommy and Daddy are about to do."

When I turned, Dorian was biting his lip to stop himself from laughing.

"What? It'd be a bit inappropriate for Little Lloyd to watch us, don't ya think?"

"Little Lloyd is bigger than you."

"Don't make fun of Little Lloyd." I stopped before him.

He took my face between his hands. "I wouldn't dream of it, but why is he covering his eyes?"

"We have something to do tonight."

He knew what I was talking about. His eyes darkened as I said the words, but still, he asked, "Do we?"

My hands stopped on his chest, playing with the fabric as nerves bubbled up in me. "That was two dates. You said a couple of dates."

He licked his lips, but I knew it was a reflex of his being in thought and not a seduction.

"There's no rush, Lan. I can wait."

"I don't want to."

He stared into my eyes for what felt like an eternity, and when he saw I had no reservations about this decision, he finally leaned in to kiss me. Slow and passionate. Relaxed, like he had all the time in the world. Like he was savoring every taste.

We stood kissing for a long time before Dorian finally pushed me back until my knees hit the bed. He broke our kiss to watch me fall, groaning as my hands skimmed up his thighs.

He continued to take his time as his hand slowly moved to the back of his shirt, and he whipped it off. It was erotic, and the glimmer in his eyes as he met my gaze again said he'd done it specifically because he knew what it would do to me. Girls were known to love that move, and at the base of it, I was like any other girl.

His chest was hard, muscular without the full six-pack. The definition was all there, but he didn't look like a model. Well, that was a lie. He was so hot he could definitely be a model, but not a pretty-boy one. He would make a great woodsy model. He only needed to grow out his beard for it.

The hair on his chest was also very unmodel-like and very me likey.

"You know—" I ran my hands up and down his torso. "—just because I've never done this doesn't mean I haven't fantasized. I'm not nervous."

He took my face in his hands and leaned down to kiss me. "Good. I don't want you to be nervous. I would never do anything you didn't like."

"Yet you're still standing here with clothes on when I would most certainly prefer you naked." I shook my head.

He released me and threw his head back laughing. "You're also still dressed, Lan."

I smirked, eyes sparkling, as I rose to my feet without hesitation and pulled my shorts down from under my dress, then the whole sundress followed it to the ground. I wasn't wearing a bra, so I was left in only my panties.

His eyes were wide as they stared down at me, attention focused on my breasts.

I settled back on the edge of the bed and leaned back onto my hands. "I think you can have the pleasure of removing that final piece. But you're now more dressed than I am."

Dorian licked his lips, basically drooling, as he stepped back and unbuttoned his jeans, moving on autopilot while his mind was focused on my skin. From the simple look in his eyes, I knew he was imagining how I would taste.

While his shoes got kicked off and jeans fell, my heart raced. I hadn't lied. I wasn't nervous. I was excited. I'd been horny for so long and now I had an outlet for it. I wanted Dorian to take care of me and the anticipation was rising within.

But the anticipation felt a whole lot like nerves racing through my stomach, tingling beneath my skin.

When his fingers slipped into his boxer briefs and he tugged down, my gasp was involuntary.

His cock popped out as if it was finally released from its prison and it stood solid before my eyes. Now I was practically drooling.

Dorian stood before me like an Adonis sculpture ready to be ogled, and I'd suddenly become the greatest fan of such art.

His chest heaved as he finally took that step closer to me. I couldn't felt my body's natural reaction to push away, slip farther up the bed. He only smirked at my retreat like he knew there was nowhere I could go to get away from him.

He licked his lips as he fell to his knees on the bed, grabbing my ankles to stop my retreat.

My heart thundered within my chest, and I had the sudden urge to shut my legs. His hold would never allow it.

Dorian dropped so he could kiss first one ankle then the

other. Then slowly up one leg and down the other, all the while avoiding the one spot we both wanted him.

I was breathing hard. Hard. So hard, my fingers clutched at the sheets to ground me in some reality as I sat perched on my elbows to watch him. He hadn't moved for my panties yet, not that it mattered. They were so soaked through, they'd become a useless barrier.

As he kissed back up both my legs, taking turns with each kiss, he stared up at me. A deviousness that was not normally part of Detective Dorian Shipman's features materialized, and I knew I was in trouble. Those cognac orbs held promises.

When he reached my knees, his gaze sparkled, and I held my breath for what was to come next.

What came next was his tongue, slithering up the inside of one thigh, then down the other. My head fell back as my hips involuntarily thrust up, hoping to reach his mouth, and my fingers gripped the sheets for dear life. I only let out a whimper as my legs tried to close but were restrained by his hold, and I think he appreciated the sound.

"Look what you've done to those panties, my suspect." His hands slithered up my thighs as he sucked on a spot low on the inside of my thigh. As his fingers grabbed the edges of the fabric, he smirked. "I think I should take these in for evidence."

I moaned as he moved higher up my thighs and sucked at a spot so close to where I wanted him. When he was pleased with the bruise he'd undoubtedly left there, Dorian pulled back enough to slowly slide my panties down my legs. I watched him through hooded eyes, my insides clenching as he brought the scrap of fabric up to his nose and inhaled deeply.

"Mm, evidence for sure."

"Dorian," I begged in barely a whisper.

He dropped the panties to the side and smirked as he laid between my legs to prevent them from coming together. His thumb played with the arousal there, spreading it down my slit and around my clit, all the while watching for my reactions.

Reactions I couldn't hold in.

I was hyperventilating. I must've been because I was hardly getting any breaths in. I meant to call his name, beg him, but the moan was incomprehensible as it left me. Dorian's chuckle didn't help. It was so sexy, my hips thrust up to beg in my stead.

"Such a good, patient, girl, Suspect. Good girls are rewarded, did you know that?"

"Please," I whimpered.

His tongue took his thumbs place as he slowly licked between my holds, ending his journey by sucking at the little nub on top, and I fell, no longer able to hold myself up.

He didn't let up on my clit, and I don't think moans stopped escaping me the entire time, getting louder then softer as breath completely left me, then louder again. I begged. At least, I think I did. I tried to. Words weren't as easy as I took for granted.

His one hand slithered up my body to play with my nipples as the other played with my opening, barely inserting the tip of his finger before easing away.

I didn't know what it felt like to come but I knew I was close, my body thrumming with the need to explode.

But he pulled away.

I cried out as he licked up my slit, teasing me, but didn't have time to complain before he was back to sucking my clit, taking me back to that edge. He chuckled against me as he finger slipped inside, and I grew more desperate with the feel of that vibration, with the sound of him.

When my body could finally take no more, his hand pressed down onto my lower stomach as his other continued to slowly fuck me. His mouth didn't let up on my clit until I was shaking. My legs, my hips, my whole body. Gone.

I was still moaning as I came down, my body shaking involuntarily as it remembered that it was no longer coming.

Dorian was watching me as his finger continued to move within me. "I've never seen anything more beautiful than when you come, Lana."

I wanted to smile but my muscles wouldn't listen to me. "Then wait until you see what I look like coming while you're inside me."

He chuckled, that sexy fucking sound. "Not yet, beautiful."

"Dorian," I cried, begged, I didn't care. I wanted him inside me.

He kissed my hip, arm still holding me down. "I need to get you ready, baby." As he said it, he inserted a second finger, and I realized what he'd meant. It felt amazing but it came with a burning stretch.

"Relax, baby." He kissed my hips, my thighs, my pussy. Everywhere while he fingered me with those two digits.

When my body finally listened, settling into the bed and reaching for that explosion again, he inserted a third finger and that burning stretch came back. My walls clenched involuntarily.

His free hand was soft as it caressed my skin, kisses still lingering everywhere. "Relax."

It took a moment but finally, with his fingers inside me and this thumb rubbing on my clit, I succumbed to the pleasure. I moaned his name. I moaned for God. I moaned every curse word in every language I knew.

He laughed as he pulled away when I was reaching for that end and slowly moved up my body, kissing and sucking as he traveled. "You're so receptive, Lan. Such a good listener. Who would've thought my dangerous little suspect would be so good for me?"

I was tired and needy, but I couldn't help the way my lips quirked into a smirk. "Should I be bad, Detective? Will that make you spank me?"

He smirked, bringing my legs up to wrap around his waist. "I think you've already been bad."

My brows furrowed and by the way his eyes shined, it was in an adorable way. "How?"

He kissed my jaw as his hands traveled up and down my legs. "The silencer." He kissed my neck. "Possession of unregistered weapons." He kissed behind my ear. "Target practice in public." He kissed the side of my mouth before moving to the other side. "All those computer hacks from years ago." My cheek. "Who knows what else from years ago." Down my jaw. "That stupid fucking place you called a home."

I giggled. So he was still mad about that. "I don't think where I lived counts as being bad."

He bit my neck. "Trespassing, Lan. Breaking and entering."

I laughed now. "Oops."

He met my stare as his hand slithered down the back of my thigh. "Yeah, beautiful." He smacked my ass. Hard. "Oops."

I gasped and moaned at once, growing wetter.

He smirked. "Such a bad fucking girl you are normally. But oh, how good you've been beneath me." He spanked me again, and I nearly came from the impact alone, fingers digging into his shoulders.

He licked around my lips before invading my mouth, tasting all of me.

I was so desperate for him, I clung to his shoulders, scraping down his back to leave my own marks, and thrust up into him. I didn't care how wanton that made me. I needed him.

"Dorian," I begged when all he did was tease his cock up and down my slit, playing the tip of his cock with my clit, before sliding back down.

"You're my girl, Lana." He eased the very tip of his cock into me. "Mine. From the moment you walked into that precinct and chose me as your victim, you've been mine."

I nodded, meeting those hypnotizing eyes. "All my firsts, Dorian. Everything I have. It's all yours."

His eyes shimmered as he slammed into me, and my back arched as the pain seared through me. "Fuck," I groaned.

He held still, allowing my body to adjust, and I'd never been more thankful for the way his fingers had teased me before, prepared me.

"Breathe, baby," he groaned into my ear.

I did as I was told and after a few moments, the pain as still there but it mixed with the pleasure and all I wanted was more. "More, Dorian. More, please. Please."

His grin pressed into the side of my neck as he slowly began moving. "So fucking good." He spanked my ass again, and I clenched around him. He chuckled against my lips. "You like that, don't you, baby? You like when I spank you?"

I nodded desperately, clinging to him.

"You like when I put you in your place?" He slammed into me. "When I hold you down?"

"Yes, yes," I moaned. "Fuck, Dorian, yes, please."

He licked down my neck, sucked on my nipples, and I was gone for.

I came around his cock, my walls clenching, wanting to never let go of him.

He groaned as he moved for my mouth again, slamming into me to find his release. "Fuck, Lana. Fuck, baby, this pussy's so good to me."

The pain was so much better. So alluring. I wanted more.

"Come with me, Lana. Come on, baby girl. Give me one more."

I tried to speak past my moans and whimpers but nothing was intelligible. It wasn't possible when another orgasm slipped through me right as he came.

I was still holding onto him, walls still clenching around his cock inside me, when I came down from the high. When I met his eyes, there was only one emotion there.

"Mine, Lana. Everything about you is mine."

"Yours, Dorian. Always."

Dorian

LANA WAS beautiful when she was teasing me.

She was beautiful when she was suspicious of me.

She was beautiful when she was angry and upset and happy and sleepy.

But she was absolutely stunning in this relaxed state I suspected she hadn't felt in many years, if ever.

There was peace over her features as she slept beside me without any worries that something might happen to her. It was the best thing I could've ever given her, and I knew I was going to become addicted to making sure she felt this way always.

I felt safe and at peace.

Not because she was beside me and could protect me—which I suspected, with her training, she probably could—but because my heart was hers now. This beating organ in my chest had never felt so at ease.

She was here, sated, with my cum still dripping out of that delectable pussy, and I wouldn't let a night of my life go by without this again.

The moon shined through the floor-to-ceiling windows of my room and illuminated her in the most alluring glow. She looked heavenly, like an angel sent specifically for me. I liked to think that's what happened. That my father did that for me.

I lay on my side while my fingers softly brushed her cheek remembering those final moments at my father's bedside.

"Promise me you'll make sure your mother finds someone to spend the rest of her life with. That you will make sure she is happy," Father demanded, his voice hoarse from all the coughing.

My fingers fidgeted, holding his hand in mine. "That's not exactly my promise, Pops. If she refuses to move on..."

"Help her. Remind her that it will be okay. That I know she loves me eternally."

"I'll do whatever I can, Pops." I let my tear slide. I put on a brave face in front of Mom and Gwen, but when it was the two of us, I didn't need to any longer. "I'm gonna miss you."

"I know, Dor. But I'll always be around. Just visit your Mom and know that I'll be watching over her."

I squeezed his hand. "I envy you, Pops. For the love you were blessed with."

"Don't," he demanded, then softened his voice so it didn't hurt so much. "Envy means you will not reach it. But you will, son. I know you're going to find a love like your mom's and mine."

I didn't want to counter his claim, both because I wanted it to be true and because I didn't want to spend these final moments with him arguing. My family would be coming in soon, so I wanted to cherish this time alone with him while I had it.

"Promise me, if I'm lucky enough to be blessed with children, that you'll look out for them," I finally said. My profession was a dangerous one, and I had no way of knowing if one day I had a family whether a criminal might go after them to get to me.

"Do not ask that of me, Dor. That is my obligation to this

family. Your children and the love of your life will all be looked after. I will make sure nothing happens to them until you can get to them."

I squeezed his hand again. "It's killing me to lose you. I can't stop talking to you."

"Don't. I'll always be around. Speak to me. I'll be listening, and I'll always be there to guide you, Dor."

Tears slipped down my cheeks, my strength faltering as I allowed all of my emotions to pour out. I brought his hand to my lips and kissed it softly. "I love you, Pops. And I promise I won't marry until I find a love like the one you have with Mom."

"I know, Dor. You're stubborn. You won't back down until you reach that goal. And that is one of my favorite things about you."

I kissed his hand again as a knock came to the door.

"I love you, Dor."

That memory hit me like a train. Pops had been right, like he always was. My all-knowing best friend.

Back then, I hadn't believed it. I couldn't fathom there ever being a love as strong as theirs, and I certainly couldn't fathom being the one lucky enough to experience it. I knew Gwendolen felt that same intenseness with her husband, but it still hadn't ever felt possible for me.

Now I knew.

It was.

My thumb brushed Lana's plump bottom lip, and she moaned in her sleep. I wanted to know what she was dreaming of. Was it of me?

No matter how much I desired to know, I didn't want to wake her. My peaceful angel.

So I went back to softly caressing her cheek.

Mom held on to Pops's hand for dear life when his chest took its final breath. She held on even tighter when it stopped moving altogether. She refused to let go for hours. Her tears were stained on her cheeks, and and she lay beside her husband, knowing he was gone and wanting nothing more than to be with him again.

That was the part of their love I did not envy.

I fought my own tears, but a few still slipped. I wasn't strong enough to hold it all back. I didn't think I'd be strong enough to hold it back if I were losing my own love.

Mom had to be the strongest person I knew.

Lana was calling my name in soft whispers, and as I came out of that memory, I realized she was awake.

"Dorian, baby, what's wrong?"

Her thumb brushed my cheek, and I realized a tear had slipped past. I'd cried? I hadn't cried for my father in years now.

"Nothing," I muttered, wiping at the tear. "Nothing," I said again when she wasn't convinced. "I was just remembering my father."

Her lips tipped up into a sad smile as she turned to face me completely, her thumb now playing with my bottom lip as my hand fell into her hair. "One day, I want to hear all about him."

"I promise."

Her brows furrowed. "I've told you before, Dorian. Promises mean something to me."

"I know. They're a lifetime commitment. They've become just as important to me since meeting you, Lan."

"Fine. Then I'll let you have that one."

My lip quirked into a small smirk as I kissed the tip of her thumb. "Then let me have this one too—you're mine forever, Lana. We'll be together, grow together, always be honest, protect each other until the end of time."

Her brows furrowed "Dorian..."

I knew what this meant to her. I knew how important it was for her to have that life she'd dreamed of and how deeply she wanted to love the man she was with. I knew there was a lot

of baggage that may come with who her family was and a lifetime of looking out for one another, but I was ready for all of
it. I wanted her. Needed to protect her and show her she was
the gem of this world.

"I promise."

Part Five

"*Some things are more precious because they don't last long.*"

\- Oscar Wilde

DORIAN LEFT. He'd gone to work the moment he'd finished his breakfast, and it gave me the time, both in cleaning after our meal and in preparing for the day, to think about this whirlwind weekend.

He'd kissed me. Taken me on dates one and two. Won me a huge stuffed elephant. Moved me into his apartment. Made love to me. And most importantly, made me my promise of a lifetime. The one I only wanted once in my existence, and I think it was the moment he learned of my family and wanted to hear me talk of them that I'd wanted that promise to come from him, even if I wasn't fully ready to admit that to myself then.

I was in the shower, readying myself for this week, as I thought about it all.

My family wouldn't be all too pleased with my decision to be with a detective. Dorian was quite literally the type of person we stayed away from. It solidified that I would never one hundred percent leave this life behind because now I was on the other side, even though I'd never do anything that would betray my family. But it did give me a quieter, less dangerous part in this lifestyle.

And I knew now why I'd never left. Part of me, the subconscious part, had always known I'd stick around.

I pictured what it might be like—Dorian meeting them. Because if this thing between us continued—and by his promise, I assumed it would—then he would have to meet them. Hell, he'd have to at least be cordial with them. I snorted back laughter. I'd brought the mafia into a detective's life. That probably wasn't a pretty look on his resumé.

Father would be open to him because he was mine, but Ivan Romanov was also a quiet man. So much would be going on in his mind. Things he would never tell us because he wanted me to be happy but would go back to his room and speak to the picture of my mother about. I'd caught him doing it years back when Carrini had shown up to take me on a date and again when I'd decided to leave. He'd always fought his need to control my life and hiding away to speak with my mother was the best way to do so.

Lukov and Ilya would be protective but the easiest to get along with. They were both goofier and kinder, so they'd do what they could to accept Dorian. They still wouldn't love having me with an "enemy," but I could imagine, with time, Ilya showing Dorian some illegal hack into someone's computers or Lukov showing him some illegal ways to make transactions, they'd grow on one another. My family would probably have way too much fun showing Dorian illegal shit that he couldn't report because I wouldn't allow him to.

But hey, who knew. Maybe the illegal shit he learned from my brothers would help him in his job at some point. It wouldn't all around be a bad thing to have an in with the mafia.

Hell, who was I kidding? It would absolutely help him. His

biggest problem would be figuring out a way to make sure everything would be able to stand up in court.

Then there was Sergei.

Sergei was going to be difficult.

He hated cops the most, and as the first heir to the mafia, he was the most serious. More than my father, though *Otets* said that was because Sergei didn't understand the love he felt yet. Both for us and for *Mat'*.

Sergei wouldn't be agreeable with Dorian in the slightest. He wouldn't even try to be for my sake like the other three. He would simply remain quiet.

Actually, that was a bald-faced lie. He would a hundred percent present his displeasure. He would throw insults at Dorian. Hell, he might even instigate a fight.

It was going to be difficult to get any of them on board as it was since they had a special dislike for the precincts in this area, Dorian's precinct specifically. I didn't know what had happened, but a couple of years ago, something had gone down between Sergei and the precinct. They'd kept it from me, and honestly, with all the shit they had going on, I hadn't really wanted to know.

But now it was something to be curious about, especially since the precinct now knew who I was related to.

Would Dorian know? He didn't get on board until a while after that incident, but maybe he'd heard stories. If not, I wasn't really sure I wanted him to know. At least, not until I knew what it was. Especially considering I was almost certain it had something to do with killing a cop.

So that, coupled with Sergei's existing displeasure that I wanted some "normal, morally sound" man, meant things would be difficult. It meant things would get awkward, too, because Dorian's friends were his team, and mine were my family. At some point, they would need to be in the same place at the same time.

Would we be able to handle a life with my mafia side and his detective side coming together? Would everyone make it out alive?

I stepped out of the shower, drying my hair with a towel as I took in my appearance in the steamed mirror. I looked happier, more alive. Now I had to keep my brothers from noticing—though only Lukov constantly visited me—because he'd know it was because of a boy, and I did not need that drama right now. It'd be nice if we could at least wait until the Mann case was over and I was fully off the suspect radar.

I was a little sore from last night, but the memories kept pouring in, reminding me of his taste, his feel, his smell, and all I wanted was more. To keep him from work and to spend the next week learning everything there was to know about each other's bodies.

But I couldn't do that. Finding bad guys was his passion, and I'd never keep that from him. Plus, I had a job too. Not one I necessarily cared too much about, so I could give it up whenever, but it was still a job. One that would keep me distracted from recounting every second of this weekend over and over and over...

I moved for his room and started dressing for the day, hoping to possibly make it to Toni's for a quick—and Lukov-less—breakfast.

NAIRI TOOK THE HINT WHEN I GAVE HER A DEATH glare as I ordered my food and coffee—*do not* call my brother.

They didn't normally track my phone then show up, so I knew it was Nairi's doing that he always showed up. And because he only ever did when she was here.

I had a hefty veggie omelette with toasted bread, maple

sausages, and hash browns to enjoy with my own company. Half of me wanted to ask Nairi to join me since I'd been coming here for years and hadn't had a decent conversation with her, but I wasn't sure how to go about that. I didn't want to encourage her affections for my brother by becoming her friend, but I wanted to become her friend.

I was just about to throw caution to the wind and call her to join me when another body plopped in the booth before me. My anger that she'd gone against my wishes and called him was about to blow when I looked up to find the unexpected before me.

"What the hell are you doing here?"

"Looking for you. I thought you were smart enough to figure that much out."

I rolled my eyes. "Aren't you supposed to be at work? You know, fighting crime, finding Mann's murderer?"

"How do you know I'm not?"

I fell back in the booth, sighing as my arms crossed before my chest. "So I'm a suspect again?"

"No."

"My brothers?"

She grimaced. "Unfortunately not."

"Then what do you want?"

"Your help," Ava answered. "You broke into computers for your family all the time. Help us out too."

My brows shot up. "First of all, I did no such thing. And second, isn't that illegal? Aren't you supposed to be annoyingly law-abiding?"

"Oh, drop the act." She took one of my toasts and bit into it. "I know you hacked into shit for your family. I won't try to prove it. I won't try to arrest you. But I know you did it. So do it again."

"I wonder how Dorian's going to feel hearing that you're asking me to break the law."

"So jump on his dick and make him okay with it. I don't care."

I gasped. "What vulgar language, Mrs. Tough Guy."

She rolled her eyes, biting into my toast again. "So you gonna do it?"

"No. But out of curiosity, what do you want me to look for?"

She smirked. "Our guys can't figure out how they hacked into the systems to change them before the murder. I need you to do it. Whoever did this was able to move the cameras and get away with it. It makes me think they'd been working in the background for a while, knew the system well enough. They didn't make any mistakes. You also know the system. Go in there, through the last few months, and see if any consistencies pop up that you hadn't paid attention to before."

"You know, Mrs. Tough Guy, if you want to progress in your career, you really should do the work yourself."

She rolled her eyes but stopped herself from saying anything as Nairi came for us.

She placed a muffin I hadn't ordered in front of me. "*Mne pozvonit' Lukovu?*"

My brows shot up. "*Ty govorish' po-russiki?*" *You speak Russian?*

The left side of her mouth quirked up. "*V Armenii vtoroy yazyk russkiy a tretiy angliyskiy.*" *In Armenia, the second language is Russian, the third English.*

Armenia? Well, now I had a frame of reference for that word Lukov had called her a few weeks ago. If only I could remember what it was...

"*Niet,*" I finally answered. "*Ne zvoni Lukovu.*" *No, don't call Lukov.* God, please don't call him. The very last thing I needed was for Ava to make him worry about me more.

Ava eyed the two of us. "Stop that. What the hell are you two conspiring about?"

"Learn the language and find out." I gave a fake smile.

"Whatever. So will you do it?"

"You speak any other languages, Ava? You want to hear it in Russian? *Niet.*"

"*Voche,*" Nairi added, though she couldn't have known what we were speaking of. "*Hayir.*"

I stifled a laugh. "Thank you."

She smiled, then turned back for the counter, where another customer was waiting.

Ava rolled her eyes. "I speak French."

"*Non.*" I said one of the only words I knew in French.

"Just think about it. You'd be helping Dorian too."

"If Dorian wanted that help, he'd ask me."

"Would he? If he knows you left that crooked life, would he ask you to jump back into it? We both know he's too sweet of a guy for that."

"You know you never answered my question the day we met."

Her brows shot up as if telling me to ask again.

"Do you like him?"

She snorted. "God no. He's far too... annoyingly moral."

My gaze narrowed. "I don't think a cop is supposed to think like that."

"Tough. I can catch the bad guys and have grey areas."

"But doesn't illegally hacking into systems make you one of the bad guys?"

"I'm not hurting anyone."

"It's still illegal."

"Yet I'm ignoring the fact that you used to do it. That you

taught someone to take your place since your family is still hacking their way through life perfectly."

I smirked. "There isn't much I like about you, Ava."

"Ditto." She stood, taking my muffin. "Think about it."

As she walked away, my lip jutted out. I hadn't ordered it, but now I wanted that muffin.

"Nairi," I called. "Can I get a muffin, please?"

She gave me an amused smile. "No dessert until you finish your meal."

I grumbled, but my lips still tipped up at her tease. Being her friend and not encouraging her feelings—that was the goal.

With my own company once more, I dove back into breakfast.

Dorian

PORTER KEPT EYEING me like she was waiting for something. Was it my relationship with Lana? Was she waiting for me to announce it? If so, it wouldn't be happening. That was none of their business.

When I didn't give her what she wanted, whatever that was, she huffed and stormed off. Lansly was off with Finnegan on the field, following a lead for another case, and I was the only one on our team in the office going through files for any evidence of Mann's murder.

"Dorian Shipman," a deep voice called from the other side of the room.

When I looked up, I met Lana's eyes.

Except they were a little lighter, older, and on a man.

He had light brown hair and a bit of stubble, but he looked like his sister.

I dropped the files on my desk and stood up. "Ilya Romanov."

He smirked. "Did she tell you about me, or have you been doing your own research?"

"Both."

"Smart man. If you trusted only what she had to say, you'd think me a bad person."

Lana had only ever gushed about her family. Should I take it as a good sign that her brother was joking with me?

"What can I do for you?"

He nodded back. "Take a walk."

My gaze narrowed. If we took a walk, we'd have no witnesses, which could be both a positive and negative. If he wanted to kill me for touching his sister, it was very bad. But, on the other hand, if cops saw me conspiring with a known mafia man, it wouldn't look good for me, so leaving would be the best route. And probably before Porter came back and saw him. Her hatred was more for the eldest Romanov brother, but that didn't mean she liked any of them.

I followed him down the stairs and out the back doors until we were on the sidewalk.

We made it half a block before he said, "So you and my sister?"

"She told you?" Lana hadn't mentioned telling her family yet.

"No. I don't think the *umnik* was planning on telling us anytime soon. She knows we don't like your lot."

"So how'd you find out?"

"You didn't think we let her leave without keeping an eye out, did you?"

"What do you want, Romanov?"

"Being a suspect in your case meant we kept an eye on your cases as well, Detective. Your recent one opened our eyes a bit more. Made us pay more attention to our sister, to you two."

I focused on the cars passing us by. "You heard about the three men?"

"We did."

"Did you read the files?" Clarification—did you hack into our systems and read the files?

"We did." Ilya didn't seem to care that he was admitting a crime to law enforcement.

"So you came to what? Check if we've locked them up? Of course I locked them up. I'll have rumors circulating soon too."

The side of Ilya's mouth lifted like my ideas of vengeance were cute. "There're a lot of things we never imagined, Shipman. Our sister with one of your lot was high on that list."

"So you're here to check me out?"

"She was your suspect not too long ago. What makes us believe she isn't still and this is your sick way of catching her." He was so calm, but his tone indicated he'd snap my neck this very moment if I said the wrong thing.

Maybe a popcorn machine wasn't enough for the protection they'd given Lana. Teaching her to fight was still the best thing they could've done, but this eternal worry for her settled my chest. I loved knowing Lana had that in her life, that she would always be taken care of.

"How am I meant to prove to you she is not?"

He smirked. "Access to your case notes would be a start."

I quirked a brow. "What? Your family think now that I'm with your sister, you can get access to anything you want?"

His lips tipped up, eyes shining, and I saw the man Lana had told me about—the one who was just as amusing as he was scary. "It would butter you up to the family. Our opinion matters to Svetie."

"I don't think I need buttering up that badly."

He snorted. "From the precinct you come from, you need more than you can give us."

My gaze narrowed on him. "*Your* brother shot my colleague. Why would we need to butter up anything?"

"Because you're the one dating our sister."

I rolled my eyes. "She's an adult."

Ilya stopped walking and turned to me, assessing me before saying, "How far are you willing to go, Detective?"

"For what?"

"The only other man Lana went out with turned out to be the wrong fit, but he was willing to do anything for her. Would you do the same?"

"You're asking if I would kill for her?" It was a loaded question.

"No. I'm asking if you would do anything for her."

"Isn't killing the highest thing on that list?"

"You're a cop, Shipman. You've killed before and you'll kill again. It won't affect your conscience the way it would a civilians. I want to know how much more you're willing to do for her."

I thought about it. Was I willing to kill for her? I couldn't believe the answer was yes when only a few weeks ago, I was talking to her about morals in our first interrogation. But the only reason I would need to kill for her would be because her life was in danger, and in that moment, I knew I'd do anything to protect her.

"What could be worse than taking a life?"

"Ruining one," he answered immediately. "Would you be willing to torture someone, to wrongly send someone to prison, to engage in some illegal activities, to kidnap loved ones, kill them instead of the person you're after?"

Holy fuck. Now, that was a loaded question.

My mouth moved to answer, but nothing came out. What could? I was a detective. My sole purpose in life was to make sure none of those things happened, and if they did, to lock up the fuckers responsible. Was I willing to become one of them for Lana? Would she be expecting it of me?

Ilya smirked like he was enjoying the war going on in my

mind. "You may think on your answer, Shipman. But know I am not pleased you could not immediately answer yes. Her last man was willing to do so much worse."

He turned back for the precinct and walked away.

It took me a moment to get my head back on straight before I followed after him. He didn't go back inside, heading to his car instead, but he did give me a final analyzing look before getting in and driving off.

I took the elevator back up this time to give myself that minute in solitude. I'd promised Lana a lifetime, yet would I be able to do some of the things that would be required to keep her safe?

Ilya showing up lit a fire under my ass to both take a deeper look into my feelings for Lana and to find out more about her past, like this other man that'd apparently been so willing with her. She said all of her firsts from her first kiss to her first time, were mine, so not much could've happened with him, but I still needed to know.

When I got back to our desks, Porter was there, rifling through paperwork. "Where'd you go?"

"I needed to take a call."

She eyed me suspiciously but didn't say more as she went back to her work.

THOUGH THE MANN CASE WAS IMPORTANT AND TOP priority, we had others on our load as well. Since we didn't have any leads in the Mann one, Finnegan wanted us to clear a few of the others. One of which was probably the simplest case I'd ever worked on.

Another... we were throwing ideas out about at that very moment.

Our team's dynamic was probably the best I could've ever asked for. Porter was always the harshest, whether for male or female leads; Lansly was always the most technical, ready to dive into searches for anything we needed and quickly produce results; I was the devil's advocate, always fighting them on whatever point was made; and Finnegan was the leader. Although still human with the possibility of his emotions getting to him from time to time, he was by far the most unbiased man I'd ever met.

The case we were working right now was a Bonnie and Clyde duo, except instead of killing people, they were... traumatizing them? The duo loved to go around to people's homes, tie them up, and make them watch as the two performed every sexual act in the book. But they were calculating and happened to know the exact positions that would affect the couples they were performing in front of most. In the most recent case, Bobbi and Macy Hendrix had been forced to watch the two lick each other's feet because Macy hated it and Bobbi had a foot fetish. The trauma deepened in every case when one, in this case Bobbi, became aroused at what he saw and the other even more disgusted and terrified.

Bonnie and Clyde loved breaking up relationships, like theirs was the only one worth having on this planet.

Bonnie and Clyde were great at getting away with things because although we had a plethora of their DNA, we had no way of actually catching them. And they didn't stick to a timeline, sometimes working two in a week and other times not attacking for over a month at a time.

Right now, we were trying to figure out how to catch them before they went around terrorizing another couple.

"Of the six couples, every single one of the disgusted partners recognized the couple, but none of them could place from where," Finnegan started.

"In order to learn of these kinks—feet, bondage, blood play—they'd need to be watching for a while. They probably already have their next couple, if not their next few couples, lined up, and they're slowly watching them," Lansly added.

"Or," Porter started, "it could be the case of a kink that gets mentioned often. Think of it—if they were to follow Macy home, they have no way of knowing whether Bobbi is as uptight as her or not. Why would they stick around just to find out they're both boring?"

"Or," I added, "Bonnie and Clyde could be listening in on conversations. Macy telling her girlfriends that Bobbi's asking for feet stuff again; Arnold telling his barber that his girl won't peg him." I gave an example from one of the other couples.

"So there's nothing crazy looking about them?" Finnegan asked. "They fit in to normal day but don't stand out."

"If we go off those two examples," Lansly theorized, "we can have a waitress and a barber or cleaner at the barbershop. Think of it—women talk most to their girlfriends, and men talk most openly to their barbers. It would be the perfect way to go unacknowledged and know everything." He turned for his computer and started clicking away. "Based on that, I can pull up bank statements for all of the victims for overlapping barber shops and restaurants."

"Perfect." Finnegan clapped. "Now to the why."

Porter shrugged. "They enjoy the turmoil it causes relationships. If they're not happy in the relationship, they shouldn't be in one."

"Or Bonnie and Clyde saw and heard from that person, in this latest case Macy, and thought her uptight, so they followed her to see if her relationship was actually like that," I rebutted. "When they saw Bobbi actually liked feet and she wouldn't indulge that kink, they knew how to act. It was their way of helping Bobbi and bringing Macy out of her shell."

Bullshit. Bonnie and Clyde lived on terrorizing these couples. They weren't trying to help for shit.

But part of figuring this stuff out was getting into the heads of the criminals. And in their heads, they may think of themselves as heroes.

"Could be," Finnegan said in thought. "Narcissists like to believe they're always doing good. We could have two narcissists."

"So which is the dominant and which is the submissive?"

"Maybe they switch. Equals. Which is why they can perform any task that many men wouldn't do."

Porter jutted her bottom lip out as she looked at me. "Aw, Shipman. You don't wanna get pegged?"

I rolled my eyes. "No, thank you."

"Lucky us, children!" Lansly called out, staring at his computer screen. "We have overlapping barber shops and the Divinity restaurant. It looks like they switch out which one gets to pick, and each one happened two days before the attack. Spot seven would be coming from the restaurant."

"Perfect!" Porter sat up. "I'll get some undercover to go in with me, and I'll complain about my love." She fluttered her eyes in our direction. "Any specific times?"

"Around noon each one."

"Finally somewhere!" I exclaimed. We'd spoken of this case every time more victims came out, so I was glad we were finally getting closer to catching these two.

And it was a nice break from constantly thinking of Mann and Lana.

DORIAN HAD BEEN DISTRACTED since he got back from work yesterday. He hadn't told me what was on his mind, and I didn't want to pry. If it was about one of his cases, he was likely trying to bring together a puzzle with a missing piece, and I didn't want to distract him.

But it also meant he used me, taking every opportunity to touch and kiss me, to push me against a wall and rip my clothes off. It was invigorating.

This morning, we took things slow, enjoying each other's company and laughing more than I would've ever conceived possible.

We showered, somehow behaving ourselves the entire time, and now we were both wrapped in towels, mine around my body and his hanging low on his waist.

"You're cute with that." I played with the scruff on his face. "I like how it feels when you're kissing down my body."

"You don't think I should shave?"

"Not completely," I said seriously, then gasped, excited. "Can I trim it for you?"

He laughed. "Your excitement about that makes me worry."

I jutted out my lower lip. "Please. Pleeeease."

He was still laughing as his face landed in the crook of my neck, and he kissed me there, that ruffled stubble sending shivers down my spine, while his hands grabbed me around the waist and hoisted me onto the bathroom counter. When he faced me again, he was shaking his head. "You have too much control over me."

My mouth opened in a smile. "Lucky me!"

His head continued to shake as he kissed me softly, then bit his bottom lip while taking me in. His hands slithered from my waist to my bare legs, the towel barely covering the tops of my thighs. "Be careful."

I rolled my eyes, but I couldn't help the giddy excitement thrumming through me. "Don't worry. I love this face. I won't nick it."

"Why don't I have full confidence in that?"

I gave him a sinister look while I took the electric razor and turned it on. "Dorian Alexander Shipman, don't test me."

He shrugged. "You nick me and you become a liar."

I began shaving his little beard so it was more stubble. "Now I really need to concentrate, huh? I can't have you thinking I'd lie. I want a future with you."

I was so focused on getting him the perfect shave that I didn't realize until his stare was burning into my profile that he was watching me so intently.

When I met his gaze, he was so serious. "Nick me all you want, Lan. Cover me in blood. I'll still be your future."

"Dorian..." I started because I hadn't meant to turn the moment so serious.

"I promise," he interrupted.

My lips tipped up, and I quickly glanced back to my work

so I wouldn't tear up. I shaved him a little more before turning the subject back around. "You know, you and my brother have the same middle name, spelled different."

"I know."

"Ah, yes. You have stalked my family."

He chuckled. "It's basic knowledge on them."

"You wanna know some basic knowledge about me?"

"Hm?"

"I prefer his spelling."

He gasped, pushing away so I didn't hurt him with any sudden movements. "Then I must change the way mine is spelled immediately!"

I laughed, pulling him back and enclosing him between my legs. "Well, you need a bit of Russian in you."

He rubbed his towel-clad cock against my bare opening. "I think you need a bit of Shipman in you."

I pushed him away, head thrown back in laughter, then pointed a chastising finger at him. "Dorian Alexander Shipman! You naughty, naughty child."

He bit my finger. "Are we saying Alexander my way or yours?"

"We can keep it your way, but my kids are going to have it the other way. Especially if they have your last name."

His eyes sparked, immediately easing my trepidation that I shouldn't have spoken of a family with him yet. "Oh? And what names were you thinking of?"

I shrugged. "Alexander is now a family name, so that'll be a middle. Spelled A.L.E.K.S.A.N.D.R."

"Yes, ma'am." He kissed me. "You know Svet is a family name for you too."

I shrugged. "A daughter's middle name, then."

"But it's a first name in the family."

I scrunched my nose. "I don't like family names as first names."

He pinched my nose. "Like mother, like daughter."

"I don't know if you should be comparing. My mother was a ball-buster."

He kissed me again. "Stop it, Lan, or I'll insist our daughter's *first* name be Sveta."

My smile was wide as I finally put the razor down, brushing the little hairs to the ground to clean up later. "Maybe we should've done the shower after."

"I can just rinse it." He moved for the faucet.

I smacked his ass as I hopped off the counter. "You need to get ready for work."

His arms wrapped around me as I was leaving the bathroom, whisper landing on my ear and making shivers pass through me. "I can make it a half day."

"Dorian," I chastised.

"Let me take care of you, Lan," he whispered. "We just showered. I think that means you need to moisturize now. I'll do anything for you to allow me to do that for you."

My eyes fell closed as I laughed. "You're ridiculous."

He pulled me for the room. "You're delicious."

I should've stopped him, but I wanted to be selfish this morning. It felt nice—being taken care of like this by him.

He took his time stripping me out of the towel and lathering my body with lotion, then grabbing for one of his large long-sleeved shirts and throwing it over my body.

He didn't allow me to reciprocate, but my fingers played their way down his chest, pulling off his low-hanging towel. He growled when I stroked his cock, pulling away and warning me with the dark look in his eyes to let go unless I wanted him to give in and fuck me. The problem was—I did want him to give in, even though I knew I shouldn't.

But I let go because we both needed energy if anything more was going to happen, and the best way to get that was some food. I gave him a final kiss and left for the kitchen, stealing a pair of briefs so I wasn't completely naked underneath. I hoped that helped control our urges a little bit.

Dorian was dressed equally as sparingly as me in only grey sweatpants that made me lose concentration. He had the bathroom cleaned, even though I'd said I'd do it, and had the washing machine going with the sheets from last night, and I knew he'd taken the time to replace it with a new set.

As the washer ran its cycle and I readied loaded veggie omelettes with everything but the kitchen sink inside, I couldn't help but get misty-eyed. This felt so normal. Being with Dorian felt like a happily ever after.

I pushed the tears away, not wanting to ruin this moment, and placed our omelettes on the peninsular island before readying a cup of coffee and a glass of water each.

I placed them all down and took my seat just in time to witness the obscene show that was Dorian putting creamer into his coffee. I liked mine black when I was the one making it, and he grimaced when he saw that.

Black is only for hard cases, beautiful. When I need something to really keep me up. That bitterness does just that.

His little comment made me laugh, and even though we didn't talk much through our meal, it felt perfect. Not awkward or forced, but like those silent meals my parents used to have where they'd be staring at each other with secret meaning the entire time. That was what this felt like.

Apparently, the food and coffee did their job in restoring energy because Dorian was ready to pounce the second he finished his last bite—not that I was going to put up much of a fight—when a knock came at the door. Who the hell was bothering us on a Tuesday morning?

He grumbled, making me giggle, as he turned for the door, and I started on the dirty dishes.

"You should probably put a shirt on," I called as he moved away.

"No. Whoever decided to interrupt us doesn't get that respect," he grunted, then screamed, "Coming," at the door when there was another knock.

I giggled, trying to keep quiet as I stacked the dishes in the sink.

"What are you guys doing here?" Dorian sounded shocked as he leaned into the crack of the opened door.

Then I heard it.

"We need to talk to you about Lana." Finnegan's voice filled the space.

And if Dorian had said "you guys," then Lansly and Porter were probably with him. Great.

I was preparing to head back to the room so they didn't know I was here when Dorian did the unexpected and swung the door open so they could all see me.

To my surprise—and Dorian's from the look on his face—the two rolled their eyes and reached for their pockets as Lansly smirked and stuck out his hand. "Told you he was in love with her."

They handed him some money as all three walked in without invitation, and I watched Dorian close the door as he tried to figure out what the hell was happening.

All three found their seats, Finnegan and Porter on the couch and Lansly on an armchair by the wall. The armchair by the floor-to-ceiling windows overlooking the city was left open for Dorian.

I cleared my throat, leaving the dishes to wash later. "I'll give you the privacy to talk about me." The bedroom was the only other place I could go, and I wasn't sure I wouldn't be able to hear them from there, but I truly wanted to give them their privacy. I trusted Dorian and knew he wouldn't let them hurt me.

Dorian stopped me with his body as Finnegan surprised us once again and declared, "Stay."

Dorian

"WE WERE GOING to ask Dorian to call you to meet us. This only saves time," Finnegan explained.

I was still holding Lana by both arms to keep her from moving as I turned for my team, eyes narrowing and nerves jumbling up inside that they wanted to lock her up. "Why?"

I wouldn't let them touch her. Hell, I'd burn any evidence they thought they had.

Finnegan held up a folder that I was just now noticing. "Walters's file. Maybe Miss Svetlana can find something we couldn't."

I met Lana's gaze. If she said she didn't want to do this, if she said she wanted them to leave, that's what would be happening.

She only nodded though. It was no shock that she'd be strong against the detectives who continued keeping her on the suspect charts, but my heart still exploded with renewed endearment. She was the bravest person I knew.

I took her hand and headed for the only seat left, pulling

her until she fell into my lap. If the team didn't like it, they could leave. I wasn't going to hide this, and certainly not in my own home. Lana was mine, and I intended everyone to find out.

The way she snuggled into me and a small close-lipped smile graced her lips, I knew I'd done the right thing.

None of them seemed shocked or annoyed or disgusted. Whatever that bet had been, apparently finding us together wasn't so far out of their realm of possibilities.

Even Porter didn't seem bothered, and she had a deeper hatred for the Romanovs. Though after those interrogations with the men who'd gone after Lana, Porter's behavior had been a little different.

"You could've at least put on a shirt," Porter mumbled as she got comfortable in the corner of the couch.

I finally stuck out my hand to take the file from Finnegan, then handed it to Lana without taking a peek. I'd seen the file one too many times and I was in the same boat as the others. If Lana could find something we were missing, it'd be the best help.

She began flipping through it immediately, skimming one page before flipping to the next. It took a few minutes of silence—which nicely wasn't awkward—before she stiffened in my lap.

Then all my attention was on her and the sheet she was focused on. There was a picture paper-clipped to it, and that's what she was staring at. "What is it, beautiful?"

I could feel the others sit up, on attention at the fact that she may've *already* found something.

Lana studied the picture another minute before she sighed and relaxed back into me. "Well, I guess I know why I was set up as the target."

"What. Is. It?" I ground out.

She didn't look away from the picture as she answered, "You guys interviewed three men who tried to have their fun with me those times." My hold on her tightened at the memory of what those fuckers had done, or tried to do, but nothing could've prepared me for what came next. "But there have actually been four guys total. Except this one was, is... different."

I shoved the file out of her hands and turned her by the jaw to look into my eyes. I could barely get myself to breathe as I searched her gaze, asking the question I knew we were all wondering but that I needed to know the answer to.

I knew in that moment that the answer to her brother was coming together, though, because I wouldn't even think before torturing this man.

Lana's gentle hands fell over my cheek. "You're still my only, Dorian. You saw the blood. You will always be my only."

Maybe, but that didn't mean he didn't do other things, try other things.

She leaned in for a soft kiss before turning back to the group. "He was different because he never tried to hurt me. He never tried to rape me or hit me."

It took me a long moment to accept that before I was able to breathe properly again. I hated everything she'd gone through and that she hadn't told me about this other guy. But most of all, I was thankful he wasn't violent with her. Three men were already far too fucking much.

I brought her closer in my embrace as my face fell into the crook of her neck, and I kissed her behind the ear telling her I'd always be there for her. I couldn't believe how strong she was, how lucky I was she'd chosen me.

Porter cleared her throat to bring the attention back to the case. "So what happened with him?"

"The others, those three you got, were recent attacks. They were seeking vengeance on my brothers by coming after me. That's why there were only those few attacks. Alfonso, on the other hand, has been a while. He was a friend of my brothers back in the day. When I turned eighteen, he wanted a shot with me. He's fucking sexy"—I stiffened, and the urge to punch a wall riddled up in me—"and I was as into him as any other sane woman would be. My brothers are a lot older though, and he was Sergei's age, so it was already hard enough to get my brothers and father to allow us to date. But we did."

Ilya had mentioned there being another guy. This must've been him. The one who would do anything for her. Anything...

"I had already been thinking about leaving, so the fact that he was in the lifestyle kinda hindered my attraction for him, but I figured, if this thing between us worked, then I'd be willing to continue the only life I'd ever known anyway. It was that argument that got my family on board—they figured if I fell in love with Alfonso the way he claimed to be with me, then I'd remain in their protection forever and gain Alfonso as a true ally."

"I thought you'd never been kissed before Shipman," Porter interrupted.

She gave a soft smile, lost in memories as she was. "I hadn't. He came to the door, picked me up like the proper gentleman, and we went out. I was nervous, though, because I'd never been with anyone before—my brothers had a way of scaring off any potential suitors—and he was so much older. He respected that. Other than holding my hand or wrapping his arm around me, he didn't push me. Other than a kiss on the temple or cheek, he didn't try for more. I was slowly allowing myself to open up to him, to want more."

I adjusted myself in my seat, clearing my throat to dissipate some of the anger bubbling up in me. As glad as I was that this one never harmed her, I didn't enjoy hearing stories of her cozying up to another man.

"Hell, I even flirted a little more than him, tried for a little more at the beginning, but he pulled away, saying he wanted to take it slow and cherish us so my family saw how important I was to him. I loved that about him. I honestly thought I was falling in love with him, but then..." She sighed, eyes clouded in memory. "Then when he eventually tried to kiss me on a date, I pulled back. I didn't know why then, and I still couldn't really tell you. I just didn't feel *it*. After that, I realized I was more infatuated than in love and more lust-driven than feeling affection. I told him I didn't feel what I thought I had, what he did and..."

"He got angry?" Porter asked.

"No. Upset, sure. But not angry. He's never tried to hurt me."

"But..." Lansly goaded.

"When we got home and they found out, my father and brothers told him to back off, that I had stated I wasn't interested. He couldn't let it go. My affections for him may not have grown in the time we spent together, but his had. His feelings went from wanting me to needing me. He became obsessed. It was the biggest problem in my leaving—my family wouldn't be able to protect me from him. But I mean, leaving made it more difficult for him to find me, so it worked out."

"So you haven't seen him since you were eighteen?" I asked, hoping the answer would help cool me.

"No." She came out of that dazed state, but she was still lost in memories. "He couldn't find me this last Christmas, but he found me on my birthday before that. And many times before that."

"And did he hurt you then?" Finnegan asked.

"Never. After I left, he'd find me every month or two and want to talk, try to take me out, basically win me over. As time went on, it became more difficult for him to find me. I mean its been like eight months now. That's the longest it's ever been. But no, on my birthday, he bought me a present like he did every year and just wanted some of my time. I didn't give it because I didn't want to encourage him, but he never hurt me."

"Did he ever seem... crazed?"

She sighed. "Yeah. That's what I was getting to. He never hurt me, but I was his. If he couldn't have me, no one could. Part of the reason I hadn't been with anyone before was because I didn't want anyone before Dorian, but it was also because I knew their safety would be on the line when Alfonso found out—because it would one hundred percent be a when and not an if."

Porter laughed softly. "And Shipman's, what? Chopped liver? Let this Alfonso go after him?"

Lana rolled her eyes. "He's a detective. He already has guys after him. One more wouldn't necessarily hurt. But to a civilian, Alfonso could really scare and ruin his life."

"So he'd do anything for you," Finnegan stated.

"*Anything*. A scary amount of anything. An anything I don't want. An anything that would lock me up with him if he could."

There was silence before Porter asked, "So how does that fit into this case?"

Lana turned the file in her hands so everyone could see the picture of Sydney Walters. "When Alfonso first tried with me, Sydney had been dying for his attention. When she saw us together, she was upset, but she gave up. When she found out I dumped him, she got excited again because he could finally be hers. But as the years passed and Alfonso still only had eyes for me... She was more than happy to oblige when I told her to keep the details of my life away from him, so I wasn't too worried when she found out where I worked. But... she still saw me as a problem. I saw her around my birthday last year too. She was upset in a way I hadn't seen before because he still wanted me."

Finnegan nodded, lost in thought before asking, "Alfonso?"

"Alfonso Carrini. You'll find a record on him, but you won't find him. He's as difficult to find as I would've been had I decided I didn't want you catching me. Match made in heaven, he said."

Porter sat back again as the story came to a close. "If she was trying to get rid of you, putting you away for murder would make you disappear for decades at least. In a women's facility, where even if he wanted to get himself locked up too, he wouldn't get to you."

As they all took in the information, I held Lana closer. All this time, she *had* been framed, and I hadn't thought to look deeper into it.

I rested my forehead on hers and whispered, "I'm sorry."

Her brows furrowed in that adorable way. "For what?"

"For not searching for more. For not realizing you were being framed this whole time."

She took my face in her hands and made me pay close attention. "You need to stop apologizing for things you could've never known. You're with me now, protecting me now. That's all that matters."

I leaned in to kiss her, losing myself in the truth of those words. I didn't care if she was a better fighter than me; I would protect her. I didn't care if I lost my job; I would work with the mafia to do so if need be.

A throat clearing pulled us apart, and I turned to my three

team members eyeing us, Lansly with amused satisfaction that he'd known all along, Porter with annoyance at our displays, and Finnegan with deep analysis.

He was the one to finally say, "We'll search Walter's things. See what we can find."

Lana

AN ARM WAS around my shoulders and about two seconds from being broken when I was crushed into the side of a body, and a familiar scent assaulted me.

Then another joined the one already there, weighing me down as I became crushed into the side of another large man.

"What do you two want?" I barked, annoyed that they were basically attacking me when I was trying to take a simple walk.

"Kidnapping you, *sestra*," Ilya said without looking down as he changed our direction and turned the corner at the end of the block.

"Whoever said I wanted to go anywhere with you?"

Lukov's laugh hit me before his words could annoy me. "That's why it's called kidnapping, Lani-Bunny."

I grumbled, but neither of them paid me any mind as they dragged me until we were by a studio I recognized. Inside the boxing space, they released the weight of their arms from my shoulders, and I felt about a hundred pounds lighter. They should've known better than to put bulging biceps on me.

"Why are we here?"

Ilya threw gloves at me without saying a word. Lukov didn't help, only winking as he put on sparring gloves and got in the ring.

I sighed. Apparently, I was boxing today.

My brothers were used to getting what they wanted. My parents, my father especially, had raised them to work for everything in life, and they'd done that plus more in order to keep the family business running and keep their men loyal.

Ilya was the tech wiz with me gone. Before, he'd been the link between mine and Lukov's jobs, a bit of tech and a bit of ops, but he'd always tried to step up when I didn't need to be part of their crimes. He'd been more than happy for the crash course of everything there was to know when I was leaving. He did well off, too, because he ended up only coming to me for help once after that.

Lukov ran operations. He orchestrated sales, prisoners, and networking. He basically kept the business that was a crime syndicate running.

Sergei was the head enforcer. Though as the underboss, he didn't need to enact so violently, easily giving the job to others, he took his greatest pleasures as the enforcer. He loved bloody fights and insisted that anyone within the organization be able to fight with no rules and no equipment. I'd been the only exception to that because I technically wasn't part of the mafia, like none of the other wives and daughters were.

And Father kept it all running. Eventually, Sergei would need to take that role, but he would never give up a chance to be enforcer, and he would always have Lukov and Ilya to help him run everything. Father and Sergei might be the bosses, but our family was loyal to one another above all else, and my brothers did and would help them forever.

So would I.

Once I threw a couple of jabs and crosses to warm up in the ring, I asked again, "Why are we here?"

"You're a very chatty kidnappee," Lukov joked.

"And you're a very annoying ass." I punched out a few more times.

"Ah, our lovely sister," Ilya called from where he sat on one of the ropes around the ring. "Such a clean, pure mouth."

"Right." I stopped participating and brought my hand up to my mouth to remove a glove. "I'm gonna go, then."

"No, c'mon." Lukov smacked my hand from my face. "Spend some time with your brothers. You know you miss this."

"You expect me to believe you simply wanted to spend some time with me?"

Ilya shrugged. "No. You're too smart for that."

"So?"

"We wanted to find out what's been going on. From your perspective," Ilya answered.

I thought about whether I wanted to lie, to pretend like I didn't know what they were talking about.

But what was the point? They'd surely hacked their way into knowing everything, including my new relationship.

"I'm sure you know more about the Mann case than I do." I threw out some more punches, ducking out of the way when Lukov swung his arm around. "My interrogations weren't based on anything but my being in the room an hour before him."

"Anything new?"

I rolled my eyes at Ilya as I punched at Lukov some more.

"Nothing new has been updated in their files. Has anything happened that they haven't put onto paper yet?"

I sighed, ducking again before throwing out a new combination, including a couple of hooks and a roundhouse kick I was particularly proud of. After getting that set out, Lukov and I circled one another in the ring. "The team came to me this morning with the file of a woman who 'had seen me with Mann in the lounge downstairs.'"

Lukov quirked a brow, allowing me to finish speaking before he attacked.

"It was Sydney Walters's file."

Ilya sat up straighter from his spot balancing on the rope, and Lukov froze. "What?" the latter said.

"Walters was apparently their witness, who claimed I had been with Mann, making out with him and going up to his room with him. I believe the team is getting a warrant to search her place as we speak."

"Carrini's never hurt you," Lukov pointed out, serious for once.

I attacked this time, wanting to distract my body as I rehashed all the new news. Alfonso would never hurt me, but I'd always wondered if Sydney would do something to get me out of the way. I always came to the conclusion that hurting me would anger Alfonso, and she would rather die than do that, so no, she'd never hurt me.

She was smart though. She didn't hurt me. She simply framed me for murder.

"I don't think Alfonso had anything to do with it," I said as Lukov and I danced around the ring, punching and defending each hit. "I think Sydney set it up to get me out of the way. Out with my freedom, there's always a chance I'll be with Alfonso. He'll never give up on me. Inside, he might stop. She could finally be with him."

"No. I remember Sydney. She was strong-willed, but she wasn't an action girl. We saw the crime scene photos. How could she accomplish that?" Ilya voiced.

"Obsession can make you do crazy things, brother."

Lukov snorted. "Like bedding a detective."

A shimmer of amusement lifted in me. "I'm not obsessed with him."

His eyes narrowed, darkening as he grimaced. "But you are bedding him?"

I fought my smile, avoiding the strikes Lukov was now throwing. My punches were precise, my moves fast, my favorite the one where I turned and jammed my elbow up. "That's all I know. It had nothing to do with me, but now it might have everything to do with me. Dorian and the guys are checking it out. I'm sure you'll see the reports soon," I huffed and nearly missed a strike into my gut.

Lukov backed away, allowing me to catch my breath as we circled one another again.

"Or you could always call and tell us," Ilya suggested. "You know, keep us from hacking in, doing anything illegal with your *cop boyfriend*."

I rolled my eyes. "If I find out anything before they get their shit written out, I'll call you."

"Your boyfriend doesn't inform you?" Ilya grimaced. "With matters of your safety on the line?"

"He does. At the end of the day, and if I ask. I don't *want* to know, Ilya, so he keeps it to himself."

"Well, today, you want to know."

"Yes, Master," I snickered.

Lukov smirked, lightly tapping my nose. "C'mon, kid. We love you. We're just looking out."

"I know. I'm a little sister though. It's my job to be annoyed."

He laughed. "Ilya, you want a turn with the annoyed one?"

I tried—and failed—not smiling as Ilya switched out with Lukov, taking the pads and putting them on. He gave me a small smile and a wink before attacking.

THE BOYS WERE KIND ENOUGH TO DROP ME OFF AT the Hollis Hotel before continuing on with their days. I didn't have to be in today, but I also wasn't needed at any of the other hotels, so I figured I'd spend the day with Elliot. I especially wanted to know if his interest in the dog-walking neighbor ever panned out.

"Ah, *cara mia*, you've come for me." His arms spread, inviting me in for a hug.

He was posted in the back of the lobby, where he could sit on one of the stools by the information desk and talk to anyone coming and going as the elevators were right across.

I snuggled into his warm embrace. Being in his arms sometimes reminded me of being a child hugging my father. Now I was much bigger, so it didn't feel as cocooning, but back then, I felt like the safest princess in all the worlds when my father wrapped his arms around me. Being with Elliot felt like that, even though he wasn't too much bigger than Ivan Romanov.

"I thought you could use the company." I took the stool beside him. "I know Tuesdays aren't the busiest down here."

"Always thinking of me. You're such a good girlfriend."

I smirked. "Are you telling people I'm your girlfriend, old man?"

He straightened his blazer. "I don't have to say a thing. They see a beautiful woman and a handsome man and assume."

I laughed, smacking him. "But since you brought up the topic of girlfriends…"

He laughed. "So you're not here for me. You're here to pry for gossip."

"About your life." I fluttered my eyelashes. "That makes me interested in you."

"This is a give-and-take, *cara mia*. I tell you, you tell me. I expect to hear more about this detective man."

The thought of Dorian brought an involuntary smile to my face. "Yeah, yeah."

He shook his head. "You're lovestruck, aren't you, child?"

I narrowed my eyes. "I said you first!"

He chuckled. "Fine. Fine. Last you saw me, I had flowers to give her."

"Mhmm." I scooted in, wishing I had a tub of popcorn.

"Her name is Cara. I was right. She's a decade younger than me. A widow for a few years now. She has two kids, both a little older than you. She lives a quiet life but is very lively. She spends a lot of time volunteering and joining groups to keep herself social. She says the biggest problem with old age is depression because of loneliness, and she won't let that happen to herself."

"You guys already have that in common!"

He laughed. "Maybe. But she's much more approachable than I am. Outside this job, I'm not a very likable creature. She's quite the opposite."

"And you would know this because..."

He knocked my shoulder with his. "Yes, yes. I've taken her out. Multiple dates now."

"Oo, multiple."

"We are old with nothing else to do."

I laughed. "How are things going, then?"

His gaze glossed over. "It is becoming difficult, if not impossible, to imagine my life without her. I feel ridiculous, but I am excited for her. She's awakened a part of me that has been dead far too long."

"Do you think she feels the same way?"

"She feels guilty because of her husband. I can see that. But she knows this is what he'd want for her. I think I would've liked her husband too. I hope he approves of us."

"So there is an us?"

"She came to my house yesterday. Started demanding the place be spruced up. Then she huffed and said it was no use, to just throw it all out, she had everything already."

My brows shot up. "She told you to move in with her?"

"Not necessarily. But it wouldn't be such a bad idea. We would have the companionship of one another. And it would make it easier when she drags me to all these groups and volunteering sessions."

I gasped. "She's getting you to get out of the house?"

"If all goes well, I may be giving up this job."

I fell into his side. "Finally."

"Now, your turn."

I sighed. Telling him about Dorian was a bit nerve-racking but worse was knowing I had to give him the preface—my life before I was Lana.

"Dorian is... amazing. And, oddly enough, had me move in with him after our first date, so maybe we chose exact replicas."

He laughed. "So things are going well with you two?"

"Better than I could've ever imagined."

"Like it's too good to be true?"

"No. That's the thing. It doesn't feel like that. It's amazing, but when something is too good to be true, it's because something *feels* wrong, even if you can't figure out what. Your gut just knows it. That's not what this is. Dorian is good. As a person, as a friend, and as my future. I don't feel afraid when I'm with him."

"So there're no problems?"

I readied myself for the possibility that Elliot could react negatively. "Well, one. He's a detective, and I'm a mafia princess."

"What?"

"My father is the Russian mafia don, my brothers next in line. Before leaving, before ever contracting to the security teams for these hotels, I was with them, helped them."

"What did you do?"

I shrugged. "Computer stuff mostly. I hacked into things, erased things, controlled them remotely, helped them do anything they needed to."

"So you're as much a criminal as any of the rest of them."

I nodded slowly. "And right before leaving, I taught my brother everything I knew so they could continue without getting caught."

"Your detective faults you for this past?"

My head shook as my mind brought up pictures of Dorian. Of him laughing and sleeping and cursing and growling. "No. He's never brought it up. Doesn't let it bother him, even though we both know he can guess what I've done."

"Then why is it a problem?"

"It's not. But it could be."

"I see that. But something tells me if he's been okay with it thus far, if he's okay with having to deal with your mafia brothers once they hear he's bedded you, then he's not going to let your past ruin this thing you two have."

I nodded. That's what I'd assumed too. "And what about you? Does it ruin this thing between us?"

He threw his arm around me and brought me in close. "Lana, love. Nothing could ever ruin this thing between us."

"You don't care that I was a criminal? Probably helped in things far worse than simple drugs or weapons? In deaths?"

"I wouldn't care if you still were."

I fell into him. "Cara's one lucky girl to have caught you, Elliot."

"And Dorian's one lucky man, La— What is your full name?"

"Svetlana. Svetlana Lyubov Romanov."

"Lyubov? Your parents named you love?"

I smiled. "As their last act of demonstrating what they had."

"Well, they knew what they were doing. You are love, *cara mia*. To me, to your parents, your brothers, to your detective. You are love."

Dorian

THE SEARCH WARRANT was barely in Walters's hand before we were storming in. She looked bug-eyed at all the men going through her town house, Lansly and Porter already upstairs as the others filled out the ground level. I didn't know where to start, so I made a random turn in a hall and found myself in her office.

Finnegan followed me into the room, putting his phone away. "That was Brinks. Apparently, Lev, Manny, and Park were found sodomized and with their hands cut off this morning. All three are dead."

A single glance in his direction said we were both very clear about what had happened—you didn't go after the don's daughter if you wanted to survive.

Ilya's visit came back to me as I stood behind Walters's desk. He'd found it amusing that I had locked the three up. I should've known they'd have their men on the inside take care of the situation.

Maybe I had known, and I subconsciously allowed it to happen. The three had deserved far worse than the loss of freedom, and I knew the Romanovs could deliver a retribution I couldn't hand out. I'd need to ponder on my greying morals at a later date when this was all over and Lana was safe at home with me.

Rummaging through the shit on Walters's desk, I didn't find anything in regards to Lana or even Carrini here. Just a whole bunch of crap about New York, delis that I was sure were fronts for organized crime and a bunch of crap about a Rose Soprano.

I scoffed. I wouldn't be surprised if that was the name Walters took on in order to join the organized crime world. As a matter of fact, she would've needed to include herself somehow because she came from a well-off family in the suburbs of Chicago and had no other inclusion. Had she made a pseudo-name in order to be included, an Italian one to stay close to her "true love," then she could be more accepted.

It didn't explain why she went by her real name with the Romanovs and Carrini though, so I wouldn't settle on that hypothesis. Hell, I wouldn't even ponder it any longer because it didn't matter to us and this case, but when this Mann shit was over, it was a very interesting avenue to look into, especially if these papers were right and there were all sorts of illegal crap we could close.

I kept rummaging and almost missed the glimpse of "Carrini" written on a sheet of paper. I pulled that one out to find the names Carolina and Cecilia Carrini written there. I scoffed. These were probably Alfonso's family members, and it wouldn't surprise me in the slightest if Walters had done her research on them. Hell, it wouldn't surprise me if she'd tried to befriend them to bring her closer to the family.

Their place of residence was listed as a home in a quiet neighborhood about an hour out of town, and I instinctively had a feeling they weren't involved in any of the shit Alfonso was. Hell, from our research, the Carrinis weren't involved in organized crime at all, telling us Alfonso had found his way into the lifestyle rather than being born into it like the Romanovs.

Maybe that fed into his fascination with Lana. If he wanted to be part of the lifestyle so desperately, he would want to marry an established mafia princess, not a civilian. Why Lana specifically had to be that mafia princess, I didn't understand.

Finnegan was going through the books on the shelves across from me, and I took the moment to wonder if she'd made this lifestyle and Carrini her entire world, if she'd obsessed over him so much it took over her life? I didn't want to feel it because of what she'd tried to do to Lana's life, but I felt sympathy for the girl.

I went back to the desk, making my way through the drawers and pulling out more shit. Journals with family names on them, some of which I recognized as mafia families and others I would get to know better once I read Walters's findings. Blades and two guns that I'd expected because there was no way she was trying to incorporate herself into that lifestyle without weapons, even if she tried to stay away from using them, and the fact that she hadn't shot Lana told me she might be trying to stay away from using them completely.

That or the fear of what her family would do in retribution. What Carrini may do.

In her mind, framing Lana the way she had had no way of leading back to her, therefore no way for the Romanovs or Carrini to find out.

She was in for a surprise when the Romanovs inevitably sent someone in the women's prison Walters was sentenced to to deal with her.

I pulled out more papers with more about New York and Rose Soprano before it all became a blur. I was so lost with going through everything I didn't realize Porter was standing right in front of me until she said, "You need to come see this."

Anxiety flooded me with the possibilities of what I might find.

I followed her as two others passed into the office to collect evidence.

I took the stairs two at a time and followed her to the guest bedroom. Or what used to be the guest bedroom.

Now it was covered in pictures of Lana, with different mannequins wearing outfits that were almost exact replicas of those Lana was wearing in the photos. On the left wall, she had side-by-side pictures of Lana and herself wearing those match-ings outfits and a wig.

Then Lansly walked out of the closet, brushing a wig over his fist. "The woman with Mann was dark-haired like our Lana, right?" He held up a bag of receipts. "I bet she threw out the outfit, but I'm sure we can find it in these."

I sighed, turning back to the walls. Finally. Conclusive proof that Lana wasn't a suspect in this murder case but another victim. Now I just needed to take care of Carrini, and my girl could finally get that normal life she'd been hoping for when she'd left her family.

I WAS ON THE OTHER SIDE OF THE INTERROGATION room because Porter didn't think I'd be able to handle myself in there with Walters. Finnegan and Lansly were on her side. I was on her side. I knew I wouldn't be able to handle myself.

They'd only been speaking with her for half an hour, but already she had tears running down her face. And not because she was afraid of the circumstances of what she'd done or that she'd been caught, but because Porter made an offhand comment about Carrini being psychotically in love with Lana. Apparently, Sydney was still in denial about the fact that the only place Carrini planned on sticking his dick was in Lana.

And that sure as fuck wasn't happening.

"You don't appreciate that Svetlana's trying to steal him, do you?" Porter baited, and it worked on me too. "You needed to get rid of her, right? What better way than making it look like she was fucking Mann, then killed him?"

"No." She shook like a deranged woman, which she was with this need for Carrini, and slammed her fists into the table. "No! She can't have him!"

"That's right," Lansly teased. "So you dressed up as her."

"Yes, yes, yes. I dressed as her."

"You were trying to be her?" Porter interrupted the crazed way Walters was about to start spewing.

"No. No. Fuck her. Alfonso's mine."

My entire body reacted to her comment on Lana, reminding me why it was a good thing I was on this side.

"Fuck her," Walters continued. "I don't want to be her. I just needed to get Alfonso to see she was trash."

"So you..."

"I just needed her to fuck up, but she wouldn't do it. He kept saying she was saving herself for him, that she just wanted the chase he gave her as foreplay for their long and happy marriage. I followed her that much, and she was never with any fucking guys! How was I supposed to prove to Alfonso that she was a whore if I couldn't get evidence?"

"Maybe because she isn't a whore?" Lansly suggested.

"No, she is! She's a whore, and if I had to find other ways to prove to Alfonso to finally get him to stop waiting for her, then I would!"

"You dressed up as Lana to fuck Mann? How does that prove anything to Carrini?" Porter asked.

"I filmed us fucking, kept it off my face. I showed it to Alfonso that night!"

"And he believed it? Isn't he supposed to be obsessed with her? He couldn't tell the difference?" Lansly questioned.

"He didn't *want* to believe it, but I've been watching Svetlana a long time. I altered my voice as much as possible to sound like her. I made sure every one of her birthmarks, moles, scars was on my body. He couldn't deny it when he saw Lana's birthmark on the woman's naked back!"

"You call Lana a whore, yet you cheated on Carrini with Mann?" Porter baited.

"No! I never cheated on Alfonso. I would never. He's my soul mate. Soul mates don't cheat. He loves me. I know it! I love him. But he needed to see that I would be the only loyal one!"

"So, what? You got the film for Carrini, then killed Mann to make sure Lana rotted in prison for the rest of her life, never getting in your way with Carrini again?"

"God no. I needed to wash that stench of a man off of me before I saw Alfonso again." She sighed at the mention of her deranged love. "I had to show it to him. I couldn't wait. I needed him to come to the realization that she wasn't worth his patience. It was a lucky coincidence that Mann ended up dead that night. I could finally get rid of that bitch once and for all."

We all straightened, Lansly and Porter turning for the mirror even though they wouldn't be able to see our reactions. If she was telling the truth, which in her crazed state, I doubted she could do anything but, then she truly hadn't killed Mann.

And we now had a new suspect with the most concrete motivation.

"Carrini killed Mann for touching his woman," Lansly interpreted.

"What? No," Walters defended. "Absolutely not. He didn't know it was me in that video."

"But he thought it was Lana," Porter stated.

"Ye—" Her eyes widened. "No. No! He would never. She's a cheating whore. He wouldn't do anything else for her." Her screams chased Porter and Lansly as they left the room. "No! He didn't do anything. He was with me all night. He was—"

Finnegan turned down the audio to the interrogation room as Porter and Lansly met us.

"If he killed Mann for touching Lana, then you could be in trouble," Lansly opened.

"I don't give a fuck about me. He's after her."

"He already killed Mann for touch—" Lansly started.

"But now he'll be angry with Lana," Porter interrupted. "If he thought this whole time she was saving herself for him, that she was pure and only he would touch her, then seeing her giving herself to scum like Mann—though anyone would've done—and now Dorian. He's going to devolve. And quickly."

"But it's been weeks. If he was going to go for Lana, wouldn't he have already?" Finnegan asked.

"Maybe. Maybe not. Maybe he couldn't find her. But now her relationship with Dorian is less private. People talk, and this precinct is as gossipy as any workspace. If he was following the case to make sure Lana wasn't hurt or to keep himself cleared, then he would've heard such gossip," Porter hypothesized.

Lansly narrowed his gaze at her. "You think like a criminal a little too well."

My breaths were becoming shallow at the possibilities of what he might do when he found her because I had no doubt he wouldn't give up on finding her. "I need to get to her."

I left the others to deal with Walters, my phone already at my ear as I made my way for the stairs.

When she picked up on the second ring as usual, there was

happiness in her voice that I would've loved any other time. "Hey, baby."

"Where are you?" I ground out, adrenaline pumping me down the stairs quickly.

"A few blocks from the precinct. I missed you, and no amount of touching myself would've helped."

"Lana." I ignored the desire such a comment spiked through me and hated to ruin the good mood she was in. "Where are you?"

"Harper and Third. Why?"

"He's out there." I sped up. "Walters said he thinks you fucked Mann. He killed Mann for it. And now people are finding out about us. I'm meeting you halfway."

"Okay," she said so calmly I wanted to rip my hair out. I might've done so if she didn't start reacting properly soon. "Just don't let any worry show on your face."

"What the fuck are you talk—"

"If he's watching me right now and sees any worry on either one of us, he'll know we might suspect him. Nothing, baby. Smile. Think about what you're going to do to me later. Think about getting between my legs or when I get between yours."

"Now is not the time, Lana." My periphery picked up every movement as I was out of the precinct now and headed toward her, though I did relax my features in case he'd already found Lana.

She was a block away, and the smile on her face didn't look forced like mine. It was easy for it to turn real when I saw her. As much panic as was spreading through me at the prospect of her in danger, she still brought me nothing but joy.

When we met at the end of my block, I finally hung up the phone, and she leaned in to whisper, "I didn't see him, so either he hasn't found me yet, or he's waiting. He was always good at hiding."

I swallowed as my hands wrapped tightly around her, forehead falling onto hers. "I won't let anything happen to you, Lana."

"I know, Dorian. Of the many mysteries in this world, of that, I'm sure."

HE TOLD me what they'd found as we walked to the precinct. Back inside, we stood close in the elevator, his hand on my lower back making me tingle all over, when suddenly, his head snapped toward me. "What exactly did you plan on doing here, Lana?"

My lips tipped up, and I scanned him like eye candy, even though I knew he wasn't in the mood right now.

His hand fisted into the back of my shirt. "There're cameras everywhere, Lana."

"Not in the custodial closets. Or the bathrooms," I argued, curious if he would actually take me in either of those places.

He quirked a brow. "Bathrooms have cameras."

"Not the stalls."

He gave a cold stare. "I'm not fucking you in some stall."

The elevator dinged open onto our floor. I pulled his arm and brought him down the hall, past the double doors, and down, down, down...

He froze, locking his body so I couldn't pull any longer, then brought me into him. His tone was made sexier by a growl as he declared, "I'm not taking you in some janitor's closet either. Behave."

"Oo." I smiled. "I like it when you boss me around." I dropped my voice. "What else should I do, Detective?"

"Stop it." He turned back for our destination and deposited me at his desk. He leaned in, aware that I was more than capable of causing trouble in this little space with all his colleagues around. So he caged me into his chair and whispered against my lips, "Be good and I'll turn the cameras off in one of the interrogation rooms."

I gave him infinite nods as I bit my lip. So my detective could be a little bad.

He laughed against my lips and made it nearly impossible to behave when all I wanted to do was jump him.

"I'll be back in a little while."

I grumbled but snuck in a kiss before he could pull away.

He winked and walked down a hall.

As I watched his fine ass leave me, Ava met my gaze from across the room. She took me in, and I wasn't entirely sure if she still hated me or if she was trying to figure out why she liked me. Hopefully, it was one of those and she wasn't simply feeling sorry for me. I didn't want or need her sympathy.

Lansly clocked my staring contest with his partner as he stopped at his desk, parallel to Dorian's. "I wouldn't be surprised if he keeps you here or at his apartment until we catch this guy."

My lips twitched up. "Not exactly. What about when he goes out on the field? Then I wouldn't be here or at his apartment."

Lansly quirked a brow. "You'd be here with everyone instructed not to let you out of their sights."

I laughed. Would Dorian be so possessive?

I shrugged as I threw my feet up on the desk. "I'd like to see him try to keep me where I don't want to be."

He grinned. "I would too."

He winked before walking back to talk to Ava. As he left, I knew even if Ava never came around to me, I could be friends with at least one of Dorian's team.

The clock tick tick ticked as I sat remembering being only a few yards down in that interrogation room waiting for their twenty-four-hour hold to be over so they could let me go. It made me smile. Maybe I should be thankful to Walters and Carrini for bringing me to this precinct. Alfonso definitely wouldn't like to hear he was part of the reason I was with Dorian.

The thought of those two made me remember a pesky little promise I'd made, and I pulled out my phone.

All I know is this—Sydney disguised herself as me with Mann so Alfonso could finally get over me. It backfired and got him angry at Mann.

I sent the text in the group chat with my father and brothers, then dropped my phone on the desk as call after call started coming in. I ignored them all, going back to getting lost in thoughts of Detective Shipman.

The calls and texts stopped within ten minutes, and I was surprised I was given such a short harassment period until a cop passed Dorian's desk. "There's a call for you on line one."

I frowned immediately and answered, "Seriously?"

"You're lucky I didn't come down there, Lana," Sergei's voice boomed into my ear.

"Don't you think it'd be stupid of *you* to come here? The detectives are all here." I wasn't sure which one exactly he had a problem with.

"Svetlana, I don't give a shit who is there. They have nothing on me. Hell, even if they did, you're my baby sister."

I huffed. "I'm sorry for ignoring your calls."

"Good." My phone started ringing with Sergei's name. "Now, pick up. I don't need them recording our conversation."

I immediately dropped Dorian's work phone into place and took mine, answering my brother once again. "*Brat.*"

"What's going on, Lana?"

"I already told you, that's what I know. I'll have Dorian send you any other information."

"Lana," he growled.

"I promise, Serg. I'll tell him right now."

He took a large breath in. "Fine." After a beat of silence, he filled it. "He treating you well?"

"Perfectly."

"Good, because *I* absolutely would kill him."

I snorted. "Yeah. I know, Mr. Enforcer. Your special problem with this precinct proved it."

"Fuck that precinct."

My hand fluttered to my heart, even though he couldn't see it. "Oh, you're such a gentleman."

"Let us know, Lan."

"Goodbye, Serg."

When we hung up, I immediately texted Dorian, *Send my family all of the information you have, please.* I added each of their numbers, then dropped my phone back on the desk, relaxing into his seat.

Sergei was the furthest from me in age and the roughest of my brothers. It shouldn't have surprised me that he had such large problems with anyone in this precinct.

I closed my eyes as I remembered growing up with my family training me, of going through interrogation resistance. I wondered if that was why Ava hated me so much from the very beginning. While Sergei and I looked alike, it wasn't clear until we were standing together, so she probably couldn't place why that hatred for me had built up so much. Then when I didn't break a sweat, her subconscious must've connected me to him. Or people like him if she'd heard of the rumors of his problem with this precinct. I didn't even think she was aware if that were the case.

"You're breaking," a twenty-five-year-old Sergei said.

"No, I'm not!" Now I broke, frustrated that we'd been at this for hours and he still wasn't letting me finish.

"Svetlana, you do not let them see the true you," he demanded. "I could see it perfectly."

"That's because you know the true me. No one else will."

"Don't be naive, Svetlana."

I wanted to be understanding of why he was being so hard on me. Otets told me he would be the worst of us all, not because he was innately the roughest in nature but because he was the one out of all of them who had been taken and interrogated, in worse ways than questions. I understood he had a deeper reasoning for going hard on me, for making sure I'd be okay in any circumstance, the easiest of all simple questions, but we'd been at it for hours, and I didn't care anymore. What twelve-year-old would?

"Sergei," I pleaded.

"You need to be prepared, Lana."

"For what? I'm not part of your schemes."

"Not all those taken are guilty, Lana. You need to be able to hold out, to put on a mask so they don't know the real you. If they know the real you, Lana, they'll use it to break you."

I huffed. "You're being ridiculous. Why would anyone want to interrogate me?"

I could say I'd been naive, but I didn't think that was fair. I was twelve years old, and much of their crimes were still hidden from me.

Sergei had been right all those years ago, of course, and the constant lessons up until I left had come in handy. He would never say he told me so because that wasn't the type of man he was, but I wasn't too prideful to admit it. Hadn't been for years when all of their lessons had paid off.

As the thoughts ran through me, as the gratefulness for my family washed over me, time passed in a blur.

Then Dorian was storming out of the hallway he'd been in and straight for Lansly, who was still hypothesizing another case with Ava. They spoke for all of ten seconds before he was coming for me.

Fuck. Did I do something that he was gonna be mad about? How? I hadn't moved. Had my brothers said something?

"Wha—"

He pulled my hand. "Let's go."

He dragged me to the same room I'd been in the first time he'd questioned me.

"Dorian, what's going on?" I got out once we were in the room, and he was pushing a chair to jam the door.

He turned dark eyes on me, but they weren't angry. They were possessive, territorial. "What was it you came here for, Lana?"

He prowled for me as I subconsciously stepped away until I hit the metal table. "For you to be inside me."

He roughly peeled my legs apart and stopped between them. "I'm here to give you whatever you want, baby. Always."

He was more sincere by the end of his declaration, which told me something had triggered *his* need to be inside me. But it was clear now wasn't the time to find out what, so I only gave him a small smile before he claimed my lips.

He wasn't soft. Not even a little bit. It almost felt like he wanted to leave marks on me.

Dorian's teeth bit into my bottom lip as his hands pulled down my pants. When had he unbuttoned them?

He ripped my jeans off, salivating as he eyed me. "Spread your legs for me."

I did as he said and the coolness from the room breezed against the wetness on my panties making my nails scrape into the metal table.

"Have you touched yourself yet?"

My head shook slowly.

"You said no amount of touching yourself would help."

I shrugged. "Figure of speech."

"You haven't touched yourself at all since we've met."

I shook my head. I hadn't even realized it until now, but no, I hadn't.

"Why not?"

"I don't know," I breathed so soft.

He began working on the buttons of his shirt until it was sitting open and his naked chest was before me. "You told me you'd touched yourself in my shirt, Lana. I thought promises were sacred to you."

I swallowed. "I technically never promised that."

He sauntered to me and slowly lifted my shirt above my head as his fingers skimmed across my skin, leaving goose-bumps everywhere. His index then played with the front of my bra, tugging at it with a wicked smirk about his lips. "What a pesky piece of fabric. Keeping me from seeing my two friends."

My breath shallowed as he kept lightly tugging on it as his other hand unclasped it like a pro. Then he tugged the thing down until I was sitting splayed on the interrogation table in only my soaked panties.

Dorian let the bra fall to the ground as he pulled off his shirt and, to my surprise, moved to put it on me rather than discarding it. I followed his unvoiced demand to put first one then the other arm into the shirt sleeves before he took a random button in the middle and buttoned it.

Then he stepped away from me, and as he drank me in, his eyes turned to a solid black. "Complete your promise, Lana."

I swallowed. "I never promised."

"I took it as one. So complete it."

"Dorian." My hips swayed, wanting his touch, but I didn't move myself to ease the need.

Thankfully, he didn't make me suffer.

Dorian moved for my legs, his hands softly pulling down my panties and shuffling them into the pocked of his trousers. He pushed the bottoms of his shirt aside and spread my legs even wider as he breathed against my cunt. "My pretty little pussy. Have you been this wet for me all day?"

"Basically," I whined.

His thumb brushed down my slit and easily slipped into my opening. Just the tip, playing with me rather than giving me what I wanted.

"Dorian, please!"

He bit the side of my thigh, eyes twinkling up at me, before moving for the wetness pooling out of me. His tongue slipped up my pussy, and I nearly dropped flat on the table, back arching with how desperately my body needed more of him.

He sucked and devoured me, eating like a starved man, and as I came close to finishing, he pulled back and bit the inside of my other thigh. Hard.

"You're mine, Lana."

"I'm yours," I breathed, thrusting my hips so he'd keeping eating.

He obliged, and said around his tongue's ministrations, "And you made me a promise. In not so many words."

"Dorian," I begged as my body rose back to that precipice.

He pulled back again, this time rising back to his feet and stepping back. "Complete your promise."

I was so lust-driven, I would've done anything he told me at the moment, so my hand didn't even need permission before it moved across my body, over his shirt, to that wet spot between my legs. I was slick, the tops of my thighs slippery, and all I wanted was to be filled.

My fingers slipped through my folds, sending shivers through my body as I grazed my sensitive clit. I wanted his mouth back there.

But I wanted to be filled so much more.

My fingers moved back down and two fingers filled my opening as my palm hit my clit, making my back arch off the table. I held Dorian's gaze the entire time which only made my pussy clench with more desire.

I moved slowly at first, then faster as my body shot to that finish line.

"Good girl."

My head fell back with the praise, and careless moans left me, and just as I was about to climax, Dorian's mouth was around my clit, sucking like his life depended on it. My eyes snapped to find him on his knees before me, and the sight alone sent me over the edge.

I cried out as I came for him, letting him eat me up.

My hand was dewy with my cum when I pulled away and I brought it to my mouth to taste.

Dorian, looking at me through his lashes, growled at the sight. "You taste amazing, don't you, sweetheart."

My head moved up and down in a haze, more concerned with pleasing him than the taste of my own cum. "I would taste better with you."

He smirked. "Is that so?"

I nodded as my pussy walls clenched, crying for his cock.

He stood as if he could hear it, and pulled his trousers down, allowing his cock to spring free. It was leaking with precum that I immediately clamped my hand around to get a taste of.

I brought said hand to my mouth and licked from my palm to my fingers. "Mm. Already tasting so much better."

He slipped the tip of his cock through my slit, tapping it on my clit and making my eyes roll back in my head. "Tell me again what you wished for coming here."

"For you to take me."

"You belong to me."

I nodded violently. "Always."

He slipped his cock through my folds, allowing just the tip to slip lightly into me before pulling back out and sliding back up my folds. "You look good in my shirt."

I was breathing hard. "Dorian, please."

He smirked as he slipped just the head in again, holding my legs out so I couldn't wrap them around his waist and pull him in. "My suspect is begging me in interrogations. Did you ever think it would come to this, Svetlana?"

I nearly passed out when he said my full name, my arms no longer able to hold me up. My hands then moved as I undulated beneath him, one slipping into the shirt and playing with my nipples as the other skimmed down to my clit. It was swollen and sensitive and at least with my hand there, his cock would need to go lower, find its way inside me.

"Svetlana..." he sang as he pushed a little more than just the head into me, then pulled back out.

"Dorian, please!" I cried. Cried. I was crying.

Tears slipped down my cheeks and I knew I'd combust if I didn't have him in me soon.

His hands dropped my thighs, pushed my hand away from my clit, and moved for the tears free falling. He laughed as he wiped them away. "Those mascara streaks make me want to shove my cock down your throat, sweetheart."

I wanted that too but not now. Now I wanted his cum to fill me. "Please, please, please, please..."

His cock slipped through my folds again, and he moved to shove only the head inside again.

But my legs were no longer being held apart, and I wrapped them around his waist immediately, pulling him in until he was shoved as deep inside me as possible.

I screamed.

He groaned so deeply into my ear, I came and another scream left me.

He chuckled, sending me back to that edge, as he held onto my waist and slowly pulled out before slamming back into me. "My girl needs to learn some patience."

I couldn't speak. Couldn't think. Could hardly hold onto the edges of this table as he slammed into me over and over and over.

I probably came a couple of times. I don't know. I think I blacked out a little. Nothing mattered to me but the way Dorian looked, gritted his teeth to keep control as sweat dripped down his body and he growled as his body stiffened with his oncoming release.

My pussy walls clamped down hard, and his head snapped back as he came. I didn't stop squeezing. Wouldn't stop until I'd milked him dry.

He was still inside me as he slumped over my body, barely catching himself on shaky arms as he hovered above me. "My fucking property, Lana. You're mine."

"Uh-uh." I lazily shook my head as my lids closed.

"Lana."

"Call me Svetla..." My mouth was tired.

"Svetlana," he growled, and my pussy immediately clenched around him.

"Mm, you like when I use your full name, huh?"

I moaned, unable to say anything else.

He smirked as he slowly pulled his cock out of me, his cum slipping slowly out of me.

Dorian stood over me like a ruler and took in his handiwork.

Then he slowly slid his index over my smooth skin until he reached my pussy. He dipped two fingers inside me, then moved for my mouth. "Suck, Svetlana."

I obliged immediately, my eyes rolling back at the taste.

"How do you taste?"

"So much better," I moaned around his fingers.

Part Six

"Children begin by loving their parents; as they grow older they judge them; sometimes they forgive them."

- Oscar Wilde

Dorian

I STILL FELT like I needed to burn this world to the ground, but being inside Lana had helped cool me down from that edge. I'd been scarily close to it.

We cleaned out mess, and I'd made sure everyone had left the desk spaces before I allowed her out, both so she wasn't embarrassed knowing all those people had heard her screams, but also because there was something about the look of mascara and sweat running down her face that I didn't want others to see. She'd made it to the bathroom to clean up without anyone around.

We were on our way back to my—our—apartment when her hand fell over the one I had on her thigh, and she gently asked, "Do you want to tell me what happened?"

When all I did was quirk a brow in her direction, she smiled.

"Something triggered you before you took me into that room. What happened?"

I sighed. Of course my girl had figured it out. What was more astonishing was that I still felt like I *needed* to be inside her, like she didn't have my cum cocooned in her panties right at this moment. And the need wasn't simply because the thought of her had me feeling like a horny teenager either, but because of fucking Walters and Carrini. Being inside her made us feel whole and like I could keep her safe from the world. "Nothing, baby."

"I thought you promised you'd never lie to me?" She didn't say it with any accusation, but that only made it worse.

I huffed out a breath because she was right. Even if I didn't want to, I had to be honest with her. "Walters let another pretty piece of information slip."

I felt Lana's eyes on me, but she didn't interrupt, her patience astonishing, though the reminder of her sitting in an interrogation room without growing restless for twenty-four hours should've made that impossible.

"She said Carrini knew about your little apartment above the ballet hall and is now looking for your new place. That she just learned of it because she found Carrini extra excited one day. That he'd been going there when you weren't home to be in your space. That he'd taken... souvenirs."

The thought of Lana's panties in that fucker's hands, up against his nose, drove me nearly insane. The only thing stopping me from doing something reckless behind this wheel was Lana beside me.

"He won't come to your apart—"

"No," I interrupted. "He's too much of a coward to show his face there, but he will—and easily can, based on his history with patience—wait until I'm not there. Until you're alone in there or until you go for a walk or something. He's obsessed with you, and he's spiraling now that he knows you've been with me."

"Dorian." Her hand ran soothingly up my arm. "He won't touch me."

I scoffed but didn't say anything because I didn't think I could put into words how terrified I was of losing her, of anything happening to her. We'd had too many close calls as it was.

I pulled into the parking garage of my complex and quickly had her hand in mine as we went up the elevator. It took everything in me to ignore the tension buzzing around the tight space. I was convinced elevators did that on purpose when you had the hots for someone in order to test people's strengths. Mine was cracking. It was ridiculous how much I wanted to slip inside her, considering I'd been in her less than an hour ago, considering I had more pressing matters to think of at the moment.

I'd needed her in that interrogation room, for reasons far past promising her we would. I needed her because it frightened me to my core that they were closing in around her, and I'd needed a way to remind myself that she was still with me.

I felt almost the same now. I needed a reminder that we were home and she was safe.

When we stepped out of the elevator and into the hall, we both sighed out like we'd been holding our breaths in there.

The second we made it past the door, I had her slammed against it, my hands hiking over her thighs as my mouth assaulted hers. Our tongues fought, lashing out to take control as my hips ground into hers.

I had her leg pushed up around my waist when a throat clearing behind me sent my heart barreling to the floor.

My gun was out and aimed in a second, Lana behind me as I focused on...

Her family?

Stood in the middle of my living space were four men, one of whom I'd met already and all of whom resembled my girl.

I relaxed, dropping my gun and holstering it once more as

Lana and I stepped further into the space. I couldn't fathom what my life had turned into that I was *relaxing* around mafia men.

I didn't release Lana's hand though. She would remain tied to me, behind me, until I found out what they were doing breaking into our apartment. Not that I believed they'd ever hurt her.

"Ivan," I opened toward the head when I realized none of them were in the talking spirit. They all eyed us with their own thoughts. Sergei looked disgusted to see how close we were, Lukov and Ilya contemplative, and Ivan, as the most shocking, accepting.

"Dorian." He nodded as if showing respect. Was this all an act for Lana? There was no way the mafia don was showing respect to a detective. Or was this because of my need to protect his daughter? Because he saw I'd do anything for her. Maybe he'd known my answer to Ilya's question even before I had. Maybe all of the brothers had, and that was why they'd allowed the relationship to go on as long as it had.

"What're you guys doing here?" Lana asked.

Nobody answered for some time, but that gave me the moment to study them.

Ivan was a good-looking don for a man in his sixties, with too many stresses and the pain of missing his wife everyday. His salt-and-pepper hair was slicked back, his stubble more salt than pepper, and his eyes the exact color and likeness to Lana's. He was tall but the shortest of the men in the family and intimidating, to say the least. But he eyed his daughter with adoration all the same.

Sergei, his firstborn and heir, took after his father's intimidating presence like it was a hair color to be passed down. He looked damn near like a replica of Ivan with dark hair, a tall form, and a lean yet muscular build. As a man in his later thirties, he was the least inviting of the lot. Unsurprisingly, considering he was the one with problems with cops, my partner high on that list. His dark eyes said he loved his sister but didn't want her anywhere near a cop, whether I could protect her or not.

Lukov, the middle son, was the tallest of the lot and the only one with no hair. He was lean like the others, but I wouldn't be surprised by the muscle that formed him. From the stories I'd heard, he was the clown of the family but also Lana's most consistent trainer. He had shimmering eyes like he was on the verge of making a joke, but the way he stood, rigid and ready, showed he was ready to burn down worlds for his sister.

And Ilya, the youngest son and the only one I'd met prior to tonight. Though they all looked alike, he was the biggest of the lot with more blatant muscle demanding attention. The look in his eyes was similar to the one his father wore—he didn't like me, but he'd put up for Lana's sake. I'd known as much from his visit to the precinct, but it was clear now where he didn't have to hide his reactions from the public, from my peers.

"Carrini's after you again," Sergei finally said, eyeing me as if it was my fault.

It was actually least of all my fault. Carrini had only ever met her because of him, only ever gone out with her at all because they'd been friends.

"He's always been after me," Lana huffed. "Just because he couldn't find me for some time doesn't mean he ever stopped."

"You're not proving any points, *sestra*," Ilya interjected.

"Actually, you're demonstrating all the more reason to come home." Sergei seethed. There was nothing but fury in his eyes, and I had no trouble imagining his strong personality against Ava's. No wonder they'd had a shootout. I couldn't imagine either one of them backing down.

"I don't *need* to do—"

"Lan," her father interrupted, voice soothing. "Come home. We can protect you there. At least until we get Carrini's threat off of you like we should've done years ago. Your brothers and I, my men. We can protect you. Your detective can do all he likes, but we have around-the-clock surveillance."

"Do I look like some kind of shipment you guys need to keep an eye on?" Lana glared.

I hardly focused on the goings-on around me because Ivan was right. I could only keep so much of an eye on her, and even with two cops on her tail, there was no guarantee she wouldn't be lost to me, find a way to lose the trail, no guarantee Carrini wouldn't just kill those cops and make his way to her.

But if she were in a mafia house? There'd be no breaking through those guys, no losing the tail, none of it.

They were arguing now, Sergei growing bigger as his anger grew while his brothers tried to take their father's approach and be more soothing. Whatever their argument was about, Lana wouldn't listen to them. Maybe before, she might have, but if she thought Carrini knew about me, was angry I'd had her— which I had no doubt he knew—she wouldn't want to leave my side. It was cute—her little protective stance against her family for me.

I interrupted Lana in her next bout of saying no. "Take her."

The following silence was deafening.

"What?" she screeched, hand tightening in mine as her free one clung to my arm.

I met Ivan's eyes, and there was more respect there than before. "You're right. You're more capable of keeping her away from Carrini than I will ever be."

"Dorian, no!" She pulled my arm to get me to face her, tears already sparkling in her eyes. "I'm not leaving—"

I cupped her face between my hands. "Yes, you are."

"Dorian." She put authority into my name, the tone women took that sent balls crawling up. "No."

"Lana, I need you out of harm's way so I can concentrate. Be with your family, spend time with them, cherish them, and the second I get Carrini, I'll come for you."

"What part of no don't you understand?"

I swallowed because I knew this next part might make her hate me, but I looked past her to Sergei. He'd be the most willing to ignore her wants. "Take her."

Her eyes widened as her brother moved immediately for us. The others didn't stop him against Lana's cries, so maybe they were just as willing to break her heart. At the end of the day though, this was about reality, and the situation came down to one thing—she needed to be away from that psychopath, and her family was the best bet for that.

Before Sergei could get her, I pulled her closer, my thumbs brushing the tears now freely falling off her cheeks as her hands clung to me. "I love you, Lana. And I'm going to come back and get you the second this is over."

Her head shook as her fingers tightened in my shirt. "Dorian. You promised..."

"Lana, I love you. I'm in love with you. A fool. I'm a detective. I'm not supposed to fall for my suspect. But here I stand."

"No."

"Baby, please. Please do this for me."

"No!" she raged. "You don't get to say that and do this! No!"

Her brother took her by the arms and pulled, but she fought against him, seething at me. It took everything in me, but I didn't stop him. Didn't move for her as she kicked her legs out and got out of his hold, only to be back in it a second later. She was an amazing fighter, but I had no doubts her brothers were better.

"Dorian," she cried, cooling in her brother's tight hold. "You promised me a lifetime."

It took more out of me not to cry as I watched her tears slide down those beautiful pinked cheeks. "I'd never break a promise to you, Lana. I will come for you. I promise."

Her head only shook as more tears slipped down her face, and Sergei carried her out.

In the silence that followed, I took a large breath in to stop myself from chasing after them, to stop myself from crying in front of the Romanov men.

"Thank you," Ivan said before following out of the room.

Lukov left without a word then, leaving me alone with Ilya.

He stepped forward and surprised me by holding out his hand. When I narrowed my eyes, he stated, "You'd do anything for her. Even the most difficult things. Welcome to the family."

I let out a humorless laugh and took his hand.

THE FIRST THING I DID WHEN I STEPPED INTO THE office the next morning was make my team promise to stay away from the Romanovs. None of them asked why I looked beat up, eyes red and bags beneath them from not being able to sleep, nor did they question my demand. Ava wasn't happy about it, grumbling beneath her breath, but she thankfully didn't fight me on the matter.

After everything they'd learned about Lana—most important, of all her good nature and resilience—I was glad I didn't have to argue a win for this.

We took the morning shooting out ideas on why Mann

was chosen as the victim. Carrini had obviously killed him because he thought Mann had been with Lana—which made me understand Lana's hesitancy to leave my side—but was that all this was? Walters said she chose Mann at random, but was that the whole deal? She'd already admitted she'd do anything for Carrini, had already tried to lie for him. Would she be lying to protect him in regards to a history with Mann too?

"We're going in circles here," I interrupted the latest spiel of Mann and Carrini laundering money or blackmailing one another or something else that we couldn't find evidence on. "Something ties Mann and Carrini. We need to look at this from another angle. Carrini's not part of a mafia, but his family has a long background in crime. Crime has a way of creating more money than should be possible, and Mann had more than any one man should. I'm thinking the problem could've been with another Carrini member that Alfonso didn't bother himself with until he saw Mann with Lana."

"Mann's been going to the Shriberton for months," Lansly added. "There could've been past interactions. On that angle, they would've been ones Carrini didn't care about until maybe he saw an interaction between him and Lana. If he already didn't care for the guy because of a family opposition, something like that couldn't stroke the beast within. Then Walters only added flame to the fire when she made that tape."

"All right," Finnegan stated. "Finally. A new angle to work with. We can start the search on previous Carrinis with a past, whether positive or negative, with Mann. The idea sounds promising."

"So why the hesitancy in your voice?" Lansly asked.

Finnegan sighed. "I have a feeling we're going to find way more connections than we'd like. Then it'll be a sorting game."

"You know what could make this a whole lot easier?" Ava

asked sarcastically. "Lana's computer skills. Especially in the system of the hotel she works for."

I tried to hide my immediate attention to her name. "No. We have plenty of men here with as good of skills. We'll have them look into it."

"But Lana—"

"Isn't available right now," I bit out.

She eyed me in the hawkish way she tended to do to intimate suspects. "Lana will know which avenues to search, what's out of place. Our guys will be going in blind. Might as well give it to someone who's never seen crime before. It'll take them ages to get anything useful."

"We can't use Lana!" I insisted, storming off as my eyes watered, remembering how I'd left her.

When I made it to the hall, I pulled my phone out.

We couldn't use Lana, but I hadn't said anything against using her family's resources.

I scoffed to myself. Resorting to the mafia's resources. I may as well have resigned today.

The first words out of my mouth when Ivan picked up were, "I need your help."

OTETS HADN'T BEEN KIDDING every time he said I'd always have my room if I chose to come back. It was the same as when I left years ago, and somehow, my style was pretty much spot-on. It was a beautiful space, a bit darker and broodier than an average female's but relaxing for me.

It almost reminded me of Dorian's room.

The tears had stopped a couple of hours after making it home, and I finally got some sleep, restless as it was. When I'd woken from a nightmare and didn't have Dorian at my side, the memories of being sent away came flooding back, and I'd been a mess all over again.

It was coming up on noon, and Ava had texted me an hour ago. She wanted to know where I was. Not that I'd believe she cared, but I knew she wanted my answer in regards to helping her. The funny thing was, now that I was locked up in this beautiful estate, I'd love to help her. To hell what Dorian thought.

I'd responded honestly because she was Dorian's partner, and though I wasn't entirely certain of my feelings for her, I knew I could trust her. She hadn't responded to hearing of my house arrest, and I wondered if she was fighting Dorian for me or happy I was out of the way.

The knock on my door, more soft than demanding, told me who was bothering my hibernation. And again, like being in this room, I was sent back to the years of growing up at Romanov Estate.

"Go away, Lukov!"

He took that to mean "come in, Lukov."

I had my legs tucked into my chest as I sat against my headboard and didn't fight him as he made his way toward me. I wanted out, but I wasn't mad at my brother for my predicament. At least, not this brother, even though he'd done nothing to stop Sergei from carting me away. It was that big oaf that needed a smack across the face with a pan.

I wasn't even mad at Dorian... too much. I understood why he did it. I still wanted to—and fully intended to—kick his ass for it, but I needed to make sure he was safe from Alfonso first. Which meant I needed a way out of here, and that would only happen with help.

I both perked up and narrowed my eyes when I saw the two cups in his hands. "How many times are you going to harass that girl?"

"How am I harassing her?" He gave that smile that could get him out of anything with any girl, even relatives. It'd worked on my mom before and worked on me now. It was charming, to say the least.

He sat before me and handed me my cup. "You're upset, and I know this is your favorite coffee, so I wanted to brighten up a little bit of your day."

I rolled my eyes. "Toni's is closed today. These next three days, if I remember correctly. Small remodel."

He smirked. "You were upset and needed a pick-me-up."

"Luk, that girl is infatuated with you. Damn near in love. Don't abuse that power." There was a back entrance to the place that led directly to Nairi's apartment on the floor above the cafe, and I had no doubts that my brother had abused her desires and met her there. The poor girl would never deny him. Why she had to fall for this asshole I called a brother—though he was the least assholey of the three—I didn't know.

"I see the coffees already working to lift your spirits if you can chastise me about her instead of being here."

I rolled my eyes and let my head fall back. "I'm gonna get out of here, Luk. He's not fighting this without me."

"Look who's so in love now she'd do stupid shit," he teased, smile almost impossible not to reciprocate.

The audacity of my brother to compare my situation to Nairi's.

I smacked him with a pillow. "The difference, asshole, is that we're in a relationship. You dangle yourself in front of her like sweets to a child with strict parents, meat to a caged lion. Irresistible yet impossible to have."

"Who said I was impossible to have?"

"You've known her years and haven't made a move. Maybe that? Though your pornos do make a great opposing view."

He leaned in with a mischievous smirk. "Wanna know what I think of when I'm watching them?"

I pushed him away, feigning vomit. "Yuck. Ugh. Lukov, you can leave now."

He chuckled as he turned so he sat beside me against the headboard, our shoulders brushing, reminding me of all the times we'd sat like this in the past. "*Sestra*... we love you. And we're overbearing, you know that."

"That's not the problem, Lukov."

"Then what is?"

"That I can't hate you for it."

He laughed. "Lucky us."

I scoffed. "Unlucky your future wives. Hopefully they have more fire in them than I do."

"I don't think that's possible, Lani-Bunny."

I sighed, pulled out of this little reprieve my brother had created. "I'm gonna get out of here."

He kissed my temple. "I'll make sure to let security know."

I smiled, knowing things were going to be difficult as it was, but also knowing I'd done it before, so I could manage it again. "I know you're ignoring it, but you should know it'd be much more helpful to use me than try to keep me in the dark."

He was already moving for the door when he called out, "Drink your coffee. She didn't work on her day off so you could push it aside."

I wanted to throw a pillow at him but obeyed instead. I'd already known he would ignore me, and he was right. Nairi knew how to make coffee like no one else. When this was all over, I needed to go back to begging her to give up her secrets.

Or make Lukov convince her to give them up.

I'D REFUSED TO EAT WITH THEM, SO MY MEALS HAD been brought to my room all day. When dinner came, I ignored the cart with the covered plate and large cups of both water and juice and decided to find my way to the dining hall. Sitting around and moping was great and all, but I needed to do something, find a way to get out of here undetected.

Since they thought I was locked up for the night, it gave me the opportunity to listen in at the dining hall. The fucking assholes, making me resort to *listening in*.

Sometimes loving mafia men was more annoying than hating them.

Passing through the corridors to the dining hall, I remembered my life here. Running through these halls with three much older brothers letting me win the race, playing hide-and-seek with my father, playing grown-up with my mother. They were the softest memories.

I never really had bad ones here. Other than not wanting to be a career criminal, my life had been complete.

Walking through the hall connecting to the family space, I saw a popcorn machine in the corner and paused. My eyes narrowed. Had they finally gotten themselves the machine?

I took the moment to deter from my journey and get closer.

It'd been used before—the few pieces of popcorn dropped around the ground said as much—but the card was still attached to it.

When I opened it, the handwriting hit me like a ton of bricks and my heart hurt.

Thank you for all you've done for her. I can never repay you.

I closed my eyes to forget this because I had a mini mission I was on, then I let the card fall back to where it'd been hanging on the machine. I turned away from it, feeling like I was walking away from my forever, and moved for the dining room.

When I was close enough to the hall, I let my back rest against the cold stone walls and listened. It was damn near impossible to hear anything because of the heavy, nearly soundproofed doors my father had installed to keep situations like this from happening.

I steadied my heart so it wasn't pounding so loud in my ears. It made it difficult to listen in. Not to mention, if someone saw me, I was so caught. They'd definitely tell my family, and though I wasn't afraid of any of them, it meant they'd go to deeper lengths to keep these conversations from me.

"We can put Artyom on the job too," Sergei's voice carried. "He can join you." He must've been speaking with Ilya because the youngest was the best with computers out of my brothers, and Artyom had always been the man they went to when I wasn't available before.

"Anything connecting Mann and Carrini. Shipman isn't sure what their connection is, and though I don't frankly care, if this helps get the fucker, then we're doing it," *Otets* added.

My breath stopped. He was helping Dorian. It felt impossible, but I'd heard the words as perfectly as if they were whispered in my ear. Low and faint but clear.

But this also meant all these fuckers in my life were completely throwing my usefulness aside. With Ilya and Artyom looking into Carrini and Mann, the job would take longer and be less precise. They seemed to forget that not only had this been my job, but I knew Alfonso in a way none of them did.

I scoffed to myself. This was the job Ava had asked me to do earlier, and now I knew Dorian would've apparently had no problems with hearing I was doing it. Though considering he wasn't asking *me* to do it, maybe he would.

I'd allowed a lot to pass recently because everything they were doing was out of love for me, but this was ridiculous. Letting me help could only aid them, and they refused even that. The fucking morons.

My blood was rushing so loudly I couldn't hear them any longer, so I dropped the pretense and banged the door open. "If you guys need computer help, why not use me? You used to use me all the time!"

"Ah, there's my beautiful daughter, always listening where she's not invited."

I grimaced. "Make the room completely soundproof if you

don't want me to listen." Though I'd find another way to hear them. "Or better yet, let me leave."

He only smiled. "If you wanted to have dinner with us, Svetlana jan, I would've put a plate for you right by my side."

My heart thundered. *Jan.* It was a term of endearment and one I hadn't heard from my father in so long.

"Where you could hide all this information and pretend like we're a happy-go-lucky family?" I didn't want to give him attitude. After Dorian, he was probably my favorite man in the world, but I couldn't help how frustrated I was. "Just... let me help you."

"No." His voice was soft, always had been in regards to me, but it was also demanding.

I turned from my father to my brothers. As I met Sergei's eyes, I knew he would never help. As the oldest, he had the most and fondest memories with our mother, and since her death, he'd been extra protective of me. Almost like he blamed himself for not protecting her more and wouldn't make that same mistake with me. It made him the most ruthless in regards to my wants, but I couldn't fault him.

Lukov's gaze was lighthearted, but it was clear as day I wouldn't get anything past him. No help from my favorite, apparently.

And Ilya... he was the most analyzing. As the computer guy after me, he understood better than the others that I could help. A part of him probably wanted to allow it, but the hard resolve in his brown orbs said he wouldn't.

I sighed. Of course all four were too smart to let me near a computer. On top of finding out Alfonso and Mann's connection, I'd find Alfonso and put myself in all sorts of danger to keep him from Dorian. The men in my life were kinda stupid, but sometimes, so was I.

I fell into the chair across from Sergei. "Sometimes I understand why people hate you guys."

They all laughed, even Sergei's permanent scowl breaking, and I couldn't help but let my lips twitch up. They were assholes, but they were my assholes, and I loved them too much not to enjoy this moment with them.

"Silva," *Otets* called out. "Get my daughter a plate." His soft eyes met mine. "I can finally have dinner with my whole family again."

My heart ached. Maybe I was an even bigger ass than them for not coming back from time to time. I'd used the excuse that I wanted out of this life, but I'd never fully gotten myself out. I could've come for Sunday dinners. Or for one a month. Something more than nothing.

I took my father's hand and squeezed, hoping he read how sorry I was in the simple touch. Hoping he knew how much I appreciated him, how much I valued the attention he'd given me and my wants my whole life, but especially since my mother passed.

His wink said he did, that he would never hold a grudge against me.

My heart pounded some more. I'd missed him more than I'd allowed myself to feel before.

"If you don't mind, Svetlana, I'd like to hear of this job you have, training the security teams in those hotels," *Otets* started. "Are you trying to make our lives more difficult?"

I laughed as Silva placed a plate and two cups in front of me with a wrinkled and genuine smile. "Welcome back, Miss Lana," he whispered.

"Thank you, Silva," I responded before turning back for my father. "And as for you, I am making nothing more difficult."

They all scoffed, but it was Sergei who said, "Oh yes. It is so much easier for us when the security *know* how to do their jobs."

I winked. "It's more interesting for me."

Sergei threw a roll at me, and I was instantly transported to nearly two decades ago when he'd do the same thing and *Mama* would get angry with him for it.

"Sergei Ivan Romanov." I copied my mother's tone, which I only had down from all the home movies I'd seen. "Do not throw your food."

Otets took my hand as they all laughed. "You truly are your mother's daughter, aren't you?"

I shrugged. "I think I have quite a bit of you in me too."

He kissed my knuckles as Ilya started telling his side of the time they'd gone to Hollis on a job and been surprised that the dumbfucks they'd known the security to be weren't the same. I remembered that day, remembered sitting in the control room with all the cameras and watching the two sides battle out. That footage had been immediately deleted with no connection to me, but I'd saved a tape for myself.

"See! Much more interesting now!"

Three more rolls came flying at my head.

$$\mathcal{Dorian}$$

FINNEGAN DIDN'T TECHNICALLY KNOW how I found Carrini's hide spot. I wasn't sure the captain of our team would necessarily be okay with using the Russian mafia for any purpose, but when Lana's life was on the line, I didn't exactly care.

I was surprised, though, that Ivan had sent me the address instead of coming after Carrini himself.

Which instantly washed away when we got to the scene and I saw two men in suits clearing their posts across the street and getting in their cars. I scoffed. Of course the Romanovs had come in first, checked for Carrini, then called it in. Ivan knew not to touch anything else though, so hopefully when he didn't find the man, he and his goons had simply left.

We went with protocol anyway and moved in carefully, and only when the place was cleared did we start rummaging through Carrini's things.

It was a pretty empty space. An abandoned spot within a warehouse that he used as one big studio apartment. On the one side were a little fridge, microwave, a rolling pantry with cupboards for snacks, and a portable sink that played as the kitchen. Attached to the other corner was a door that led into a bathroom with three stalls and three sinks that Carrini had brought a portable showerhead into and attached to one of the sinks. With the drains on the grounds, the man could shower in the corner, and the water would wash down. The damp floors proved as much. We would need to check how the utilities in this space were still working, but my guess was he was paying for them in cash, pretending to be the owner of this "developing" lot. It would take minor technical skills to forge those documents as long as proper checks were never done. And if Carrini was paying well and on time, no proper checks would've ever been done.

With the "essential" rooms taken care of, Carrini used the rest of the empty space however he saw fit.

On the wall by the bathroom was a bed, messily made like he'd jumped out and hadn't had time to clean it. He must've been tipped off to the Romanovs coming for him and left in a hurry because, based on the cleanliness of the rest of the place, I was convinced he was a bed-maker. A pristine bed-maker.

There was a round table with papers and photos thrown about between the kitchen space and the living space. It looked messy, like they were haphazardly thrown there, but on closer inspection, everything seemed to have a place on the table.

By the couch in the middle of the space was a coffee table with files stacked up and a super eight film digitizer. On the wall across from the couch was a projector.

Most of the space didn't have much littering it. There were rugs around almost all of the room to block off the echo and cleaning supplies by the makeshift kitchen, but that was the extent of the space. A clothing rack held a few pieces by his bed, but Carrini definitely used this place as a hideout.

"Nothing here has to do with Mann," Lansly called from

where he shuffled through the papers on the round table. "But I'd say Lana's account of his obsession was pretty accurate." He held up picture after picture of my girl.

Porter scoffed from the other end of the round table as she caught sight of one in particular. She held it up. "Yeah. Maybe an understatement."

The photo was a bunch of cutouts glued together. It depicted Lana, Carrini, and three kids, which looked familiarly like the two of them. He must've taken his and Lana's baby pictures to make it. The thing was fucking framed.

I turned away from them and let my attention rake over the coffee table I stood in front of. The stacks were neat, and I'd bet everything I owed that they were categorized.

I turned on the super eight to see if he was watching anything, and if so, what the last thing was, and was surprised when Lana's laugh instantly hit me.

The video was years old, that much was clear from the younger Lana on the screen, but it was one of the two of them.

I froze on my way to take a file and shuffle through it.

Lana was beaming in the video, truly enjoying her time with Carrini. He kept taking her hands and spinning her around as they danced on a bridge in a park somewhere.

I was hypnotized watching my woman continue to spin back into that fucker's arms as they whispered to one another, smiles broadening.

Finnegan cleared his throat beside me. "Moments like these, even if few, would've fueled his obsession. After this date, he wouldn't have been able to interpret a life where they both didn't feel excited and in love with one another."

"I know," I mumbled, unable to break my stare.

In the video, Carrini started pulling on Lana's hand. "C'mon, Svetlana. We need to get going."

She gave him that teasing smile that won me over the very day we met. "I don't wanna go."

No wonder Carrini had fallen so hard. I'd known from the very beginning that I was a fool to fall for her smiles, but I'd done so anyway. Had I been more sick in the head, I might've been liable to get a little crazy for her as well.

"It's our first date, Svet. If I want your brothers to allow another, I need to get you home on time."

She pouted, and I fell for her a little harder in this moment, watching the projection.

Then the camera moved, and Carrini was no longer in view as he brought it closer to Lana.

"Look at that beautiful face." He recorded her. "How am I supposed to deny it anything?"

She gave a wicked, delicious smirk. "Don't."

He growled. "Don't play games with me, Svetlana. Your brothers will kill me if I touch you on the first date."

She grumbled and pushed away the camera, but there was still a hint of her smiles as the camera fell. "Fine."

The film stopped then, but I didn't move.

Lana had said they'd had good moments before she realized she wasn't entirely into him. She'd said her first date was great. I couldn't be upset about it. Especially knowing even with how happy they looked in that video, they didn't do anything and things didn't last. I still had all of her firsts—from kiss to orgasm to love.

And most especially because I had a past too, and she never judged me on it. She never got angry about the fact that I had girlfriends, women I'd been more than intimate with. She was allowed her own past too. I was only glad it was as innocent as this video, no matter how much it tugged on my heart to watch it.

Finnegan cleared his throat. "If he constantly watched this

video, it was also a constant reassurance that her feelings were there. That she was only playing hard to get. Not to mention, he may have more."

I sighed. "I know."

With the light from the super eight brightening the place, I finally sat and took a file from the coffee table, Finnegan doing the same with another one.

Mine was dedicated to the employees at Shriberton Hotel. "He kept track of everyone who worked there, the men especially. I bet it was to make sure they didn't touch Lana, but he could've had an in with one of these for Mann."

It was quite frustrating not knowing what Lana's family had found out about their connection, how they'd found this place at all. All Ivan had done was let me know of the hideout, and while I was thankful for it, some extra information would've been nice as well.

Finnegan shook the file he held. "I have Hollis."

My gaze snapped from the picture of one of Shriberton's more attractive male security to my captains, then to the folders on the table. I took another. "Artsoc Hotel. Those are the three she regularly contracts to."

Porter met us at the coffee table, taking a file as Finnegan took another and said, "These are less descriptive, but they're of some of the other hotels around town. He made sure he had any possible threat in a coworker or other contractors figured out."

Porter snorted. "Too bad that's not what he had to worry about." She was extra focused on the papers she was flipping through, her brows furrowed as she skimmed it.

"Whose do you have?" I asked her.

She turned it back to the first page and flipped it for us to see. There, staring back at me, was my face. It wasn't my detective portrait, though he had a small version of that clipped to the folder, but a close-up candid taken as I walked in the city.

Finnegan sighed. "We were expecting he'd have something on you."

"I know." I grabbed another. "Even better if Porter goes through it. I'd probably miss something important, thinking it's nothing since its about me."

Porter looked shocked that I was allowing her to look at any dirty laundry Carrini might've pulled on me, but I ignored it as I opened the one in my hands. "Sergei."

Porter's head snapped up. "Let me se—"

"Ah, ah, ah." I held the file close. "You have mine to focus on. It's the most important, after all."

She growled, nostrils flaring, but stepped back and opened my file once more.

Finnegan opened another file. "I have Ivan."

I took another. "Lukov."

"Ilya," Finnegan finished.

We flipped through some more to find files on the rest of my team and members of the Romanov's closest confidants. I stacked the files together, keeping Sergei's on the bottom so Porter didn't try to steal it and get distracted from reading mine, and Finnegan did the same with his stack. When we turned, Lansly was almost done filling his box with all the things on the round table so he could inspect it all in the office.

The place was clean. None of the drawers held anything, nothing under the mattress or bed, nothing behind appliances or stuck to the doors in the bathroom. Nothing under the couch, between the cushions, taped beneath any of the tables or chairs. Nothing behind the projection screen on the wall or hidden within the covers. No squeaky floors that we could tell held something beneath and nothing on the walls that looked out of place. We'd keep surveillance on the place unless Carrini decided to come back—which I highly doubted—but for now, these files he read through and added to on a daily—because I believed his obsession meant he had to keep up with them all like he was inputting data for a large corporation.

Finnegan dropped his files into an evidence box, then I threw mine in there, making sure to place the lid on quickly so Porter's sneaky hands didn't get any ideas. I saw the way she'd eyed it before I covered the box.

Then I walked it to my car with Finnegan.

As I dropped the box in the back seat, I couldn't help needing to turn back. Finnegan was stopped talking to a few cops by the front doors when my phone rang. My heart pounded with how desperately I wanted to hear Lana's voice.

I was both relieved and disappointed that it wasn't her.

Then glad once more because it was a call from the second-best woman in my life.

"Mom," I said into the phone, turning away from the hideout.

"Hi, sweetie," she cooed into the device. "I'm sorry if I'm bothering you at work. I just missed you and wanted to hear your voice."

A smile lifted my lips for the first time in a while. "I miss you too, Mom. I'm sorry I haven't been around recently."

"Nonsense. Heroes have too many people to take care of. I understand that."

I laughed. "Trust me, Mom. I'm no hero."

"You are at work, right? Because it sounds to me that you're starting an argument, and we both know I'm too stubborn to give in before you."

The darkness around my heart cracked off, and I was thankful to her for it. "How are you? You sound happy."

"I am, Dor. Extremely."

My smile broadened, but she didn't need to know it as I

said, "Ugh. Please tell me it's not because of a man."

"Dorian Alexander Shipman!"

I laughed. "I can't wait to meet him."

"Me either. And what about you?"

"I can't wait for you to meet Lana either, Mom."

"Lana," she teased. "So that's the name of the woman who's taking all that real estate in your mind."

"So much I've forgotten to call. I'm sorry."

"Don't be, sweetie. The honeymoon stage is exciting. Thrive in it. I am!"

"Goodbye, Mom!" The very last thing I needed was to hear about my mother and her boyfriend. She wasn't old, so I knew she could have a virile sex life, but it was possibly the very last thing I'd ever like to know about.

She only laughed. "Goodbye, Dor. Come by whenever you have a little downtime."

"I promise."

When she hung up, I turned back to the warehouse. Finnegan was in the car, but I couldn't get in yet.

How long had Carrini had this place? Had he been so close, so meticulous about all the people in Lana's life, for long? Would the profile regarding his obsession for her be correct? Would he end up hurting her if things spiraled too far? He hadn't done so before, but that was before the rest of us were in the picture, before I had touched her.

I sighed, taking in the abandoned building a final time before getting into the passenger seat.

Finnegan started the car, and we were off to the precinct to sort through this shit and hopefully, mercifully, finally be over with it all. I couldn't wait to get back to my girl, to hold her and never let her go again. To kiss away every hurt she ever experienced and to make sure she trusted my word above all else, trusted my promises to her meant everything to me.

I WAS LEAVING the gym with two goons assigned to my tail. I'd been punching away at a bag, imagining it was Alfonso, and for a couple of hours, I'd been at peace with all that was happening in my world.

Then I left the space, and everything came crashing back on me. I was in the midst of eyeing areas of the home I hadn't tried to sneak out from before when I turned the corner to see Lukov.

And behind him were Nairi and... Ava?

What the fuck was Ava Porter doing here? How did my brother allow her in?

Lukov's little smirk with his shining eyes told me he was waiting for more harassment jokes. "You've got company."

"*You* let a cop into this place?"

"I let my friend into our home." His hand landed on Nairi's back, and she froze, probably trying to memorize the way his touch felt on her body. "She brought a friend."

I eyed Nairi, narrowed my gaze at Ava, then watched the

former girl once again. "You here to finally teach me how to make those coffees?"

She gave a soft smile that seemed to hold Lukov's attention a little too tightly. "If I did that, I wouldn't get to see your stunning face at the shop any longer."

She leaned into Lukov as she spoke like she was doing so subconsciously, and though all of her attention remained on me, I couldn't help but take note that my brother wasn't focused on our conversation at all. Maybe Nairi was infatuated, but my brother looked... I couldn't even allow myself to think it.

He was pressed against her, hand still on her back, like he was ready to get in front in case of an attack, even though we were in the safest spot in the whole state. It didn't look like he was conscious of the fact there was barely any space left between them, but the pinking of Nairi's cheeks said she was very aware.

I turned to Ava, choosing to follow that line of thought another day. "And you came because?"

She gave a smile anyone could read as false. "Come, now, Lan. You're my partner's girl. I thought the three of us were really becoming a girl gang the other day."

My ass.

The other day Nairi and I had been discussing getting backup, but Lukov and the goons didn't need to know that.

Nairi coughed softly, causing my brother to step impossibly closer like it was a gut reaction, and though I could tell it took everything in her to ignore his movements, I caught the look in her eyes—we needed to speak privately.

It was an interesting turn of events—Nairi and me against Lukov rather than them against me.

"Right." I gave a cheery smile that I was sure convinced no one. "Let's go to my room, then."

My hand fell into the crook at Ava's elbow, and I reached for Nairi when Lukov finally snapped out of his thoughts. He met my gaze and must've seen the shimmering of "I'm so teasing you later because you totally have a crush and that's why you're always grabbing coffees from Toni's" because he stepped away from Nairi abruptly and smirked. "Have fun, ladies."

He was off before we could say any more, but Ava must've picked something up, too, because she quirked a brow at me that said, "Yeah, they totally have the hots for each other, and it's disgusting."

The look made me both smile and remember that I still didn't really like Ava Porter.

I turned us down the hall for my room and was back to being followed.

"What's up with the goons?" Ava asked.

"Apparently, I can't be trusted in my own family home," I said with offense.

Nairi giggled from my left. "Lukov mentioned once you broke out of the house because you were bored and almost got three people killed because 'they should've been able to keep an eye on you.'"

I smiled at the memory. It wasn't that I was simply bored. It was because I'd wanted to head to an art exhibition and hadn't been allowed because of the people who might show up to said exhibition, so I'd snuck out. It wasn't my fault their stalkers couldn't keep track of me. "I didn't realize you two talk so much."

"We don't." Her cheeks burned, longing filling her soft brown eyes. "But when he was trying to get me to tell him when you were around, he warmed me down with some stories about you."

"Ah. And I thought he simply got your number by flirting."

She laughed. "No. He didn't flirt. Doesn't flirt. Ever, I don't think."

I quirked a brow in her direction. "He's flirted with you in front of me, Nairi."

She shrugged. "To annoy you because what sister wants to see that. It's not real."

Ava snorted on my other side, and I had half a mind to do the same, but I could see that being the truth. If Lukov didn't flirt when they were alone, I could see why Nairi would think it was all for show. Did she think the way he stood with her back there was a show too? Because I could guarantee that hadn't been anything but his desire to be close to her.

I cleared my head. Now wasn't the time to think of their love lives. I needed to figure mine out first.

When the door to my room closed, leaving the goons in the hall, Ava dropped the act and pulled out a computer from the inside of her sweater. It was stuffed in the back, her jacket covering the bulge.

"They didn't frisk you? How'd you manage that?"

"Brother dearest wouldn't let anyone touch coffee dearest here." She smirked. "I'm surprised he didn't frisk her himself just to touch her."

"I asked them not to touch Ava either," Nairi added. "Lukov... wasn't happy, but he listened."

My smile broke out. Oh, Lukov was getting teased hard-core.

I turned for her. "And how did Ava convince you to come?"

She shrugged. "She wouldn't have been able to make it through with the laptop without me. I like you. I wanted to help."

"Even though it goes against Lukov's wishes?"

Her gaze went dejected for a moment, but she remained determined. "Men don't always get what they want. Mafia men especially need that lesson."

I chuckled. "I think I like you even more now." I opened the laptop, knowing what Ava wanted from me. "And how did you know he'd let you in? That he'd listen if you asked not to be checked?"

"I didn't. Ava said she knew he'd listen to me. I didn't believe it, but I guess it worked." She shrugged. "I guess he does owe me for all the times I've called him about you."

As I tapped away on the computer, opening Shriberton's systems virtually, I narrowed my eyes at her. "Yeah, thanks for that, by the way."

Ava scoffed from where she lounged on my bed. "Please, he didn't do it because he owes you. I could damn near smell the desire wafting off you two out there."

Nairi flushed as I quirked a brow at Queen Bitch.

"When we found out about your family, I did a little searching. Especially when I heard Lukov's name in your gibberish conversation the other day," she answered. "I found out middle brother Romanov likes to frequent Toni's. Exclusively. I put my bets on the fact that it was for more than the coffee. Especially if the pretty barista mentions him in a gibberish convo."

Nairi turned a deeper red, and though I didn't want to contribute to the poor girl blowing up, I lit the flame. "Are you afraid? That he might want you? Afraid to join this family?" I couldn't blame her.

Her gaze was clouded and faraway. "No."

Something in the way she said it made me believe the answer wasn't for Lukov's sake. There was some other reason being in this mess wouldn't terrify her. Interesting, fascinating girl.

I dropped my attention back to the computer instead of continuing on with the conversation because as much as I wanted to learn more about these women risking the wrath of my family to help me—though I had no doubts Ava was here for selfish reasons—I needed to make sure Dorian was safe first.

I worked quietly while Nairi pulled out a journal to write in, and Ava pulled out paperwork she'd had folded in her little side bag—one too small to hide a laptop—to do. I first got into Shriberton's systems, then made sure no one knew I was there. I didn't need them thinking they were being hacked right then, especially since Dorian's team had asked the hotel to send all requests to them instead of me for the time being. The very last thing I needed was Dorian catching wind that I'd gotten on.

After two hours, I'd made my way quietly into the systems and gone through a nice amount of footage with the girls, but I had weeks, if not months of shit to go through to see if Carrini and Mann had past altercations, so I'd be finishing off on my own. I needed to get the girls out before Lukov came looking and questioning. I hid the laptop under my pillow before walking them out.

We were in the foyer, the two almost gone, when Sergei came storming toward us. "What the fuck is she doing here?" he roared, scaring even me.

Ava didn't look perturbed in the slightest. "Scared my presence will hurt you, coward?"

My eyes widened at her audacity just as Lukov and Ilya made their way into the space, the former moving instantly behind Nairi.

"Sergei," Lukov started. "Calm do—"

"Do not tell me to calm down, brother!" He stepped forward, but Ilya stopped him before he could touch Ava.

I knew he hated the precinct, but this much?

"Yes. Listen. Calm down and crawl back up your father's ass!" Ava snickered.

"Ava!" I reprimanded. "Stop baiting him."

She turned incredulous eyes on me. "*He* shot me in the chest!"

"Sergei!" I exclaimed.

He snickered, fighting past Ilya. "I'm sorry I missed your heart."

Ava got in his face, completely pushing Ilya out of the way. "Are you confessing, bastard?"

He got closer, hand locking around her jaw. "Our word against yours."

"You guys!" I wanted to pull them apart, but they were so angry I was afraid one wrong move would merge them together and turn a fire-breathing dragon on me.

But at least now I knew what that problem between the precinct and Sergei was. And it was a pretty damn big one.

"I shoot you right here, right now, and no one will ever find out," Sergei spit into the tiny space between them.

To my shock, Nairi stepped up. "Yes they would. Let her go."

Sergei's jaw ground, and his hand looked to tighten around Ava, but before he could roar at Nairi, Lukov joined her. "Let go of her, Serg. She's Shipman's partner. Lana's connection makes her untouchable."

"Fuck Shipman!" Sergei seethed.

"Sergei." I finally stopped before them, though there was no space to get them separated. "Sergei, stop it. Whatever happened with you two, you have to drop it. For me."

"Go ahead, *Sergei*," Ava baited some more. "Drop it." Then whispered so low I only heard it because I was standing right beside them, "Then I'll end you."

"Sergei, please," I interrupted his retort.

He took a large breath in while his fingers dug into her cheeks, short nails piercing skin, then finally, he released her, stepping back before storming off. "Get her out of our home, Svetlana."

I breathed a sigh of relief, turning back to the two women. Ava was pissed, but she reined it in well and turned for the front door.

More of my attention was on Nairi. She'd stepped up to the next don of the Russian mafia. That took balls harder than steel.

I'd always thought she and Lukov were from completely different worlds, but maybe my assumptions were completely off about the girl.

"Thank you, guys, for keeping me company," I said by way of goodbye.

Ava nodded and headed out while Nairi turned a soft goodbye to my brother. She was stepping away when Lukov's hand landed on her back as he said, "I'll walk you out."

Meeting the eyes of the only other person left in the room, Ilya grinned. "This house is like a fucking soap opera."

The comment made my lips twitch as I turned back for my room. I could stick around to tease Lukov when he came back, but I decided to let it go for now. Maybe I'd underestimated why those two weren't together, and I didn't want to push up unpleasant thoughts for my brother.

Plus, I had a shit ton of work to do.

I'd go to dinner because I owed it to my family after the hundreds I'd missed in all the years, but otherwise, I planned to have my bedroom door locked and my head stuck in a laptop.

I HAD A LOT OF GUILT FOR MISSING THINGS WITH MY family. It'd always been the most painful part of being away. But I hadn't missed anyone as greatly as I'd missed my father.

He'd called and checked in on me constantly, and I always called on birthdays and special occasions, so I never went long without speaking to him, but things were different when we were together. Already in the few days I'd been on house arrest, we'd laughed and played games and trained and taken so many pictures I almost felt like we made up for all the pictures I'd missed over the years. My favorite was the one of my father and me, arms wrapped around each other as we beamed.

It was in looking at that picture that I decided to go to him before hunkering down with my secret laptop for the night.

He was in the gallery room. It had always been *Mama's* favorite room.

He was staring at a portrait of him and *Mama* looking like they were king and queen. *Mama* looked ethereal in it.

The door shut silently behind me, but he would know I was there. He didn't move though.

I cradled into his side, hugging his arm as I stared up at the portrait. "I've never been able to imagine what it was like living on without her, but I especially cannot imagine it now."

"It is a pain like no other, Lan. Worse than anything you can imagine." He scoffed to himself. "And yet, I still hope you feel it one day. In the far, far future."

"You hope I feel it?"

"I certainly don't want you leaving this earth before Dorian."

I chuckled, then snuggled into him. "Can you tell me a secret, *Otets*? One that was only for you and *Mama*?"

His hand caressed the one I was gripping him with, but he didn't break his stare from my mother's. "You are more like your mother than you believe, Svet."

"How's that?"

"She didn't want this life either."

My eyes widened. "But she chose it." She wasn't from a mafia family. She chose to come into it.

He shook his head. "She chose me, Svet, not the life. She took it on so eloquently because of how amazing of a woman she was, but she hadn't wanted it. It is why I had given the okay with Carrini all those years ago. I was selfish. I'd promised your mother it would be your decision, so if you fell in love with him and stayed with us, I got what I wanted, and it was still your decision."

"The boys don't know?"

He shook his head. "Your brothers assume, I think. They were much older than you when she passed, so they picked up on certain things you wouldn't have. But none of them have brought it up. I think they see no problem with it, and I cannot blame them."

"Because if they fell in love with a civilian, they'd want to selfishly bring them into the life too?"

He shrugged. "I've never called myself a good person, Svet."

I reached up and kissed his cheek. "You're the best person, *Papa. Mama* chose this life. If she was as much like me as you say, then you wouldn't have been able to stop her. Hell, she would put herself in danger specifically to prove that she was going to be in the life with you no matter what."

He laughed, shaking his head and closing his eyes with the joy. "Fuck, Svet. Just like your mother. How else do you think we got together?"

"What do you mean?"

"I rejected your mother, Svet. I loved her, and I wanted her to be safe from this life. She was the one who got involved enough to make me come out and claim her."

I'd heard of how they'd met, the innocent interaction. I'd heard of how they'd fallen in love. But I'd never heard of this.

"You rejected her!"

He met *Mama's* eyes in the portrait again and had a faraway smile about him. "The hardest thing I've ever done, Svet. Though, I'll admit, things were easier when she didn't take no for an answer. I knew that she loved me as much as I did her. My fucking firecracker."

"Your fucking neck," I teased.

He sighed. "Yes, my beautiful, perfect neck."

I interlocked my fingers with my father's. "You want to be with her again, don't you?"

"Every. Fucking. Day. And soon, I will be again."

"You know," I tried to lighten the mood. "Some variation of Svet will be my daughter's middle name. First name if Dorian gets his way. But I also hope we have your first grandson."

"Why's that, *moya doch*?"

"You're the best man I know, *papa*. My children are going to know it too."

"You do not have to name them after me, Svet. As long as your mother's name is there, I'll be there."

He threw his arm around me, and I snuggled into his side. "You're right. Sergei's probably gonna take Ivan anyway since it's his middle name."

He chuckled. "And Ilya called Viktor a long time ago."

I grumbled. "Fucking bastards."

He kissed my crown. "*Ya tebya lyublyu.*"

"*Ya lyublyu tebya yeshche bol'she.*"

"*Nevozmozhnyy.*"

"*Navsegda vozmozhno.*"

IT WAS FOUR IN THE MORNING, AND I WAS EATING licorice as I stared at the screen on my secret laptop. I'd been going through recordings from the past few months for hours now and had jotted down a few points that looked maybe a bit off, but I wasn't sure if any of them would connect. For now, I was only searching though.

It was quiet in the house, even though there were men up and patrolling both in the estate and outside. They were silent though, always had been.

It made sneaking around—and, in turn, sneaking out—all the more difficult, but I'd always enjoyed the challenge when I was younger. I didn't sneak out often back then, mostly only to see if I could manage it, but every time had been exhilarating. Even the ones where I was caught.

I was already approaching December, and I had every inconsistency with the cameras that I recognized jotted down. They were always at times I hadn't been working, so I would've never noticed. Since I wasn't part of their security per se, it wasn't my job to go back and look through their footage, so it was stuff I would've never seen.

But I was the one who'd set up their cameras, so I knew where they should be. If Alfonso had moved them, then he'd done a perfect job of moving them back so I wouldn't noticed. I hadn't noticed for months.

His little game of constant cat and mouse that he believed we were playing.

I went to switch days, going further back in time, like I'd been doing for hours now, but paused. My brows furrowed.

There, trapped between a disrupted video footage of the

day Mann had come up to talk to me—though I hardly remembered it—was a file.

When I clicked on it, a password box popped up.

My fingers hovered over the keyboard. What the fuck would Shriberton put a file in the middle for? Why would they password protect against their own security team?

I nibbled on my lip, going back to the video. It was the first time I'd met Mann.

The first time Alfonso had seen Donovan Mann flirt with me, follow me around the room, fuck me with his eyes.

I took in a large breath and went back to the file, typing in my birthday for the password.

Wrong.

I typed in Elington Bridge, the first date we'd gone on.

Wrong.

Elington didn't work either, and neither did any dates that stood out to us, so I stopped to think. If Alfonso had left this here for me, then he knew I'd be able to figure out the password.

So I closed my eyes and remembered us. Our first date and snuggling in his car and whispered secrets and painful confessions and... when he tried to kiss me on what became our last date.

I typed in the theatre's name, and the file opened.

I shook my head at the screen. Was that his way of telling me that hadn't been the end of our relationship? Sitting here waiting for the video before me to change from the black screen, I couldn't believe I'd allowed this obsession of his to continue for so long.

As I stared at my computer, the screen went from black to Alfonso's face up close and smiling. "*Mi bella,*" he cooed into the camera. "I knew you'd be the one to find this. We always worked so perfectly together, eh, my girl? I've been chasing you for a long time. I thought I'd finally give you the thrill to chase me."

He stepped back a little, raising his arms out, and I swore the room looked like one of the Shriberton Hotel ones. "You've hurt me, Svetlana. But still, I wish to give you nothing but love. And what better way to show my love than to rid of the one in our way?"

My heart stopped. Dorian? He had Dorian?

When Alfonso stepped all the way back, I settled back down. Not Dorian. He didn't have Dorian. I repeated the sentence in my head to keep from freaking out.

On the ground, tied up, was Donovan Mann.

So this was the night of the murder. This had probably happened after the security and I had left and Sydney had shown Alfonso the video. I knew he wouldn't have been able to wait but never would I have expected him to record the whole thing.

And for me.

For me to watch and enjoy.

Watching his beautiful—yet crazed—smile as he moved for Mann's crying form and cut him free, I tried to think about a life had our relationship been more like the one he thought we had.

I would've never cheated, so the video would still be faked by Sydney, but I know I would've loved the gesture of his killing Mann because he touched me. If I were more deranged in the head, I'd touch myself right now, knowing he'd made this video for me, made *me* play cat in finding it. Maybe I'd record myself getting off on the violence I knew was coming and leave it for him to find. I could imagine, in an alternate universe where Alfonso and I fell in love and we were a danger to this world.

But that hadn't happened.

And now I was stuck in bed about to watch a video of a murder that took place almost a month ago. A murder that Alfonso might've even known I'd become a suspect in since I'd been the last one seen in his room, but he'd allowed as punishment for me. A punishment he could watch from the sidelines but was ready to jump in and protect me if need be. Because that had always been Alfonso. He'd always protected me. Even when I didn't want it.

I scoffed to myself. And to think, his little plan was part of the reason I'd met Dorian. I had him to thank for it entirely.

Alfonso stared into the camera before he brought down his knife for the first attack. "*Bella*, why would you touch him when you have me?" Another stab. "The things I was going to do to your body... mmm, I think I shall carve my name into you so you never forget who you belong to." Another stab. "No one will ever touch you again, *mi bella*. We will be eternal." He moved for the camera and pulled the top of his shirt to the side. "I am already marked, my girl."

Carved under his collarbone was my name.

Carved.

Forever branded as a scar.

His eyes sparkled as he stared into the camera, into my soul. "When I find you, *amore*, I'm carving my name beside that sweet little pussy so you never forget who it belongs to."

I watched him go back to Mann, go back to stabbing him and talking to me until the place was splattered with blood, until he was splattered with blood from head to toe.

He took his final moves for the camera as my heart raced with the horrors of what I'd seen. It wouldn't have fazed me so much if I didn't know it'd been done because of his obsession with me, if I didn't know he'd do the same, if not worse, to Dorian.

He stopped before the camera. "*Amore mio*, you see what I

had to do for you. And I will do it again. To any man who ever touches you again. You are mine, Svetlana."

I couldn't breathe. He couldn't touch Dorian like that.

I threw the laptop to the side, the video closing as it fell, and quickly changed clothes. I had no idea if security would be waiting for me to try the air vents as a way out, but it was my best shot right now. I needed to get to Alfonso before he got to Dorian.

LUKOV'S NAME flashed across my screen. It was insane to think that I'd gone from not having any contacts with the mafia to having the four top Russians as some of my most important callers.

"How is she?" It was how I'd been picking up all of their calls.

"A dead woman when we get our hands on her." That was the opposite of the answer I'd been receiving.

My heart dropped. "What happened? What did my girl do?"

"More like what did *the* girls do," he ground out, anger bubbling in his words.

"Who're the girls?" Lana didn't tell me about any friends.

"Your little partner was here the other day, Shipman. I was stupid enough to let her pass through without a full-body search. I know that's how Lana got access to a laptop."

My heart sank a little deeper. Since when were Porter and Lana friends? They'd never liked one another, Ava even more so since finding out which family Lana belonged to.

"What happened, Lukov?"

"Ava stopped by, and suddenly, Lana has a laptop that she used to look into the systems at Shriberton. She must've left in a hurry because she left her notes on the bed. She found the key points that linked everything together through their security footage. This was the exact reason we hadn't allowed her access before."

"What did she find?" I swallowed. If he was this mad, then I was going to be scared out of my mind. And when all of this was over, I was going to kill Porter.

"We're coming now with her stuff. She's gone though, Shipman. She's gonna use herself as bait to get him without us."

I didn't have control over my body as I turned and punched the wall, my hand aching but my nerves barely registering it. "How long?"

"We'll be there in ten minutes. She must've left a couple of hours ago, I'm not sure. Sergei's figuring out which of the security lost her trail. He'll deal with them."

It was eight o'clock in the fucking morning—where the fuck was she?

"Fuck," I grunted.

"Precisely. Oh, and Shipman," he called. "That bitch better not be there when we get there. I'll finish what my brother started if I see her."

I was damn near ready to finish what his brother started. "Whatever. Just get here."

I stormed out of the hall I'd been in when I got the call and straight for the desks my team were at. My fist hit the table, my attention on the only female. "What the fuck is the matter with you?"

She quirked her brow. "I'm going to need specifics."

"You brought her a fucking laptop? You knew she'd find something and get to Carrini before he could get to me!"

Instead of looking ashamed, she perked up. "She found something."

I seethed. "Apparently. And her brothers are on their way here with her notes to see if we can get it too." I got in close. "If something happens to her because of this, Porter, I'll finish what Sergei started."

Her eyes darkened and nostrils flared at the threat, but she only gave a single nod.

My heart pounded the entire time we waited for them. And all the while, I heard my father's voice in my ear telling me she was going to be all right, telling me I would be able to feel if she were in true danger because that was how true love worked. He was such a sap for those things before. I'd made fun of him for it constantly growing up, but I understood now. He'd been so in love with my mother that he hadn't been able to stop the feelings from spewing out. I felt that now for Lana.

I missed him now more than ever. Wished he was around to meet her. He'd love her. Call her my firecracker.

He'd always said I was a hero, but sometimes I was too good. He'd delight in having Lana bring out the bad in me. He always said life was more interesting in the grey areas. Lana brought out all of my grey areas like Mom had for him. I couldn't wait for Lana to meet Mom, so Dad was there in spirit to meet her as well because that was the one place we knew he'd always be—with Mom. Even if she moved on, which he'd wanted on his deathbed, wanted her to be happy, Dad would always be there.

The clocks ticked in slow motion. Time passed with my heart beating so wildly I wasn't sure it was healthy, but finally, they were here.

Porter refused to leave like the boys had requested, but she promised not to be a nuisance and to remain on the other side of the office when the men stormed in.

I was surprised all of them hadn't shown up but knew they had other things to coordinate as well. The two younger brothers walked into the place like they owned it with three men behind them, and both men's gazes darted straight for Porter.

They were both storming for her when Finnegan and Lansly got in the way.

"You can settle your differences another time," the captain ordered. "Right now, let's go through what your sister found and find out where the fuck they are."

Ilya scowled but dropped the notebook on my desk. I had the thing opened to the first page immediately, my team coming in behind me to get a look.

"We already went through it. There's that stuff, and there's an encrypted file with a password that we're still trying to get in to," Lukov informed. "Let us know if you can come up with anything. We'll be here to fill in the blanks."

I flipped to another page. Then again. "What the hell is all of this?"

"Exactly," Lukov muttered.

Ilya pulled out a computer. "This is the laptop she used." He glared at Porter one more time before beginning to click away. "She'd been analyzing the security footage at Shriberton, which is what those notes are based off, and whatever that file is, she found within the Shriberton security."

"This shows she went backward from the kill date." Finnegan pulled the notebook. "But all that's stated is blind spots. Why would she write about blind spots?"

I pulled the notebook back. "She works the cameras too. She saw something out of place and was marking when they happened. How do these help though?"

Porter took the book. "The goal was to see if any consistencies popped up. This was before we knew of Carrini though. So her goal was probably to see what consistencies Carrini left behind when playing around with the footage."

I took the book again, flipping some more. "Hm. Her dates changed back."

"That's it!" Lansly declared, pulling the notebook from my hands. "She went backward in time with all of her checks, dating the ones she found discrepancies. Then she started moving forward around the time of the encrypted file. Probably where Carrini put it in order to tell her when all this started. He knew she'd be the one to find it. From this moment." He turned the notebook. "What happened on December twenty-ninth?"

Ilya moved quickly, typing away at the laptop until he pulled up the cameras for that day. He turned it so we all watched as Lana moved through the lounge during the day in order to grab a water. She was sweaty, presumably from training the security, and minding her business.

And in the corner was Mann. He noticed her instantly, then moved for her.

We couldn't hear what was being said, but he spoke to her, obviously flirting, and she clearly rejected him. That must've fed Carrini's obsession.

But Mann didn't drop it and turn away; his gaze remained on Lana as she left, salivating at the mouth as he fixed his junk, then turned back for his table.

Lansly flipped through the notebook pages once again. "She saw that, then started working forward again. After that, cameras started changing position. Carrini had seen that. It was the inciting incident. He likely didn't do anything because he thought Lana couldn't be less interested, but when Walters showed that video..."

"Okay, so how do we find her? See this file?" Lukov asked. "This helps your case, not ours."

My jaw ground. It didn't help my case. All I cared about was getting Lana back.

"But it does." Lansly dropped the notebook and moved for his desk. "It proves that the anger at Mann had been building, that Carrini had been watching Lana for a while. He was obsessed, and when he couldn't have her, he needed something of theirs." He rifled through the dozens of papers on his desk, all from what we collected at Carrini's. He finally pulled a photo. "Here. This!" He turned it. "This photo has the most crinkles in it. If I had to guess, when he couldn't go to the location, he'd look at this photo. This means something to them. Or at least, to him it does."

Lukov snapped the photo from Lansly's hands, and the two brothers took a closer look. They were shaking their heads until Lukov straightened. "That's the skylight. That's Bringley Theatre."

"What?" Porter asked as Ilya immediately started typing into Lana's laptop.

"Bringley Theatre. It's an abandoned, ripped up space Lana always thought was romantic. They went there on one of their last date. He told us after that date that he'd promised her forever," Lukov explained as one of their men pulled out his phone to inform the others.

In the meantime, Ilya got through the file and turned it to show a video file.

"*Mi bella*, I knew you'd be the one to find this," Carrini's voice started as we looked at him. He had a crazed look in his eye as he continued speaking to Lana.

When he stepped back, he was in a hotel room with Donovan Mann tied up. He took his time cutting away the ties so Mann would fight, then stared into the camera as he made his first attack, speaking to Lana the entire time.

We all stood there, my team and the Russians, and watched as Carrini inflicted every single injury, as he showed Lana what would happen if another man touched her.

This was what got Lana to drop everything and find him herself. If she let any of us in on it, we'd hold her back and she knew I'd be in his line of fire. My girl was trying to protect me.

But I needed to protect her more. He was obsessed with her, not me.

"Let's go." I moved without waiting for the others when the video ended with his final words to Lana.

But they were right behind me, Finnegan declaring, "You tell your friends to wait. We do this the legal way. That way Lana is safe, and Carrini is brought in without any of you getting in trouble."

Both brothers and their three goons scoffed, and I couldn't blame them. We took the stairs down quickly, all moving for our vehicles as Lukov texted me the address and I sent it to the rest of my team. We all knew the Romanovs weren't going to be taking orders from cops. And especially not when their sister's life was on the line.

I didn't care though. I was finally one step closer to getting my girl back. I only hoped she hadn't been with Carrini too long now.

ALFONSO WAS thirteen years older than me. At eighteen, he'd been thirty-one and the finest specimen to walk this earth. At twenty-four, he was thirty-seven and still the finest specimen to walk this earth. I hated to admit he was attractive in a way most couldn't be, in a way even Dorian wasn't.

But that didn't mean I wanted him.

That ball had dropped a long time ago and never came back up—my desires for Alfonso were gone.

But I was still human and couldn't help the way my gaze dropped to take him in slowly, from those boots he always had tucked beneath his trousers up to those suspenders over the nice shirt to his gorgeous smile.

He was waiting for me in the middle of the room, the lights dimmed but the skylight brightening the space. The shadows cast him in a glow that made him irresistible. At least to anyone who didn't have a history with him.

Part of this entire problem was Alfonso knew he was attractive, knew I found him so. What he couldn't process, though, was that the attraction that had been so strong years ago had faded.

"*Mi bella*." He smiled. "You've come to me."

From the look of the seat at the end of the illuminated area, he hadn't exactly been standing here waiting for me. I hadn't concealed any noise coming in, so he'd know I was here. But before that, he'd been sitting and remembering me. He had a blanket lying on that chair that had been over his knees, a material for him to play with while looking up at the skylight, that I remembered from one of our first dates. I'd left it in his car, and he'd obviously cherished it since. I'd been hiding in the beams at the corner of this building for hours before he showed up and nearly an hour after. I'd wanted to take my final moments with him in because as much as I hated him, he was a big part of my life.

I shrugged as I moved closer. "You always knew this would happen."

His hands landed in his trouser pockets. "That your desire for me would grow with every day of the chase until you were unable to stay away any longer."

"Is that what's happened?" I stopped directly under the skylight.

He moved slowly until he was only a foot away, his hand soft as it moved a piece of my hair back. "Isn't it, *bella*? You're finally ready to start our life." He leaned in, his fingers softly grazing my cheek. "But I need to know, *amore mio*, what has happened these past months? If you wanted the release, why find other men?"

"I was never with Mann, Alfonso. Sydney made that up to break your attachment." And unfortunately, it hadn't worked.

His brows furrowed. "I saw your marks, Svetlana."

"You will find the same marks on her. She needed to make sure you believed her."

His brows furrowed deeper, then released with his sigh as his forehead fell over mine. "He never touched you."

"No," I said. "You never had to kill him."

He grimaced. "He deserved to die for ever wanting to touch you. He obviously desired you if he fell for her ways."

"So you killed him."

His thumb brushed my bottom lip. "You saw how I gutted the fucker. For you, *amore mio*, always for you. He needed to be dealt with. I saw the way he lusted over you for months. He had it coming."

"The same way you planned on gutting Dorian?"

A low growl left Alfonso. "You're in his apartment, *amore*. How am I meant to believe *he* hasn't touched you?"

"You aren't."

Alfonso's nostrils flared, his hand wrapping around my jaw as his other hand landed on my hips. "He's had you? Taken all of my firsts?"

I swallowed, brushing aside the irritation of Alfonso calling them his firsts instead of mine. It made me remember how I realized my desires for him were mere infatuation, why I'd stopped what we had—to him, I was always his property. And not in the same way I called Dorian mine or me his, but in a total ownership way. I was nothing but an extension of him, could never be a person myself.

"He's had all *my* firsts, Alfonso. They were mine to give."

"They were mine to chase!" He seethed.

"You mean yours to capture, Alfonso. I was never given the opportunity to make decisions with you. What I had was yours."

"I allowed you the time to become comfortable with giving it up."

"Because you wanted my total submission, not because you respected me as your woman."

"You are my woman!" His hand tightened around my jaw. "I did not have to do any of it. I could've demanded your submission. I was good to you."

Yes, on the outside, he was good to me. He would buy me things, be sweet, take me places. He would open doors and make promises and keep every single one. He was the only person I didn't want promises from and the one who had proved above all else that he would keep mine, to a dangerous degree. To a point where my opinions no longer mattered.

Six years ago, he promised we would be together forever, that he would never stop romancing me, that he would always be mine and I his. Six years ago, I told him I didn't want that.

For six years, his promises had gotten more and more dangerous, and now they were the catalyst behind Dorian's safety. I could no longer exist knowing Alfonso wanted me. I now needed to live knowing Dorian did, a life where Alfonso wasn't a threat.

My hand slithered up his arm until it sat over the one gripping my jaw. "I chose Dorian, Alfonso. I love him."

"No!"

His eyes widened when I winced, hand finally releasing me. "I'm sorry, *amore*. I would never hurt you. You know I would never hurt you."

"Going after Dorian hurts me."

"I will drop it," he declared. "Come away with me. Start our life, and I will stay away from him."

He was lying. It was clear in his light eyes that he wouldn't allow Dorian to breathe, knowing he'd touched me.

"You don't want that, Alfonso. You don't want me with you while I think of him."

His head shook violently. "He is nothing." He moved for me quickly, hands softly cradling my jaw this time so my eyes had nowhere to look but into his. "He was a tool, a means to an end. I understand, *bella*. Before you, I had women, plenty of women. I understand that it hurt you to know I had touched others, been touched by others. You were teaching me a lesson. I understand. I am pained you did it, but I love you. I will never stop loving you. It will be you and me, Svetlana. Until the end of time."

My eyes teared because those last declarations were the exact things I'd always wanted to hear.

He just wasn't the man I wanted to hear them from.

My hands pulled on his, trying to pluck his fingers off my face, but he fought me. "I'm Dorian's. I will always be Dorian's."

His jaw clenched, eyed darkening. "I will not allow it."

"I won't let you hurt him."

"No, *bella*. It is you and me. We will be together. I will make sure of it. Even if it is only in death."

"You would kill me? I thought you promised you'd always protect me."

"I will kill *us*, Svetlana. I will ensure our lifetime."

"But you promised to protect me, to never let anyone harm me. You count as anyone, Alfonso."

"Some promises are meant to be broken."

My heart sank.

I never wanted promises from him, but that didn't mean it hurt any less when one was broken. To know he cared more for his control than my happiness.

"No, Alfonso." My eyes blinked with tears I didn't understand. "Promises are endless. They are made for a lifetime."

"And my biggest one was that we would be together." His fingers clenched, scraping against my face. "I will ensure I keep it."

Dorian

IVAN AND SERGEI were just getting there with their men when we pulled up. Thankfully, otherwise I was sure they would've gone in without us, without me.

I needed to be there for my girl, keep my promise that I would always be there for her. She was mad at me at the moment, thought I'd given up on it, but I would never do such a thing. The one thing I valued more than anything in this world was my promises to her. Like she'd told me at the beginning of our meeting, the last ballad was the best. And I'd promised her a lifetime, which meant our last ballad would come upon our deaths. We still had a hell of a long song before then.

Everyone merged at the back of one of the Romanov SUVs as the trunk came open, and my team was privy to a hell of a lot of weapons. Weapons I had no doubt weren't registered.

While some of their men began arming themselves, the Romanovs passed around shirts for all of their men to change into. The material was rougher, not bulletproof but close to it.

My team had our vests on and our police guns, so we stayed silently on the sidelines and waited. Porter narrowed her eyes at the entire show, but she wouldn't be able to do anything about what she saw here today. Sergei's smirk in her direction said he knew how deeply that infuriated her.

When the brothers stripped to change, I was shocked that the only tattoos they had in color were those of flowers. Ilya's in particular caught my eye. There was a rose where his left tricep met his shoulder, then petals falling diagonally down his back to his right hip. The bright red of those petals was enticing, and I wondered about the meaning of that tattoo more than the flowers of his brothers.

"Are you checking him out?" Lansly teased Porter with the way she was staring at Sergei's back.

She grimaced. "Those tulips are newer than the ink he had when I'd been under. Need to remember them specifically for research. I'll find something on the fucker."

When they finished, closing the trunk and readying themselves, the Romanovs came for us. Sergei didn't stop like his family did but moved straight for Porter and aimed the barrel of his gun at her chest. "Give me a reason, princess."

Finnegan's gun landed on the side of his head before Porter could snark back. "Give me one, lowlife."

I pushed Finnegan, then Sergei away. "That's enough. Everyone's ready. Let's go."

They didn't argue with me, and I was eternally grateful for it.

We ran up to the theater in groups, the mafia men breaking up into four groups and my team breaking in two, Porter following behind me as Lansly and Finnegan moved left. We all had our earpieces in, and we were ready to end this. To end Carrini.

None of it mattered. The groups, the earpieces, none of it, because when we got inside, we were met with one large room. They hadn't been kidding when they said this was an abandoned, ripped up space. There was only a chair under the skylight which I knew was for Carrini with the way a blanket sat beside it.

We wouldn't be able to hide and maneuver toward him so the earpieces were useless, and there was no sections to hide off into for the groups to split up.

There wasn't even a way to surround him. The side of the theater he had his back to was enclosed so the only way to get there was to pass through the large open space. We wouldn't be able to do that without giving ourselves away.

Not that it mattered.

The way he held Lana, his hands on her shoulders with the knife in one hand placed dangerously at her throat, he knew.

I held my breath. He knew we were here and he wasn't about to lose her again. Not in this life.

My heart beat erratically. If he knew, she knew. And she wasn't doing a thing about it. She knew we were here, that I wouldn't allow her family to come in without me, and she wasn't moving.

That was the smart move, but still, every instinct in me wanted to yell at her to get away from him, not that she could safely do so with the knife so close to killing her.

The Romanovs agreed to allow us to take Carrini in and at this moment, I was regretting being a cop, regretting that I'd had no way of fighting Finnegan when he declared that was the only way to do this. It meant none of the men could kill him outright when they had the chance, when Lana wasn't in the way.

"Your family's here to see us bound, *amore*."

Bound. As if she would marry anyone but me.

We didn't try to hide then. The window above didn't light the entire space, but I had no doubts he could see us. He knew we were there as he turned Lana around in his arms, holding her against his chest with the knife so close to her neck that blood was seeping down.

I nearly lost it then.

I couldn't do anything. I knew any movement *I* made would only anger Carrini more, so I had to rely on her family, but everything in me wanted to rip that man apart for touching my girl.

"Don't be foolish, Carrini. She is spoken for," Ivan opened.

My breath left me. What the hell was he doing? We needed to indulge his stupid fantasies to keep this at bay, not rage him on anymore.

"By me," Carrini grimaced.

"By the cop," Ivan remarked, making matters worse.

Lana winced, though I knew she was trying to hold it in, as the knife pressed into her.

"That's not true, *amore*." He bent into her, covering his face with her hair, so any shot would hit her before it hit him. "Tell him. You're mine."

Come on, Lan, I thought. *Tell him whatever maniacal thing he needs to hear.*

But all she did was look at her father.

They were having a conversation with only those simple stares. Nothing telling about them, something done only by two people who loved each other so much, they'd made their own secret language.

"*Amore.*" He growled into her ear.

She ignored him as her brows furrowed softly toward her father. She wasn't confused. She was upset. That was the furrow she wore when she didn't like something but accepted it. She'd worn the same furrow when we'd been in that alley and she'd accepted that I would only see her as a mafia princess. She'd worn it when I thought she was trying to trick me about her freezing hands in our first interrogation.

I stepped forward, instinct telling me I didn't like whatever it was Ivan was telling her, whatever it was she were accepting.

That move caught everyone's attention. Carrini focused his glare at me.

His eyes were dark, deranged.

And he held my future in his hands.

"You," he growled, holding tighter to Lana though—thankfully—the knife didn't bite any deeper into her.

"Let go of her, Carrini," I said calmly, giving the three members of my team and the four goons that had come with the Romanovs time to wrap around the building so he was finally surrounded, so we had some leverage to disarm him and take him in without hurting Lana.

"Why would I do that? She belongs to me." He kissed the side of her head, and my stomach recoiled. "I will do as I please with what belongs to me."

Lana was still looking at her father as she mouthed something I didn't understand, something in Russian, and he winked. This felt like acceptance. But of what?

"I belong to Dorian, Alfonso. I always have and always will."

My heart thundered. She'd said it before, and it was stupid for her to rile him up with it now, but I couldn't help the endearing hold those words had over my heart.

"NO!" The maniac shouted.

"I belong to him," she said.

"Lan." As much as I loved the sound, I needed her to stop baiting him.

"Everything about me. My heart, my soul, *my body*. He's done unspeakable things to my body."

His free hand gripped at her waist. "Don't speak like that, *bella*. Your father is right there." There was barely controlled rage within him.

Ivan didn't help. "She's an adult, Carrini. Don't try to hide behind some facade that she is naive to pleasures, the same pleasures you wish to give her. And if she's decided those pleasures will come from the cop, then they come from Dorian."

Everything felt frozen in time as the Italian and the Russian stared at one another. In Carrini's eyes, I understood one thing—Ivan Romanov was giving his blessing to me when he'd never given it fully to him.

"NOOO!" The call was loud, aggressive, frightening. Carrini's eyes grew wide with rage, and Lana took that moment to shove her hand into the crook of the elbow holding the knife to her, and pushed it away. Just enough space for her to duck out from the sharp end and lay flat on the ground, like she knew what was coming.

Carrini didn't seem to pay attention to that movement though. His whole focus was on Ivan, and he didn't seem to be thinking as he flipped the knife in his hand toward the Don.

Ivan didn't move.

It all happened quickly, but the Romanovs had instincts. It's what had kept them alive all this time.

But he didn't move.

Shouts rang out from everywhere, and I recognized my voice along with those of his sons, recognized us moving to get him out of the way even though none of us would make it in time. But Ivan didn't blink.

Not one movement as the knife pierced through the shirt that I now realized was slightly different than those of his sons. He'd opted out of wearing the protection they had. He opted out of having that barrier as the knife struck his chest.

And he fell to his knees.

To hell with what Finnegan wanted. Carrini wouldn't make it out of here alive, and I would make sure nothing happened to my new brothers.

From this moment on, I would help them.

In a way I wasn't able to help their father.

SHOTS RANG OVER and over and over and...

My brothers' guns were the only ones going off, leaving holes all over Alfonso, but the only thing I saw was my father on the ground, blood starting to seep out of him.

I had crawled over to him, had his head rested on my lap a moment before I was surrounded, a hand on my shoulder as my brothers enveloped us.

"*Otets*," I cried.

He gave that soft smile. "No, *lyubov*. Don't cry."

I agreed to this. I knew my father wanted nothing more than to be back with his love, knew it by the simple look he'd given me before. I'd agreed to that look because I could not imagine being away from Dorian as long as he had *Mama*, but...

"*Papa*," I cried.

His eyes fell closed, then opened again, catching Ilya and Sergei's attention above him. "*Moi mal'chiki.*" His hand shook as it cradled first one, then the other's cheek. "You two need to stop being so serious. Be softer, allow a woman into your lives. I promise it is the best thing to happen to you."

Tears fell down both of their cheeks, but they were otherwise strong, giving our father a single nod of acknowledgment as they each took his hand and held on tight. They didn't want to let go. Even Sergei, who was so rough and tough all of the time, didn't want to let go of our father.

Otets turned to Lukov next, finally releasing Ilya's hand to cradle Lukov's cheek. "You, *moi mal'chik*, already found your woman. Get ready, *syn*, because she will take you on a ride. But stay by her side. You take care of her."

Lukov's head shook as tears fell down his cheeks. "*Otets.*"

If this wasn't about Nairi, then I had no idea who my father was giving his blessing for. Who was the woman my father had dubbed good enough to become my sister?

Otets's thumb brushed Lukov's cheek. "She will only make you stronger, *syn*. Promise me my grandchildren will look like her."

Lukov nodded as more tears slipped down.

Then Father's attention was on me, the blood pooling all around us.

"*Doch', moya lyubov.*"

My head shook. This was my fault. I could barely see with all the tears slipping down my face but took solace in the soothing nature Father's thumb brushed my cheek.

"I have been ready to go since I lost my Sveta, *doch'*, but I couldn't leave you behind until I was certain you were taken care of."

"*Otets...*"

"I can overlook his being a cop because I know how much he cares for you, Svetlana. Be good to him. Make that life you always dreamed of, and know your brothers will always be around."

"*Papa…*" My tears fell in chunks.

His breathing was beginning to shallow. "Do not cry for me, *moya doch'*. I am finally going to be with my wife again. It is all I have wanted for fifteen years now. But I needed to make sure you four were okay, otherwise *Mama* would kill me. Make sure you found that life you'd always been searching for."

"*Papa*," Sergei called. "*Pozhaluysta.*"

Otets's breathing shallowed as my head fell against those of my brothers, the four of us caging our father from the horrors of this world.

"*Ya tebya lyublyu.*" Father's words came out as a whisper. "*Ya lyublyu vas moi deti.*"

Then his chest stopped moving, and I shut my eyes to erase this day from my memories, even though I knew it would forever burn in the back of my thoughts.

"*Ya tebya lyublyu papa,*" I whispered as I heard the same thing muttered by my brothers. "*Ya tebya lyublyu papa, ya tebya lyublyu, ya…*"

Part Seven

"You will always be fond of me. I represent to you all the sins you never had the courage to commit."

- Oscar Wilde

SHE STOOD by the floor-to-ceiling windows of our apartment, staring out at the view like she'd done every day for the past three. Almost like watching over the city would bring her father back.

She didn't cry much anymore. She said as much as it pained her, she was glad he'd gone because the one thing he'd wanted more than anything in this world had been to be back with his wife, and now he had that. She hurt as his child but she accepted the circumstances. I knew the feelings would come and go. There would be days when the grief struck harder until missing him was a normal part of her day and the tears stopped like they had for her mother.

I knew the feeling of losing a loving father and was glad to be there for her, to help her cope through this.

I stopped silently behind her, arms wrapping around her waist to pull her into my chest. She never fought my holds, falling into me effortlessly.

Ivan had been carried away by his men, then given a proper funeral three days prior. In the days between, I'd made sure my team and any law enforcement stayed away from the Romanovs' involvement in Carrini's death. I would make sure the three sons weren't tried for killing Carrini. I would protect them. They were family now.

"It makes me a horrible person, doesn't it?" she whispered, staring out at the city.

"What does, beautiful?"

"He's happier now, with *Mama*. I know he is. He was never as happy as he'd been those first years of my life because he didn't have *Mama* anymore. This is what he wanted. Which means I'm happy it happened."

I kissed the side of her temple. "No, baby. You're not a horrible person. You're a loving daughter. You can grieve someone and be happy for them all the same."

She sighed. "I cannot believe he stayed on that long after she passed. I cannot imagine living after losing you, Dorian."

My lips tipped up, and I kissed her temple again. "You may feel a bit different when we have children."

An amused scoff left her. "That's quite a while away. I won't be having any children out of wedlock. And I won't let pregnancy be the reason I marry."

I grinned fully now. There was my girl. "You won't." I stepped from behind her, then turned her body to face me. I slowly pulled out the box I'd been carrying for two weeks now.

"Dorian..." Her brows furrowed, more concerned than aware. "What is it?"

I cleared my throat. "I don't think any of us could've protected your father, Lana. I think he was ready to go." As she nodded, I opened the box in my hands so only I could see inside. "But I will do what I can to protect your brothers, even if I do not agree with their lifestyles, because that's what family does for one another."

That furrow between her brows eased. "Dorian..."

I turned the box so she could see now. "Your father came to me two days before what happened. He gave me this, said he knew you would forever be taken care of and he did not need to stick around any longer. That he loved his sons, but you were his little girl, his little Svet."

"She's still angry with you, Shipman." Ivan broke me out of my thoughts.

I was so lost in going through everything we had on Carrini that I hadn't heard him come into the precinct. Hell, I didn't even know how he got in.

It was late, and I'd decided to stay here tonight rather than go home. I had a change of clothes, and there were beds in the back that I could use, so I'd be fine. At least until we got Carrini. It was too difficult to be in that apartment without Lana.

"Better angry and alive than the alternative," I responded from where I sat on the couch, papers all around me and a laptop propped on the coffee table before me.

Ivan sat on the table in front of me, restricting my access to some of the papers. "I must confess, I knew you made her happy before, but I still didn't like you."

"I never expected you to."

"I like you now, Shipman." He scoffed. "Shipman. To think, my grandchildren will bear that name." He shook his head. "My daughter will bear it."

I dropped everything around me and met his gaze, completely alert now. "What?"

"You do intend on marrying her, do you not?"

"Absolutely."

He gave me a quirked brow know-it-all look. "Then she will bear your name."

I cleared my throat. "I guess I'm just shocked that you're so open to it."

"I am not in favor of your occupation, but what has always

mattered to me above all else was how you cared for her. Your letting us take her showed me."

"So what are you doing here? I get reports of how angry she is with me over the phone too."

He laughed. "Yes. She's cussed you out in five or six languages now, I believe. And she only speaks three of them. The others she specifically learned to call you names."

I laughed now. "That's my girl."

His laugh sobered, and he wore what felt more like a sad smile. "Yes. Your girl." He cleared his throat as he pulled something from his pocket. "That's why I'm here." He opened the black box in his hands and stared down at it. "My goal in life was always to make sure my girls were taken care of. I failed my wife when she passed, but I refused to fail my daughter. She was allowed to live the life she wanted because that was what she desired, but I always kept an eye on her. I was waiting. And it probably annoyed me as much as it annoyed Walters that she wouldn't find someone already. My boys are special to me; I love them so much, but they can take care of themselves. They have their sister to vet women for them. I needed to make sure my little Svet was taken care of before I could meet Sveta." He handed me the open box. "I hope your love transcends all matter, Dorian."

I couldn't move. This was the least expected thing to happen that I could've fathomed.

But finally, I forced my gaze away from Lana's father and down at the diamond ring staring up at me. It wasn't very large, but it sparkled and was the perfect amount of bling for a finger.

I met Ivan's gaze once more and knew for certain—he was giving me his blessing.

Her eyes were brimming with tears when I knocked out of the memory and witnessed her awe as she took in her mother's engagement ring in the box. "Dorian..."

I dropped to my knee. "Svetlana Lyubov Romanov, I knew

it the moment I saw you that you would be trouble. And that's all you've been since then. Not because of your family or your obsessive stalker but because of what you've done to my mind, my heart. I cannot breathe without you, Lan. I wake up every day excited about life because of you. I go to sleep imagining a life with four of our own kids. I may not have agreed with a lot of what your father did, Lana, but I do with one thing—I cannot live my life without my wife. So be my wife. Please. Make me your husband, carry my children, give me that life you always dreamed of."

Lana dropped to her knees before me and took my face between her hands. She laughed softly around her tears as she voiced, "Svetlana Lyubov Shipman. Has kind of a nice ring to it."

My grin slipped ear to ear. "It has the best ring to it. I fall asleep every night repeating it to myself."

She leaned in close so our lips brushed. "Me too."

I SHOULDN'T HAVE BEEN SO antsy. He'd met my family without a problem. Meeting his shouldn't have been so nerve-racking.

Except it was extra nerve-racking.

His family was normal. I didn't know how to do normal. Whereas he'd known how to deal with my family because they'd had a very common interest—getting rid of Alfonso.

I wouldn't be able to meet Gwendolen today because she was visiting her husband's family across the country, but Dorian's mother lived right here in town.

Caraline Anne Shipman.

I didn't know too much about her, but I was aware that she was slightly upset that we'd done a courthouse wedding and nothing grand. Though "slightly" may be a loose term. Dorian didn't exactly want to explain how his mother felt about it.

But we'd won her over when Dorian explained that he couldn't bear the thought of my continuing without his name. And when he mentioned he wanted me pregnant as soon as possible, suddenly, Mama Shipman was completely on board with our situation.

But the real reason was because of our dads.

He'd lost his a few years ago, and I'd just lost mine. We didn't want to do anything big without them. And I certainly didn't want to walk down the aisle without my father. Not so soon after losing him.

In the future, maybe for our ten-year anniversary, we could have a wedding. One our kids could also be a part of.

"Relax, baby." Dorian smoothed his thumb over the top of my hand. We'd just stepped into his mother's home, and two dogs were barking to inform her of our presence, one Caraline's own and the other she watched when her neighbors were out.

Before she could make her way to us, Dorian walked us through the living space and into the kitchen.

Where I paused suddenly.

"Elliot?" I gawked at the man sitting by the island next to the beautiful woman rolling dough for cookies.

Caraline's head snapped to us, and she beamed. "Oh, darling, you're here. Oh, and with such a beautiful bride by your side."

I tried to snap my attention to her as she rushed us, bringing us both in for a tight squeeze, but it was hard to do with old Elliot sitting there with a beaming smile on his face.

Caraline took our hands each and examined the rings. "Oh, how lovely. Dorian said this was your mother's, Lana dear. How beautiful."

I met her gaze and allowed the smile that naturally came when thinking of my parents' love to lift my lips. "Thank you."

She cupped my cheek softly, her eyes warming. "Dorian told me, my love. It is a devastating pain."

I knew Dorian had told her about my father. I'd been the

one to okay it. I was part of the family now, so I wanted them to know about mine. And part of that was knowing that my father had died because I'd had a stalker.

"Dorian's been perfect helping me through it."

She scoffed as she made her way back to her dough. "He better be. He dealt with his own loss on his own. He never let us in."

"Don't worry, Ma. Now when you want something from me, all you have to do is have Lana ask me for it."

They were laughing between themselves, but my attention was back on the other man. "Elliot, what..."

My gaze shot between him and Caraline.

Caraline.

Cara...

I released Dorian's hand and stopped before the island he was seated at. "Did you know? The entire time? Did you know who Dorian was?"

He gave a cheeky grin. "Not necessarily the entire time." He met Caraline's sparkling eyes, and I knew she'd known this whole time too.

"He knew my name was Shipman, dear. And when he heard my son was a detective. And his name. He pieced it together, then informed me. It is how I was so calm with learning of your background. If Elliot thought you still impeccable, then you were certainly good enough for my boy."

My glare at Elliot softened. "Fine. I won't be too mad at you."

He snorted. "Too mad? Give me praises, *cara mia*."

Caraline smacked him for teasing me, and I felt a sense of security within this family.

"This is the Elliot you've told me about?" Dorian stopped beside me, analyzing Elliot. "And both of my favorite women in the world love him?"

Elliot sat a little straighter. "I hope that means I can do right by your father, son."

He smirked. "I think if both Ma and Lan love you, then Pops and I don't really have a say."

"Does this finally mean you've quit though?" I asked Elliot.

He shrugged. "There're things to do around the house to take up my time. And I get enough socialization from Cara and the places she takes me that I don't need it for that aspect any longer."

"Good." I grinned.

"I'm sorry that means I won't be around any longer."

I shrugged. "At work, maybe. But I can always come here and tease you then."

"Oh no," he grumbled. "Now it can happen at any time."

We all laughed, then Caraline met my gaze. "I'd like to meet your brothers as well, dear. If that is okay?"

Dorian's hand landed on the small of my back, reminding me that Caraline wouldn't want to meet them because she was scared but because she loved family so much that she'd want to incorporate them as well.

I smiled. "I'll make sure they come over whenever you decide."

"Perfect, dear."

"Things really are perfect," Elliot commented. "Now I have free rein to question your boy all I'd like. I'll make your father proud with what I come up with."

I snorted. He knew my father had already met Dorian; knew he'd given his blessing; knew he was gone but forever with me. I was more than happy that Elliot was the man in mine and Dorian's lives in place of our fathers.

Ignoring his threats to my husband, I watched Caraline take out the cut outs for the dough. "Do you need any help?"

"Need? Never. Want? Always."

That sent a renewed sense of adoration through me. She didn't need me around, but she wanted me around. All we ever desired in this world was to be wanted, and I was wanted by her.

I gave Dorian a chaste kiss, reading the twinkle in his eyes saying he caught on to that as well, then moved beside Caraline.

As I was cutting a cookie in the shape of a star, Dorian turned to Elliot, "You can question me all you like, Elliot. As long as I can question you in turn."

Elliot stiffened. "Maybe I shouldn't be too hard on you."

We all laughed, and as I met Dorian's eyes, I knew that no matter what, we had a lifetime of memories ahead of us.

Nairi

WHEN TONI'S WAS EMPTY, it was both heaven-sent and the most boring part of my existence. I had my journal out while I sipped on a cup of coffee to pass the time.

I allowed the quiet of the room to give space for my mind to bring all of the baggage to the forefront and dump it on this page. Right now, my mind was focused on my uncle.

Then all of that came crashing down when Lukov came storming into the shop.

My entire body reacted, perking up to his presence. But he looked so different than normal. He looked angry, and though I'd seen him angry before, it had never been trained on me.

"Luk—"

"I trusted you!" he roared.

My brows furrowed as the whisper left me. "Lukov."

"I trusted you, Nairi!"

"What are you—"

"You brought her a laptop, knowing we weren't allowing her to use one."

I stood straighter. So he found out. So what? He'd locked

his sister away and cut off her communication. I wasn't going to apologize for giving Lana a bit of that freedom back.

"You used my affections for you to walk through with it, and because of that, she went and offered herself to the one man we were trying to keep her away from."

I froze. What the hell was he talking about? "Is she hurt?"

He was pressed against the other side of the bar so tightly his body was liable to break through and storm into me. "You're fucking lucky she's not." He leaned over it, hands wrapping around the counter by my hips. "You're lucky she got out and Carrini's dead."

"I'm lucky?" I muttered, then louder, "Don't you think if you'd given her a laptop from the beginning and allowed her to help, she would've included you in everything and not snuck off?"

"Nairi—"

"I'm not lucky she's unscathed. You are. Maybe that'll teach you about locking women away."

His nostrils flared, and just before he was about to say something, he pushed away and stormed around the space between tables. Then his sharp gaze snapped back to me, and he moved quickly, this time coming behind the counter.

I backed up instinctively, even though I knew he wouldn't hurt me.

Although I didn't. I hoped he wouldn't hurt me because of my projected feelings. I didn't really know anything.

When he was only an inch from me, my back against the counter, he raged, "You're right. Lana's fine. We're lucky. But you know what we're not lucky about? My father! *He's* gone, Nairi."

"What?" The whisper left me barely audible.

"Carrini wasn't going to let her go, and we weren't... my *father* wasn't going to let anything happen to her." His eyes brimmed with tears he didn't allow to fall. "He's dead because Lana snuck out; because she found that information; because you used me to get it to her."

"Lukov..." I started breathlessly, shaking my head because this was all wrong.

"He's dead, Nairi!" he ground out. "Dead."

"I'm sorry, Lukov, I really am." He would never understand how sorry I was that he'd lost his father. "But that wasn't my fault. If this Carrini was as obsessed with Lana as Ava said, he was never going to let her go. He would've ended up killing your father and all of you to keep Lana to himself."

His fists clenched where they sat on the counter by my hips, caging me in. "Would he, *kyank*?" It was the first time he'd said that word with disgust. "You have that little faith in us to protect the women we love?"

"Luk—"

"Nairi," he interrupted. "I think you've done enough to my life. Carrini's no longer a problem for Lana. You don't need to contact me upon seeing her any longer. Was that what you wanted?"

My head shook, but words were difficult to get out. I didn't want to lose him, but I wasn't going to cower as he blamed me for everything. "This is what happens with obsession, Lukov. He spiraled. Instead of blaming everyone else, how about you take the time to remember how much your father loved your sister, how much he loved *you*?"

I'd met Ivan Romanov three times. Once when he came in to pick up an order Lukov had put in. He'd sat patiently at a stool and watched me make the coffees, chatting with me so freely and sweetly. The next time when he'd joined Lukov coming in to order. He'd eyed us the entire time, then when Lukov stepped out to take a call, had teased me for my "little crush." And finally, last week, when he'd come in to talk to me at closing, he'd sat at the booth Lana normally took and had dinner with me. It'd been the best night I'd had in a long time. He'd told me all sorts of stories, of his family, his time with only his wife, and specifically about Lukov. Then he'd given me a box of things that I hadn't had the guts to open yet.

I was going to miss him too. Maybe not as dearly as his children would, but those three visits defined something deep in me.

"Don't bother telling me about my father."

I didn't say anything more. He was upset, and I would never blame him for the feelings jumbling up inside.

He scoffed and shook his head, head falling lower until our lips almost touched. "I trusted you, Nairi."

"I still trust you." My voice was barely audible to my own ears, so I didn't think he heard it.

He scoffed again, then pushed away.

As I watched him leave for what felt like the final time, tears fell down my cheeks. Both because I would mourn his father deeply but also because of the finality that shook the air with his departure.

Translations

<u>Russian</u>

Otets - father

Mat' - mother

Sestra - sister

Brat - brother

Umnik - smart ass

Lyubov - love

Moi mal'chiki - my boys

Syn - son

Doch' - daughter

Moya - my

Pozhaluysta - *please*

Nevozmozhnyy - *impossible*

Navsegda vozmozhno - forever possible

Ya tebya lyublyu - I love you

Ya lyublyu vas moi deti - I love you my children

Ya lyublyu tebya yeshche bol'she - I love you more

Armenian

Kyank/kyanks - life/my life

Voche - no

Don't forget to leave a review!

Thank you so much for finishing your read! Don't forget to leave a review or rating on all platforms as it helps me as an author more than you can ever imagine!

Amazon and Goodreads ratings help the most but feel free to talk about it everywhere else too—including social medias, blogs, Youtube reviews, and most importantly—word of mouth, and more.

About the Author

Nelly Alikyan is a girl from the Los Angeles Valley who moved to Boston for school and found she prefers the East Coast. But really, London is where she'd like to be since it's her favorite city ever. She's the only reader in her family—not her only cause as the black sheep—and has dreamt of being a writer for as long as she can remember.

When she's not working on her books or in the real world, she's on Youtube at Nelly Alikyan!

For more books and updates:
www.nellyalikyan.com

instagram.com/authornellyalikyan

tiktok.com/@authornalikyan

youtube.com/NellyAlikyan

amazon.com/author/n.alikyan

goodreads.com/authornalikyan

facebook.com/authornellyalikyan

pinterest.com/insinpublishing

Acknowledgments

Loving detective shows meant I wasn't always into the bad boys. We all fell for it, right? We love the bad boys, the mafia men, but something about watching the detectives in those shows made us root for them too. Detective Hottie is one of those guys.

This book came to me after watching a lawyer make a random TikTok. Yes, a lawyer made a TikTok giving some advice. I don't remember what it was, but the moment I saw it, Lana and Dorian were in my head.

My thanks go out to all the same people. My mom, for always supporting me; my siblings, for always finding it insane that I can do this; to everybody in my life who encourages my work, who's so bewildered at my ability to do this. I'm one lucky girl to have such supportive people in my life.

And of course, thanks to those hot detectives that make it so much easier to believe in loving the good guys. Currently, I'm specifically thinking of Elliot Stabler from SVU and Derek Morgan from Criminal Minds, but I know there're more. I think all of us are in love with those two (though I know some of us love the nerdy of Spencer Reid too - now that I think on it, I'd say he's more a Lansly even though that hadn't necessarily been my intention when writing Lansly).